A NICE GIRL LIKE ME

ABIGAIL BOSANKO

TO MY MOTHER,
ANN

Acknowledgements

The Whisky Society of the novel is not The Scotch Malt Whisky Society of Queen Street, Edinburgh, but a fiction inspired by it.

Thanks are due most of all to my husband, who insisted on taking me out when all I wanted to do was stay in and write the same sentence over and over again and then delete it.

There are individuals in the whisky industry who have inspired and helped me, in particular Annabel Meikle, a good friend and a fine nose, and Richard Gordon of The Scotch Malt Whisky Society who gave me an imaginative amount of freedom to do my sales job as well as commissioning my first pieces of writing: whisky tasting notes. (This novel exceeds the brief, I fear.)

Thanks go to Arthur Motley for buying the first cask of pink whisky, and the second and the third, and Charlie MacLean, whose whisky tasting notes are still the most delightful and edifying thing I've ever read in a bar. Anne Armstrong, whisky broker, I hope you will forgive the little liberties I've taken to suit the plot. Jennifer Anderson and Laura Hinchliffe, thank you for the TV credits, and David Forcada Muñoz for the flat in Barcelona.

Thanks also go to Rachel and Campbell McAulay for failing to find me a Glasgow lawyer – someone I could take out to lunch and ask for advice on the character and golf handicap of my hero. My second novel ended up being set in Edinburgh, just like the first. However, the lawyer I met was charming so I don't mind one bit. I would like to thank him, even though he believes that's not at all necessary.

Special thanks to Eugenie Furniss, my agent, and Tara Lawrence and Jo Coen, my editors, for their extraordinary patience and determination that I could, and would, write this second novel. Your bracing editorial notes had many a late night dram spilled on them.

A NICE
GIRL
LIKE ME

Prologue

The Society existed not only to gratify the aficionado,
but to introduce the pleasures of whisky to the novice

The Scotch Malt Whisky Society – An Honest Tale

My best friend, Flora, is a professional whisky connoisseur.
For around three hundred pounds you could spend some time
with her at the Whisky Society in Edinburgh, sampling fine
single malts while she explains the art of nosing and tasting.
For free, she gave me some advice on how to appreciate a fine
dram. 'Nose it first and think about the aromas – vanilla and
flowers, for example, or pear drops or peat smoke. Taste it,
add water, nose it again, taste it again. Keep going. Then, if
you want, you can add ice. In fact, mix it with whatever you
like and don't let anyone tell you you're doing it wrong.'

Most whisky drinking takes place between midnight and
sunrise among young people in clubs, who drink it with ice.
They generally live in warmer climates than Scotland –
around the Mediterranean or in South America or the Far
East. There is more whisky drunk in Paris than in Glasgow;
there is more whisky drunk in Spain than in Scotland.

In Scotland, you're supposed to drink it 'properly' – no ice,
no mixer, no DJ and if you're a girl, don't even bother. In
Scotland, we live in a bracing northern climate and whisky is
seen as a man's drink.

3

Don't you believe it. Flora and I are a bit sick of being told that girls don't drink whisky.

Flora says that in a proper whisky tasting, you should sample five different single malts. Start off with a plain, dry lowland, move on to a flowery, fruity Speyside, then a rich, dark, sherried kind of Speyside, then something more robust from the highlands, and finish off with a heavy, smoky, deeply satisfying Islay. It's important to taste your whiskies in the right order. Never start with a powerful, dizzyingly heady malt because after that you won't be able to taste anything else. You've got to work up to it gradually. Start with the light-weights. Flora likens her current boyfriend to a fourth whisky – a satisfying highlander, but not the last one she intends to try.

She says that when I got married I did everything in the wrong order. I missed out all the other interesting men I should have tried before settling on Andrew. It was like start-ing with the really serious whisky you're meant to save till the end. 'And he's so much older than you, Emily,' she told me. 'You should have worked your way through some of the younger ones first.' I did – sort of – but their immaturity only disappointed me and I got bored. I was looking for something more challenging, something that could sustain my interest, something that would take my breath away.

When I found Andrew, there was just no going back. Everyone else became a poor substitute for the real thing. This is an absolute truth. Once you've tried the real thing – a very fine, properly matured single malt – everything else pales in comparison. You look back on the sticky whisky blend of callow youth that you cheerfully mixed with Diet Coke and you think: 'yuk'. How much more interesting it is to love a complex, darkly promising whisky whose first taste leaves you reeling.

You can make up your mind about a man very quickly. I married Andrew six weeks after we first met and our marriage was a shock to everyone. As Flora pointed out, the only thing we had in common was a reputation for commitment phobia.

Eighteen months of happy wedded bliss later, I went for an interview for a marketing job at the Whisky Society (Flora prepared me with intensive private coaching). It was a very convivial panel interview held along the bar and it went on for hours until I could barely remember why I was there in the first place. I didn't do too badly, though, and I know I definitely drank my whiskies in the right order. At the end of the evening the woman chairing the panel ordered me a taxi and as we shook hands at the door she said: 'Oh, Emily – before you go – you will take the job, won't you?'

My husband was delighted by my news. He said he was proud of me. I could really make a go of this new career and wasn't the staff discount excellent? That weekend he bought me flowers and we went out to dinner. It was a double special occasion: my new job and our First-and-a-half wedding anniversary. We were still untouched by disaster then and deeply in love. I can get achingly nostalgic when I think about it.

Before starting my new job, Flora, happy with her high-lander, asked me if I ever wished I could try some of the things I'd missed. What would I do if I met someone else and found him irresistibly attractive? 'What would you do, Emily, if you really, really wanted him?'

But I could never imagine wanting anyone but Andrew.

At the start of my story, I was living happily ever after.

taken from Flora's notes

The First Whisky:
LOWLAND
an apéritif

good for beginners
light & refreshing, keep it chilled
take it with ice
great to sip when you're getting ready for a night out
try it with Canada Dry and don't let
your average barman put you off

Some Lowland Malts:
Rosebank
(rare, distillery closed)
St Magdalene
(very rare, closed & bulldozed)
Bladnoch
(closed and reopened – hurray!)
Glenkinchie
(our local, just off the city bypass)

'Whisky-tasting is something of a misnomer, since most of the work of evaluation is done by the nose, and not the palate. Professional whisky tasters are themselves called "Noses"'

Malt Whisky, Charles MacLean

Chapter One

I worked in a Georgian townhouse on Charlotte Square, which was busy night and day, cellar to attic. The Whisky Society operated like an upmarket club with its bars and sitting rooms, library and dining rooms and flats on the top floor for overnight stays. However, most people joined in order to buy from the society's list of rare single malts which was sent out by mail order to its twenty thousand members all over the world. It was a very specific kind of Edinburgh club – a whisky warehouse with Adam interiors. The closest we ever got to being like the clubs I had known in Paris or Barcelona was in the smoky, crowded lower basement which played music long after midnight and always kept ice on the bar.

The availability of ice was kept secret from the older, more sedate members who were settled in front of the fireplace in the drawing room three floors above.

I liked it that, in the evenings, we held whisky-tastings in the drawing room and people would come along and sample what was on offer and chat to the staff. It wasn't usually me who did the talking. Flora did. We had been close since we were little, and it was fun working in the same place. In the two weeks since I had started my new job, I had made new friends too. There was Dolores, the receptionist, who was the same age as me and knew everything that was going on and everybody's comings and goings. She always sat at her little desk near the entrance on the ground floor, whereas I was on the top floor, in the main office.

It was the end of January now and very busy because of all the Burns Suppers. Private dinner parties went on all the time, but in January, Robert Burns took over. When I arrived at work that wintry morning, I could see that the whole place was glowing. The hall was warm with red roses. 'You have to have roses for Burns Suppers,' said Dolores. 'It's traditional. "My love is like a red, red rose."' She buried her nose in the bouquet on her desk. 'These are from Graeme,' she told me. 'I bought them on my way to work so he could give them to me.' Poor Dolly; love always fell very far short of her expectations.

I climbed the spiral staircase that swept grandly round the hall all the way up to the top floor. I could hear the noise of the office before I saw it. There were too many people crammed into too small a space. The place was humming with activity and all the phones were ringing. A brand new list of whiskies had just been mailed out and everyone was phoning in with orders. Flora had told me it could be frenetic when a new list 'hit', as she put it, and it would be a few weeks before we could resume a quieter rhythm of work. I made my way to my desk.

A whisky office is just like any other office, only with more whisky. I started my day by selling it on the phone. Longish conversations about oak casks and age and types of maturation and special bottles for presents and all sorts of questions and chat and gossip. There was also a lot of corporate business to attend to – phone calls about private tastings for private dinner parties and all the ordering and organising that went with that. Everyone around me was busy, rushed and animated, and I wondered whether that meant we were all very hardworking and successful or just disorganised and panic-stricken. I hadn't quite worked it out yet.

The company was owned and run by one Kitty Gillespie, an indefatigable whisky enthusiast who loved her work so much she stayed here most of the time. She actually liked the office to be chaotic because she believed chaos was creative. The Accounts department did not always agree with her and often stayed late just to try to restore some order. Although Kitty was a successful businesswoman, I was beginning to realise that the Whisky Society had always operated on a whim and a prayer.

Mid-morning, the phones seemed a little quieter and I caught up on some admin. I went to my filing cabinet and began nosing whiskies. I had to write a short comment on the smell of each one as part of my training. I was supposed to do a few each day, but here I was in a mad rush to catch up. Rosebank, St Magdalene, Linkwood, Glenmorangie, Knockdhu. I stopped for a rest. You can't really try more than four or five whiskies without having to stop and rest your nose. (Well, I couldn't, but then I was still a novice in the whisky industry.) I wrote some emails, made some phone calls, typed a few letters and went back to it. Highland Park, Ardbeg. Then Kitty appeared and looked at my list. Kitty was in her late fifties, tall and thin with red hair and bright, alert eyes. She wore chiffon scarves and flowing skirts and bold, modern silver jewellery. She reminded me of an actress

11

I had seen in a production of *The Prime of Miss Jean Brodie* at the Royal Lyceum.

'How far have you got, Emily?'

'I'm up to Ardbeg.'

'Don't try the ten-year-old until after you've tried the seventeen-year-old. The ten-year-old is much more pungent. Always remember you have to work your way up to the heaviest malt. I'll help you out,' she said. 'Here, pass the bottle.'

Kitty was a very hands-on sort of manager. We took turns and did two more and got as far as Laphroaig. 'That's enough for the time being,' she said. 'I think Flora wants a word with you. She's wandering round the building looking for a quiet place to sit and test some samples. Give her a call on her mobile.'

Kitty left, walking purposefully through the office on a wave of red chiffon and I rang Flora. 'Where are you?' I asked.

'Downstairs in the blue sitting room. We could get through this batch in an hour. Are you free to come now?'

'I think so.'

'Bring my notes, would you? I left them on your desk.'

I pushed several bottles aside to get to my in tray. There was a selection of miniatures in it. Empty. We were only looking at labels today. And there were Flora's notes, together with some clean tasting glasses – proper tulip-shaped ones for nosing spirits. 'Can you bring them with you?' asked Flora on the phone. 'I might not have enough here.'

When I found her, she was sitting with her feet up on the chaise longue, happily rootling through her box of samples. She was smiling to herself and the dimples appeared in her cheeks. Flora's baby photos must have been cherubic because even now she seems to retain a miraculous, wide-eyed sense of wonder as if she is thinking: isn't the world an amazing place? She hates her dimples, but I think they suit her.

'Emily!' she exclaimed. 'There you are!' She reached for the first little bottle stacked in a row beside her on the table. 'Come on, let's test these.'

I watched while she poured. 'Lovely colour,' she said. 'Bright and clean. Matured in an ex-bourbon barrel.'

Even I knew that much. You can tell by the colour. Rich gold means it could be a first fill. With each subsequent filling, the whisky grows paler. And then the really important moment: Flora held the glass to her nose. I copied her, trying to learn. After the initial nose prickle had worn off it smelled of vanilla.

'Definitely first fill,' said Flora. 'Come on, Emily,' she added, 'what else would you say about it?'

'Lemony?'

'Lemony, grassy, herby . . . '

Flora said she could discover eighty per cent of a whisky's identity just by looking at it and nosing it. Flora was a connoisseur; I only did sales and marketing. Occasionally our paths crossed. Kitty Gillespie was keen that we should work together more often and so Flora was trying her best to teach me a bit more about the job.

'Typical Linkwood,' she announced, putting her glass down.

'What does the label say?'

'Linkwood. I'm right. Lucky guess. I love that Linkwood. Spit it out, Emily.'

I shook my head and swallowed. 'I can't. It's so disgusting, spitting it out.'

'You can't taste eight cask strength whiskies and expect to touch-type the tasting notes afterwards. Use a spittoon. And make sure you nose it with water. It makes all the difference, you know.'

Flora had an exceptional nose, originally trained by a Grand Nez at a famous French institute of perfumery in Grasse. Not one of the very fine noses in the whisky industry could identify a Diorissimo or a Dolce e Gabanna, although they were all very good on Dufftown. Experienced whisky industry men had declared themselves awestruck at Flora's ability to name an elusive element in a complex malt, but a good nose is a good nose. No argument. They just quietly admitted to themselves that the girl can nose.

She poured me another glass. 'Do you like this one? I do. Robust, fresh, good. Try it and then nose this one. It smells like custard.'

'I don't get the custard. Condensed milk?' I suggested hopefully.

'I get rice pudding.'

'If you say so.'

'I do. With nutmeg.'

For Flora, talking about scent was part of her everyday professional conversation, but it applied to more personal subjects too.

'How's Ben?' I asked.

'Somewhere in the Bay of Biscay. It won't be long before he's home now.' She hugged herself happily.

Flora had fallen in love with Ben because he had the right natural balance of ambergris, dark fruit, fresh air, musky saltiness and surprising floral notes. The only problem was he spent a lot of his time at sea.

'And how's Andrew?' she asked.

'Very well, apart from the usual long hours. I've painted the whole house just waiting for him to come home in the evening. But at weekends we do the decorating together.'

She looked at me carefully. 'Is your nose a bit tired? After several whiskies, it can get confused. I'm not saying you haven't got a good nose. We could walk round the block, stop for coffee?'

'No, I'm fine. Let's keep going. Next box. Is this the dodgy lot?'

'It is indeed. Don't think we'll find anything in here, but we ought to check, just in case.'

This particular box of samples had not come to us via a bona-fide whisky broker; instead it had been abandoned on the hall table, left there by one of those over-confident young men from the Home Counties known in the whisky industry as 'wine boy'. Piers (for that was his name) had come up to Scotland on a shooting trip and had fancied doing a bit of whisky business on the side. Regrettably, he had been fobbed off with a box of dodgy samples in a bar in Aberdeen. Whiskies with green highlights from copper intrusion; orange highlights from rusty nails penetrating the cask; old sherried whiskies with a lot of sulphur; spirity whiskies that had refused to mature.

'Not very nice at all,' said Flora. She quickly discarded nine of the little glass bottles and then stopped and looked very hard at the final sample. 'Wait till you see this,' she said quietly.

'What is it?'

'The odd one out.' She held it up to the light, putting a sheet of white paper behind it to see the colour more clearly.

'It's pink!'

'Yes, it's pink.'

It was the colour of pale rosé wine, and in other lights perhaps salmon pink, blushing in the glass. 'What kind of whisky is that?'

'It's a real find,' said Flora happily. 'It's turned pink because it was re-racked – you know, poured into another cask – and in this case the cask was a port pipe. It picked up some of the port character from the wood and some of the colour as well.'

'Is that bad?'

'No, not at all. It's good, I'd say. It certainly noses well. Icing sugar and vanilla and almonds,' she said, eyes half-closed. 'Thick slices of Battenburg cake.'

'I get the vanilla.'

'A rare, very fine rosé whisky. Beautiful. No one has ever marketed pink whisky, you know. You never usually get it this

15

pale anyway. No one sees the point of selling it as it is. It's generally hushed-up and blended away.'

'But it's so pretty.'

'I know, but whisky has a very traditional, masculine image and the belief is that if pink malt was ever put on sale on the open market, it could undermine the status of whisky as a man's drink.'

I added water and sipped my cool, pink scotch. 'And nobody wants that to happen.'

Flora drained her glass without spitting. 'We're buying this,' she said decisively. 'We're definitely bottling this one.'

'How do you know people will want to buy it?'

'Would you buy it?'

'Yes, but I'm a girl.'

'Precisely. I think this would be great in the summer list as a long, cool drink. With ice.'

'The old barman might not like that.'

'No, but the bar manager will. She'll love it. Can you put together some notes on it for the boss to take to that sales meeting next week?'

'What sort of notes? Tasting notes?'

'Yes, and a few lines on how it came to be pink. Just keep it very simple because I know there are going to be vodka people at the meeting and vodka people know nothing about maturation. You can make vodka in the morning and drink it in the afternoon.' She shuddered slightly. 'Unlike scotch whisky, which takes years to mature. The vodka company will be taking the notes back to Vodka HQ for a meeting with their alcopop team, so keep it in short, simple read-aloud sentences. Just say something about how this particular whisky has spent most of its life in an American barrel before it was finished in a port cask.'

'An American barrel?'

'Yes, because scotch whisky is matured in casks that have already been used to mature something else. You can't make

16

scotch in fresh oak, remember? You need secondhand wood or there's too much vanilla and you'd end up with something more like Kentucky bourbon.'

'When will we be bottling it?'

'As soon as we can, before the port influence gets any stronger.'

Flora tidied away the glasses and I went back upstairs to my desk and got down to work. All around me, people were wrapping up last-minute special bottles that had to go out with the courier. All those corporate gifts for Burns Night. The courier was an hour late and, beside me, Maisie and Fiona were taking it in turns to ring up and find out where he was.

In the middle of all this, Andrew phoned. 'How's it going?' he asked.

'Great. I'm really busy.'

'How many bottles of whisky have you got on your desk today? I always love to know.'

'Er, seven. No, eight. How many have you got?'

'Believe it or not, I do have a bottle today because a new client is being nice to me. How many bottles of whisky have you got in your filing cabinet?'

The courier arrived. 'Andrew, I'm really, really busy, you know.'

'Oh, go on, just tell me.'

'At least forty in each drawer. About a hundred and twenty bottles.'

There was always a little silence at this point while he enviously considered my whisky collection.

'I've only got paper in my filing cabinet,' he said.

'What would you like?' I asked. 'The courier's finally got here. Can't you hear the cheers? I'll send you a bottle as a corporate gift from me to you. Old sherried? First-fill ex-bourbon cask? That's the one with lots of vanilla. There's a good chewy Laphroaig here. What about a lovely, fudgey, smoky Highland Park? I suppose we've got that at home already.'

'What was the first one I tried when I met you after work last week?'

'That's Flora's favourite to headline the next Bottlings List.' In a hurry, I yanked open the bottom drawer of the filing cabinet and the bottles clanked together. I could hear him laughing down the phone. 'It's a twenty-four-year-old from St Magdalene distillery which closed in 1983. Excellent lowland, now extremely rare. Here's Flora's note about it. She says it was originally made with water from a holy well dedicated to St Magdalene, patron saint of repentant sinners – so it'll be good for your soul, Andrew. The official tasting note for the Bottlings List has a very long title. It's called "The Elusive Scent That Lingers After An Elegant Woman Has Gone". I've told Flora we can't get all of that on the label so she's going to have to think of something else. And according to my own tasting note here—'

'Are you doing those as well now?'

'At the tasting sessions. When we get a new list, we taste everything and make notes in the margin and I said that it was very tingly at the start and faintly smoky around the edge with a very long finish, and Flora said that it was a very sophisticated whisky and rather alluring.'

'Alluring?'

'Yes, and if we're being blunt about it you could say it was rocket-fuel strong, being natural cask strength, that is sixty-two per cent alcohol by volume and an old-fashioned one hundred degrees proof.'

'You've sold it to me.'

'Good. It'll be with you in about an hour – if I can get it to the courier in the next ten seconds. I'm stuffing it in a box right now. I'm writing your name and address on the front: for the attention of Andrew Drummond. To Andrew, love from Emily. Kiss, kiss, kiss. There. Done. Right, I'm giving it to the courier as we speak. And these others too – same building on George Street. Thank you! And remember,

18

Andrew, don't leave it lying around the office or you'll lose it. Keep it in a safe place. You know what lawyers are like.'

The last thing I did before leaving work was to check my emails and find another message from him: St Magdalene arrived safely and is now under lock and key in my filing cabinet. See you tonight. xxx

I got home at seven and, unusually, he was home before me. His coat was thrown over a chair and his keys and change scattered on the hall table. My footsteps echoed as I walked down the hall on the newly exposed floorboards, bare light bulbs hanging from the ceiling. I couldn't go anywhere in our new house without thinking: lighting, curtains, carpets, paint that wall, sand that floor, must get rid of that old junk. I turned the corner into the living room (hideous flowery wallpaper that was definitely coming off tomorrow) and there was Andrew, sitting on the matching flowery sofa, flicking through a newspaper. (Must get rid of that sofa.) He got to his feet when he saw me. 'Emily,' he smiled.

My husband, Andrew Drummond, was tall and broad with thick dark hair which he aimed to keep short but kept forgetting to get cut, and the kind of face that is described as having character. In other words, he had a broken nose and a scar on his chin (only rugby, a long time ago). I always thought he looked – to use an old-fashioned word – handsome.

'So how was the whisky today?' He smiled broadly. 'Had a good day at the office, dear?'

'Oh, it was really good again! We tried this very rare pink single malt.'

'Pink whisky?' he laughed. 'You've only been there a few weeks and already our national drink has become very girlie.'

'Yes, it's pretty. You'd like it.'

'Pink whisky.' He shook his head and pushed his fingers through his hair, the way he always did when something baffled him.

'It got re-racked into a port cask,' I explained. 'That's why it's pink and there's port on the nose as well. I think we're going to bottle it, even though it is a bit too girlie for the established market.'

'I don't think my dad could cope with a pink malt. I don't see it going down well at the golf club.'

'Golfers are not the target market, to be honest.'

'Pink whisky . . . ' He still looked very amused by the idea. 'So when are you going to launch that? Gay Pride Week?'

'We want more girls to try whisky.' I walked over to stand beside the fireplace. He had come home early and bothered to light the fire. What a desirable quality in a man. 'Traditionally, women just don't drink whisky. The industry would love to unlock that market, and they've done quite well in other countries but failed spectacularly in the UK, especially with single malts which at the moment is the only growing sector. Here, marketing teams just stand around like spotty adolescent boys at a party, wondering how to chat up the girls.'

'So, is this your pet project now? You and Flora are going to show the whisky industry how to talk to girls?'

'We can try a few ideas out at the Whisky Society. It's a small place and perfect for this sort of experiment. Nothing may come of it but it'll be fun to try. Anyway, I really do like the pink whisky. It's quite robust, despite its girlie appearance. Very strong. There is a bit of nose prickle.'

'Is that a technical term?'

'It is, actually. Then quite hot in the mouth and really good with ice.'

'Ice? That's sacrilege.'

'No, it's not, honestly.'

'Did you bring any work home?' he asked, hopefully.

'Not tonight. I've caught up on the ones I needed to taste for the list.'

'You can try some of my St Magdalene if you like.' He disappeared into the kitchen and came back with two glasses of the special bottling of rich lowland. Single cask, first fill. We sat down together on the sofa. I put my feet up and made myself comfortable. 'This is just overtime for you, isn't it?' he said.

'I'm really excited about the pink whisky. Wait till you taste it.'

'Emily, you're turning into a complete workaholic.'

'I'm not as bad as you. How was your day, anyway?'

'Clearly not as much fun as yours.'

'How come you're home early for a change?'

'I was supposed to have a meeting with my opposite number on a case but her firm postponed it. Great relief, I can tell you.'

'Is your opposite number a real pain?'

'She wants my head on a plate.' He drank, then lay back and stretched out on the sofa. 'But she cancelled,' he said cheerfully, 'and it's Friday night so we can forget about it.'

I sipped from the glass he had given me and felt deeply contented. 'I like coming home when you're here.'

We moved here a month ago. It's a large Victorian house with a lot of original features. When we first got the keys, we walked around it holding hands like children in a strange place who are told to stick together and look after each other. This was our first real home together. I can't count the penthouse flat – that was definitely his. There, he had lived in lofty splendour with sleek metal furniture and smoky glass tables and a couple of kitsch leather sofas.

I turned to look at him in his new environment, surrounded by flowery wallpaper, and there was a dazed expression on his face and a faint smile, like a sportsman playing on with mild concussion and doing his best to keep up. 'I live here,' he said to himself. 'I actually

'But we don't have to live with the wallpaper.'

He's been repeating it often and surely it won't be long now before it finally sinks in. 'I live here with Emily, my wife.' Then the customary pause while he makes a show of pinching himself. 'My wife.'

'You must be used to that bit by now.'

'No,' he said, 'it still amazes me. Emily, I think we should change the alarm code to something more memorable like 1980. That year is burned into my memory.'

I knew what he meant. The burning moment had happened as he'd watched me write my date of birth on the form for the marriage licence: 27th February 1980. It wasn't as if he hadn't known my age but he hadn't actually worked out the year, and seeing it there in black and white really brought it home to him. I remembered him saying, 'You can't have been born in the eighties.' (Pause, calculation.) 'Christ, you were, weren't you?'

When I was at primary school, Andrew was being a twenty-something lawyer in London. I think he may even have been one of the original yuppies. In fact, of course he was, because he still had all the furniture when I met him. He brought it back to Edinburgh with him the summer I took my A levels. By the time we met four years after that, his style had still not moved on, but it would have to now because I was hoping for some light and airy redecoration. Some new ideas.

'Shall I get us ice for this whisky?'

'No,' he said firmly. 'I know you've had an intensive few weeks, but believe me, Emily, you're just a beginner. I've had years of practical drinking experience.'

'It's nice with ice.'

'Persevere without.'

'I accept that you've had years of practical experience, but maybe you could do with a change.' I made a half-hearted attempt to get up and he stopped me. 'Stay here, Emily,' he said, kissing me. 'Why not just stay here a bit longer? Drink your whisky,' he added, 'before it gets cold.'

I subsided back into the cushions. Kissing him, I remembered something Flora had said once about how it was possible to fall for a man just because he smelled right behind the ears. It was, she said, a primitive but aromatically complex indication that he would prove to be a good match.

'This whisky is rich in every sense of the word and resolutely high in alcohol despite its respectable maturity. A generous whisky with a wealth of experience to offer. The nose is deeply satisfying – a swirl of vanilla, orange, honey and dark fruits soaked in brandy. Take a sip and all these flavours emerge in concentrated intensity. Mouth-feel is delicious. Develops and lasts'

Cask No. 55·11   *A Wealth of Experience*
Alcohol: 61.2%   Proof: 107°   Outturn: 190 bottles

The Scotch Malt Whisky Society Bottlings,
Winter 2000

Chapter Two

The weekend didn't get off to a great start in that Andrew had to leave early Saturday morning to play golf in some kind of corporate competition. Lawyers versus Surveyors. I spent the morning 'playing houses' as Flora called it, turning our chintzy living room into a paler, more interesting place. The last of the wallpaper came off in satisfyingly long strips, then I pottered around with a tub of Polyfilla, poking at the pock marks in the plaster and smoothing over the cracks. It was an absorbing sort of job and I made slow, minutely detailed progress. At lunchtime, Andrew phoned from the clubhouse to say that the surveyors had won and all credit to them, but they did have a lot more time to practise than lawyers. If he could knock off work early like most surveyors he knew, it would have been a different story. 'I should have stayed at home,' he said ruefully. 'I should have stayed at home with my lovely wife instead of embarrassing myself on the golf course.'

'Come home now, then.'

'I can't. We're here as guests. I'm supposed to be enjoying myself for hours yet.'

'Oh, just come home, Andrew.'

'I ought to stay a bit longer – at least for the presentation.'

'You know you'll be bored to tears.'

'But I'm being officially entertained.'

'I wish you were here with me.'

There was the pretence of a pause while he wrestled with his conscience, which immediately hit the floor and gave up. 'Okay,' he said. 'You've persuaded me. I'll skip the presentation and come home now.'

'What will you tell them? Will you have to make an excuse?'

'It'll be a very thin, transparent one. Apparently I have a reputation for being uxorious.'

'For being what? Is that an insult?'

He hesitated. 'Sometimes.'

'Don't listen to them.'

'Right. I'm leaving now.'

I went back to work and found myself thinking that there were very few occasions when Andrew and I could have come across each other. It's not as if I like golf. Even if I had wanted to take up the game, his club would not have allowed me to play at weekends as he did. The rules were quite clear: at weekends, you couldn't play without a penis. Those lacking in the essential golfing organ were offered a discount on the fees by way of compensation. These unfortunates could play golf, but only on weekdays and only if accompanied by someone with the right sexual organ. Women were not allowed in the clubhouse under any circumstances, no matter how many male members might be there to accompany them on this the most hallowed part of the course.

The scrape of the knife down the long, slow length of a hair-line crack. I searched the walls of our living room for faults and I filled in the gaps.

Andrew always said that before he met me, his life had been very predictable: a straightforward progression from infant school to high school, from university to law firm. In those forty years, there had been very few surprises: been there, must have missed that. His social life had revolved around after-work drinks on Fridays, married friends' dinner parties on Saturdays and golf on Sundays (handicap: 12). Weekends could also be punctuated by hill-climbing and late-night whisky-fuelled drinking sessions with people he knew from school. If you are a male, forty-year-old Edinburgh lawyer, your world can be very neatly arranged. However, such a world can be thrown into fantastic, tumultuous chaos by a chance meeting with 'a naïve, pretty girl, half your age, who knows sod all about what you're really like'. (This according to Kate, his fiancée – or ex-fiancée – who had committed her feelings to paper and hand-delivered them with a slap across the face that I had heard all the way upstairs in the bedroom.) Kate's bracingly angry letter had told Andrew exactly what sort of a man he really was. He had shown it to me before we got married, just so I would know.

I met Andrew at his cousin's wedding at the Dalmahoy Hotel. I was a bridesmaid in a strapless, candy-pink flouncy dress. I didn't notice my future husband until we came face to face during an eightsome reel called 'The Kelso Fling'. This is one of the more hazardous Scottish country dances where everyone gets to dance with everyone else and there's a lot of fast spinning involved and people fling each other all over the place, but if you use the best hand-hold (thumb hold, not finger clasp) then you can spin around very fast in total

27

confidence. As each new partner reaches for your hands, you know instantly whether or not he knows how to do that thing with the thumbs. On a dance floor of forty wedding guests, maybe only two people will know, but if one's a man and one's a woman and they're dancing 'The Kelso Fling', eventually they will meet. And that is how I remember Andrew. He was the only completely secure, really fast spin I had all night. Unfortunately for me, after that I came up against my Uncle Donald, who was a keen but clumsy hand-clasper. We took a corner far too quickly and I twisted my wrist. I had to sit out the rest. Andrew came and talked to me while I nursed my hand in an ice bucket. He brought champagne. He said that if I had to sit with an ice bucket, I should at least have the champagne to go with it.

I didn't think anything would come of my attraction to him, this admittedly older man, but I still found myself trying to impress him. I made out that my life was wonderfully exciting. When I wasn't tramping through the jungles of Papua New Guinea, or bungee-jumping off cliffs in New Zealand, I was assessing an attempt at eco-friendly tourism on a beach in Bali. I had returned to Edinburgh to take up a great job offer, but a sudden change of plan had had me flying straight out to Paris where my current unfixed abode was a flat on the Rue Soufflot, with friends from school. I love Paris, don't you?

Andrew admitted he was very impressed. I was clearly a talented young woman with a brilliant future. I had felt myself positively glowing at the praise. When I asked him if he had been anywhere himself recently, he apologised in advance for being boring. He said that, compared to me, his life had been pretty unadventurous. He didn't do sudden changes of plan. 'What's stopping you?' I asked.

He kept glancing around. I realise now that he was looking out for Kate. She never came, although she had been at the wedding service that afternoon. I think they had had an argument. When it got to ten o'clock, Andrew finally began to relax. It must have been Kate's deadline. I could just imagine her saying: 'Look, Andrew, I'll see how I feel. If I'm not there by ten, I'm not coming.' By eleven, we were getting on famously.

'Would you say you were flirting with me now, Emily?'

'You've got to flirt if you're a bridesmaid,' I said quickly. 'It's stated in the wedding handbook that flirting is the bridesmaid's most important function, whereas you –' I poked my finger at his chest – 'have no excuse!' I told him this was the last Scottish event I would be going to for a long time. I told him I was emigrating to New Zealand.

'Friends of mine wanted to do that,' he said, 'but they were turned down. Not enough points to get in. They were too old at thirty-two.'

'It's easier when you're twenty-one, like me.'

'Twenty-one?' he echoed.

'Yes, I've just graduated. Well – a few months ago.'

'Right,' he said slowly. 'Good for you. Well done. Let's drink to that.' And he raised his glass of champagne to me and took a big gulp. 'Just graduated,' he repeated.

For a moment he sounded like my Uncle Donald (who was by this stage drunkenly playing air-guitar on the dance floor): 'Well done, Emily,' Uncle Donald had slurred to me earlier. 'Of course, exams aren't the same as they were in my day. I did O levels. What do you call them now? GCSEs? Highers or Higher Still or some such crap? Oh, you've got a degree! You're kidding! But now that you mention it, you do look older than I remembered.'

'What's your degree?' asked Andrew.

'French and Marketing.'

'And now you're living in Paris. How long do you think you're going to stay there?'

'I don't know. I was doing a course in Teaching English as a Foreign Language but I've dropped out. I don't think I want

29

to teach in New Zealand. I want it to be a whole new start. A whole new life.'

'Sounds good. I wouldn't mind one of those.'

I held out my hands in a gesture I'd seen the university careers advisor use: 'There's a life,' I said, cupping the air in front of him. 'It's yours. What are you going to do with it?' and I opened my hands as if to drop it into his lap.

He made a wry little smile and watched his imaginary life plummet to the ground. 'Splat,' he said. 'What a mess.'

'Imagine you didn't drop it,' I insisted, 'and it's still there in your hands. Now, what are you going to do with it?'

He groaned. It was as if he'd asked himself the same question a million times before. 'Well,' he sighed, 'if that's my life, I've already used up half of it, haven't I? So all I've got is this . . . ' and he stared at his empty right hand.

It was broad and strong-looking. 'It's a perfectly good right hand,' I said.

There was a long silence while he contemplated it, then said, sadly: 'It's my birthday today, you know.'

'Is it? Happy birthday!'

'Thanks.'

'I know what we'll do,' I told him firmly.

'What will we do?'

'You will let me write my phone number on your hand.'

He laughed out loud, and while he still found it funny, I got a pen out of my pink satin bridesmaid's bag. He started to mumble about how I didn't need to make my point quite so literally, but he let me open his fingers and write my way into the palm of his hand. 'Emily,' he said, watching me, 'how old do you think I am?' He said it quietly and seriously.

'I don't know. Does it matter?'

'I'm nineteen years older than you.'

'You're forty?'

'Yes. Forty.'

'Well, happy birthday, because honestly, you don't look

that old.' He cringed when I said that. 'What I mean is, age is irrelevant, isn't it? If you enjoy each other's company.'

'I don't think age is irrelevant.'

'Don't you? Well, I suppose it might be relevant in some ways. Here, I'd better write my name down as well, in case you're suffering from memory loss. Emily. There. Done.'

He looked at my name written on his right hand – all over the second half of his life – and he seemed bemused by it. 'Thank you,' he said.

'You'd better wash it off before your fiancée sees it.'

'Yes, I'd better. She might not realise it's a joke.'

I wasn't very sure what to say to that, so I said nothing. And then he pressed me, just a little. 'It's a joke, isn't it?'

I drained my glass of champagne. 'Well,' I tried, 'it's meant to make you smile.' I poured out the dregs of the bottle. 'What I mean by it, really, is that . . . well, I suppose what I mean is that I've enjoyed your company. There. That's all it is. And you've enjoyed being with me – at least I think you have.'

He smiled, kind of sadly. 'I have,' he said, 'although that's not necessarily a good thing.'

'Why not?' I leaned towards him. 'Listen, Andrew, I've got an aunt who's thirty-five. Would that meet your age require-ment? Would you rather it was her you fancied instead of me?'

He was taken aback when I said that. (So was I, to be honest. He's engaged, I told myself. He's forty. Pull yourself together!) Andrew kind of jerked his head up and looked at me differently. 'No,' he said, eventually. 'I wouldn't.'

I started back-tracking quickly. 'But you do have a fiancée, remember.'

'Ah yes,' he said. 'Kate.'

'Yes, think about Kate. She's your fiancée. If you fancy me, it's only a passing fancy.' (Oh God, what do I sound like? That's it. I'm not going to drink any more.) 'I mean, you love

31

Kate, don't you? You don't just fancy her, you love her. Think about Kate.'

'Kate is . . . ' He paused. 'Kate is a very patient, generous and even rather noble-spirited sort of person and . . . ' He stopped, as if he knew he shouldn't tell me, but recklessly, he would. 'And I've been told by a mutual friend that Kate has only ever failed at one thing in her life and that's me.'

'What do you mean, she's failed at you?'

'She's failed in her efforts to improve me.'

'You mean she wanted to make you a better person?'

'If only,' he smiled. 'If only, if only.'

I invited him to one of my leaving parties and he came. With Kate. It was the Glasgow leaving party at my friend Josie's house. Josie already knew Kate from the Kelvingrove book club. She told me Kate and Andrew were supposedly living together but for practical reasons they lived apart. Kate was in Glasgow, and Andrew was in Edinburgh and they both worked very long hours. No wedding date had been set because there was a serious disagreement about who should move cities, and neither would contemplate the halfway house that would be the Falkirk Compromise.

Kate had a confident smile and glossy blonde hair tied in a knot at the nape of her neck. She was one of those elegant women who walk tall and thin, and when I was introduced to her I couldn't help feeling short and fat. I was wearing a strappy denim dress with flip-flops and a bracelet of painted melon seeds. Kate wore a silk shirt, well-cut trousers and exquisitely beautiful shoes. She walked around my leaving party like Gwyneth Paltrow rehearsing a perfect Versace Glasgow accent. You knew she'd get an Oscar for the role of a brilliant, beautiful, ice-cool lawyer. I asked a few people about Kate and found out that she was everything I had thought, but not ice-cool. I knew this because Josie had seen her angry.

At a drunken book club meeting only the week before, Kate had reduced someone to tears over one of those Mars and Venus-type guides to relationships. (I hadn't known Dolly then, of course, but her choice of book seems entirely in character.) 'Kate just demolished her argument,' said Josie. 'Every single point. Bang! Bang! Bang!' Josie thumped her fist into the palm of her hand to demonstrate. 'Just knocked it right out of her; kept on about how it was all just a list of excuses.' It seemed Kate had actually snapped her fingers in front of the girl's face as if to wake her from a trance. 'Wake up!' she had shouted. 'Wake up! Wake up!' Clearly, here was a woman who had built her career on a triumphant ability to state a case.

At the party, Andrew and I were in each other's company for most of the evening, although we hardly shared a word alone. I saw no sign of the inner turmoil he later claimed to have been feeling. He rang me the next morning and we met again, just the two of us, for lunch in a restaurant he said I really ought to go to before leaving the country. We met every single day after that and he ended his engagement with Kate that very same week.

I still had all these big plans to emigrate, but secretly I wanted him to beg me to stay. He never did, though. He just looked ghastly when I talked about going. He listened to my plans with a fixed smile on his face and when I crossed another day off my special Southern Hemisphere calendar (with its July snow-scene) he made lame jokes about his world being turned upside down. Then, one night when I was telling him about tramping over mountains outside Queenstown, he said, with false brightness, 'It sounds wonderful. You go for it, Emily. There's no good reason why you should stay here.'

'There's you.'

'No, I am a reason why you should emigrate.'

I've got to tell him, I thought. Say it quietly. Admit it. 'The thing is, Andrew, if you wanted me to stay, I would. I don't want to leave you.'

His face softened into the expression Flora called 'that completely gooey way he looks at you'. The slightly sardonic smile (which was his guiding attitude to life) tended to disappear when we were together. But then he replied, 'You should still go, Emily.'

'I want to be with you. Do you want me to stay?'

Seeing the look in his eyes, I was definitely hopeful, but then to my dismay he moved away from me and pressed his hands to his face, pushing his fingers through his hair. 'Oh, God,' he groaned. I was appalled. I didn't know what to do, but then I realised he was laughing to himself. 'Oh God, where's a bit of jaded cynicism when you really need it?'

Andrew always claimed that falling in love with me came as a profound shock. It undermined everything he believed in – or rather, had not believed in. It was, he said, almost like finding faith, almost like proof of the existence of God, or some other such absurd, unlikely notion. He told me he sometimes wished his love for me had been unrequited because then he'd only have had one intellectual crisis to cope with.

When he told me he loved me, it was the most fantastic feeling I had ever had in my life. Suddenly, with him, all sorts of things seemed possible. My own commitment phobia had usually taken the form of 'leave early or be left', but with Andrew I was so completely wrapped up in my feelings for him, and so tightly swaddled in his love for me, that I couldn't bear the thought of leaving him even for a moment.

He proposed to me when he dropped me off at work one morning. I had just leaned over to kiss him goodbye when all of a sudden he seized my hand and said: 'Emily, will you marry me?' He said it quickly and emphatically, as if he had to get the last word in, as if he had to win an argument.

'Yes,' I replied.

We stared at each other. Did that really happen? Did we just do that? Then, embarrassingly, I found myself crying and he started saying a lot of very emotional things he couldn't remember afterwards – not without prompting, anyway.

We decided to keep things low-key and elope. I still had my address in Paris, so we made arrangements to go there and get married at the local Mairie. The legal requirements turned out to be more complicated than we had thought – you can't get married in a hurry in France – and so before the wedding, we took our first holiday together. We attempted, between wine, sex and food, to talk very seriously about our future and what difficulties we might face, given the age difference and so on. Andrew insisted we make an effort to have second thoughts. He was adamant that a pre-wedding honeymoon could function as a time for calm reflection, a sort of 'cooling-off period'.

Did you ever hear anything more ridiculous in your life?

We spent two weeks exploring rural Périgord in a state of clammy excitement, then we took a high-speed train back to Paris and got married.

The vows sound less intimidating in a foreign language, and in a French civil ceremony pretty much all you have to say is 'oui'. You don't have to repeat a lot of long-winded, serious promises, which was a relief given Andrew's standard grade French and my extreme nervousness. After we had said 'oui', we paraded arm in arm down the steps of the Mairie in the Place du Panthéon, feeling triumphant. We had dared and won. We blew a lot of money on dinner and got drunk on expensive champagne. It was fabulous. We were ecstatically happy. We loved each other to death. I promised that I would never, ever leave him. It was a sort of spontaneous, post-nuptial vow in English that I made to him later in bed. He said he was very touched. He said that if I never left him, it would be the best thing to never happen to him.

My friends were pleased for me although some, like Flora and Josie, had reservations about the age difference. But they were all nice about it – they had to be, really, because we were married by the time I told them. Andrew's friends were incredulous and some of them were pretty rude. They couldn't believe he had walked out on Kate and got married all within the space of six weeks. But others just nodded to themselves, as if they had always known something like this would happen.

Kate was bitter, but fortunately not twisted. After the delivery of her furious parting letter, she had remained dignified and aloof and for that I was profoundly grateful. If I'd been Kate, I would have had me shot. But Kate just let it be known that, for a while at least, she would prefer not to be in the same room as Andrew and so we were never invited to anything that Kate might also want to attend. This ruled Andrew out of quite a few things, which upset him a bit because he was a sociable kind of person.

If Andrew still spoke about her it was only on the very rare occasions we had dinner with some of his grander legal colleagues and her name came up in conversation. Andrew would praise Kate for her success and point out that she had worked hard for it. The others around the table would nod, then the talk would move on to other topics. Books, theatre, music and opera (some remembered my mother's singing career), then on to travel and holidays. Villas in Tuscany, gîtes in France. Andrew would try to bring me into the conversation. He once mentioned that I had studied French as part of my degree, and that I spoke Spanish too, and that I had won a prize when I graduated. Someone suggested, teasingly, that he sounded like a proud father at a school fête, but he managed to laugh that one off.

I stepped back. The light was fading now and I couldn't see quite so clearly any more. I wasn't sure if I had just smoothed over a crack or vandalised a perfectly even surface.

There was the sound of a key in the door. Andrew had returned. Whatever excuse he had given them for leaving early, it had delivered him safely home. I went to meet him in the hall. 'I'm glad you're here,' I said, putting my arms around him.

'So am I.'

We kissed. 'What was that word they said you were?'

'Uxorious. It means being excessively fond of one's wife.'

'How can that be an insult?'

'Exactly.'

'She taught me the art of nosing. She was my mentor. She is the Nose of Noses'

Charles MacLean, whisky connoisseur,
speaking of Sheila Burtles, research analyst,
formerly of the Scotch Whisky Research Institute

Chapter Three

On Monday morning, hurrying to get ready for work, I had to climb over an obstacle course of packing cases just to get to the wardrobe. Our bed was like a barge floating in a sea of wreckage. Some of these boxes were destined for long-term storage in the loft; others were waiting to be unpacked. Each box had a vague description of its contents scrawled on the side in thick black marker pen, like Andrew's Old Stuff or Emily's Junk. Here were all the things we had managed to ignore because we had always had so many other more interesting things to do.

One box had been rammed up against the chest of drawers. I tried to haul it out of the way so I could open the top drawer just wide enough to tug out a pair of knickers but the box didn't move. On the side Andrew had written: Records A–D. I called to him as he was shaving in the bathroom.

'Andrew, this box weighs a ton!'

'Does it?'

'Can you help me? I can't move it. I need to get my clothes out of the drawer.' Then I heard the shower running. Great timing. Okay then, I would just have to take a few records out and make it lighter. The brown tape sealing the top had already been cut open (explaining why the peace of Sunday afternoon had been shattered by AC/DC 'Live at The Hammersmith Odeon').

I lifted out some of the old vinyl albums and there, between Aerosmith and Anthrax, were about a dozen letters from Kate. Some printed out emails too. I knew all about this correspondence. It had never been deliberately hidden from me and I wasn't surprised to see it filed in a box along with Andrew's Old Stuff.

'Emily!' called Andrew from the shower, 'there aren't any towels!'

'Can't hear you!' He appeared in the doorway, dripping wet and shivering. 'Towels are over there,' I pointed.

He grabbed one and came to stand beside me. 'Were those letters in that box?'

'Yes.'

'I thought they were in with albums G to K. I don't know why I keep them. I should throw them out.'

'It's up to you. They're your letters.'

'Not exactly fan mail, though.'

'I'm sure some of the early ones must be.'

'I think it's time I got rid of them.'

'Do you file all your ex-girlfriends' correspondence in with your records?'

'No, only Kate's. No one else wrote to me.'

'Maybe you made a subconscious decision to file her with Death Metal.' I put the letters away, slipping them down the side of the box out of sight. Andrew pushed the box into a corner of the bedroom. 'I'll get rid of all these tonight,' he said. 'I don't want to keep tripping over them in the dark.'

He disappeared to iron a shirt and I finished getting ready.

'I should have moved that box for you,' Andrew muttered, coming back into the room. He was making a mess of doing his tie.

'Andrew, we've really got to go in ten minutes or I'll be late. Can you hurry up? It's nearly eight o'clock.'

'Okay, I'm nearly ready.'

I have this thing about being late. I get all agitated if I think I'm not going to be on time. I tend to turn up early for everything, just in case. Punctuality is a jealous god and demands regular attendance. My mother is exactly the opposite. She thinks life is more exciting if you're late. You get to lie in bed for longer, drive faster, race from the stage door to your dressing room and throw all your clothes on the floor. And the later you are, the more thrilled everyone is to see you. She says no one with my mania for punctuality could ever hope to be a star.

We rushed about, skipped breakfast and just made it out of the house on time. Andrew set the burglar alarm with the memorable date of my birth, then we set off on our morning commute across Edinburgh.

The Burns Supper season was over now. It was February, and the flowers on Dolly's desk at reception signalled that spring was near. Tall blue irises and yellow tulips. 'I love spring flowers,' she said. 'They're so cheerful. I'm going to get a special spring bouquet for Graeme to give me for Valentine's Day.'

'Are you going to buy the card too?' I asked.

'No. He always buys me a card. Always. Last year, even though he had to stay late at the office for a retirement party

41

and didn't get home till after midnight, he still bought me a box of Milk Tray from the all-night garage at the bottom of Dundas Street.'

'How long have you been together, Dolores?'

'Five years. Sometimes I think we're too close, that we're more like best friends than girlfriend and boyfriend. That's why I buy us flowers. You have to keep the romance alive, don't you?' She sighed wistfully.

At that point, the phone rang and Dolores left her tulips to answer it. She waved me off as I walked upstairs. Flora was waiting for me, hopping up and down impatiently. 'I'm glad you're never late,' she said. 'Kitty asked me to come in early today.'

'You mean on time.'

'She wants to talk to us about the pink whisky. She said it might be fun to do something "rather amusing" with it. She wants to see us both in her flat. Go and get those notes you did and meet me up there. Top floor. First on the left. There's a stuffed Scottish wildcat on the drinks cabinet outside the front door.'

I had never been inside Kitty's flat before, although Flora went there once a week for a whisky-nosing masterclass. I was nowhere near that standard and wouldn't be for years – if ever – but I knew that an invitation for me to visit Kitty at home was significant. It was Kitty who had founded the club at Charlotte Square more than twenty years ago and her membership card clearly stated: Number 1. Kitty must have a good reason for wanting to talk to me, and not just Flora, who she regarded as her special protégée.

I fetched my notes and climbed the stairs to the top floor. First on the left and there was the Scottish wildcat, a lithe, slinky-looking creature, its claws flexed as if ready to let rip on the polished surface of the old drinks cabinet. I knocked and walked into the hall. It was painted a dramatic shade of red.

'Emily, is that you? Down the hall, turn right.'

I followed the sound of Kitty's voice, glancing at the pictures on the wall. Scenes of Victorian highland nostalgia were hung next to contemporary paintings that exploded with electrifying colour. At the end of the hall was a huge black and white photograph. At its centre was a single drop of liquid and emanating from it were ethereal clouds of swirling smoke.

'That, my dear,' said a voice beside me, 'is a photograph of a smell.' I was now in the Gillespie presence. 'The smell of a fine whisky.'

'Is it possible to take a photograph of a smell?'

'Volatiles are just molecules floating in the air, but a microscope camera can capture them on film.'

'I've never seen a picture of a smell before.'

'Neither had I until recently – at least, not as art – but last year I went to an exhibition at the Miró Institute in Barcelona. There was an artist who had photographed the aroma of a coffee bean, and I thought it was such a curiosity that I asked him if he would do the same with a drop of whisky.'

Behind her, Flora nodded at me encouragingly.

'Which whisky is it?' I asked.

'It's a drop of Lagavulin sixteen-year-old that I bought in Duty Free.'

'We haven't had any casks from Lagavulin for quite a while, have we?'

Flora's face fell. I looked at her expression and it said: No, don't go there.

'They need it all for themselves,' said Kitty smartly. 'Got to sustain their brand. They're not likely to sell a cask of sixteen-year-old whisky to us, are they? Out of the question. They'd be mad to do that.'

I ignored Flora. 'Why?'

'Because they need every drop of it to pour into their own bottles of phenomenally successful sixteen-year-old whisky. They can't spare any. There's nothing unusual about that, Emily. It happens all the time. We own some casks, and there are others we buy through brokers and third parties, but it is increasingly difficult for us to buy from the people who actually own the vast majority of casks in Scotland. The few big companies that comprise the whisky industry in Scotland.'

I glanced at Flora, who just folded her arms and stared straight back at me: Now look what you've done.

'It's only going to get worse.' Kitty sighed. 'Come on, Emily. Come and sit at the table.'

'How will we keep going then?'

There was a quiet pause. 'I don't suppose we will.'

Flora actually bit her lip. Kitty sat down, perfectly calm. 'Last week the Whisky Conservative Marketing Board told us that we may no longer refer to a whisky by its proper name. We are no longer allowed to reveal the names of distilleries. We can't call a Macallan a Macallan, for example. It's a brand name and we do not have permission to use it.'

'But how will people know what kind of whisky they're buying from us?'

'We'll have to start using code numbers. If you've got any better ideas let me know. In the meantime, I'm going to cheer myself up by having some fun with this pink whisky. I suggest we do the kind of exciting, innovative little project that no one else in the whisky industry would dream of doing.'

There was a glass of pink whisky on the table. As a professional whisky nose, Kitty Gillespie knew that taste and smell are always clearest in the morning and that this could sometimes make for a bracing start to the day.

'I'm feeling inspired,' said Kitty, nosing the pink malt. Then she raised her glass as if she were making a toast and gestured towards a portrait on the wall opposite.

'Know who that is?' she asked, taking a sip. 'That is a portrait of Elizabeth Cumming, known as "the Queen of the Whisky Trade".'

Ah yes, Flora had told me before my interview that Elizabeth Cumming was Kitty Gillespie's great heroine. In the 1870s, Cumming had taken over the family distillery from her late husband and had driven it to unprecedented success. In 1893, she had negotiated the original great whisky business deal and merger with John Walker & Sons, and for over a hundred years Cardhu had remained at the heart of the Johnnie Walker blends. Kitty Gillespie could, and frequently did, make a good case for her belief that Cardhu was the most successful whisky in the business.

'And now Cardhu single malt has been blended away,' said Kitty. 'They've diluted it with other whiskies and called it a pure malt instead of a single. They've bastardised it, but kept the Cardhu name so they can still cash in on its reputation. Elizabeth Cumming must be turning in her grave. She would never have risked sullying the status of her product. She was a businesswoman with an eye to the long-term security of her distillery. She didn't lose it in the merger, you know. She negotiated her rights. She always looked to the future.'

We sat in respectful silence. 'However,' she said, brightening, 'I think Elizabeth might have enjoyed a dram of this pink malt. The style of it, the taste, the finish. The colour isn't just a novelty either, there's definitely port on the nose. It's good, Flora. I like it. And it's feminine, of course, like Cardhu. Cardhu was always described as a lady's malt because it was sweet and floral and silky on the palate. It's a delicious whisky. And now it seems everyone wants it and there's hardly enough to go round.' She seemed to grow sad again for a moment, then: 'Right! And now to the point!'

Kitty appeared galvanised. Flora and I sat up straight.

'In brief, girls, I want to make a little mischief with this pink malt. I want a feminine whisky with a sense of humour, because, by God, I need to keep my sense of humour now! I'm prepared to throw a lot of money at this project on the condition that you – that's you, Emily – come up with the most radically feminine marketing plan you can possibly imagine. I want pink, I want flowers, I want a brand new label. I want a smoothly fashionable bottle with a softly curving bottom. I want a whisky that's going to shock the boring old farts in this industry into a pink fit of apoplexy. I want to shock their little Argyle socks off.' She finished her drink. 'All right, my darlings?' she asked. 'Can you do that for me?'

I could scarcely speak, so overwhelmed was I by her vision.

'We'll do it,' said Flora.

Back outside Kitty's front door, I leaned for a moment against the drinks cabinet, feeling breathless. 'She means it, doesn't she?' Flora nodded. 'I'm not going to waste a chance like this. Where in my whole career will I ever again get the chance to do a product launch as radical as this?'

'Nowhere,' said Flora. 'Never.'

'I even get to dream up a new name because we're not allowed to say where the whisky comes from. What will we call it?' Behind me, the Scottish wildcat stretched out her claws. 'Wild Cat Whisky.'

'Wild Cat Pink Whisky.'

'Scottish Wild Cat Pink Whisky.'

'Just call it pink whisky,' said Flora.

'No.'

'Pink Wild Cat?'

'No.'

'How about we have one of those focus group things where we get people's opinion?'

'No. After a few drams it would be a slightly out of focus group anyway. And we don't want agreement. We don't want a vulgar common denominator here. What's wrong with Wild Cat?'

'Can we just ask Josie, then? She's coming to see us this afternoon today anyway. I know you like the Wild Cat name but perhaps we should get a few more suggestions, ask for some industry opinion – just someone to bounce ideas off.'

'All right, but no one from the whisky industry.'

'He might know a bit about the whisky industry. He's into all sorts of things – drinks industry things generally. Vodka, rum and gin, tequila – you name it, Jack likes to get involved.'

'Jack? Who's Jack?'

'Jack Buchanan, friend of Ben's. I know him quite well. He does vodka mainly but we forgive him. According to Jack, single estate rum is going to be the next cool, fashionable drink. That's what he does – predict market trends. He's got himself a really sweet gig just swanning around the world visiting distilleries and then reporting back and selling his information. Shall I ring him? I know he's around because Ben's meeting him tonight for a drink. They could come here, couldn't they? Why don't I ring him?'

'Okay, you ring him. I'm going straight out to Sainsbury's to buy curvy bottomed bottles. See you later.'

I ran down the stairs and waved a cheery goodbye to Dolores at the door.

The slightly-out-of-focus group began at five p.m. in the drawing room bar. Josie was to be our first potential consumer encounter. Jack wouldn't be arriving until a bit later. Blonde, petite Josie, our friend from Glasgow, sat neatly in an armchair, wearing this season's little white T-shirt with Chanel logo. It contrasted perfectly with her fashionably short Armani skirt, revealing long, glossy-stockinged legs. For her visit to the Whisky Society she had concealed in her Louis Vuitton handbag a cherry-flavoured vodkapop, and only reluctantly put it aside when I suggested a brief whisky consumer test.

'I never drink whisky,' Josie said as I set out a row of bottles in front of her. 'I just don't like it.'

Josie was what was known in marketing terms as a 'hostile prospect'. If we could find what might tempt her to try whisky, then we might learn something about the elusive target market.

'What do you normally drink in a bar?' asked Flora. (She was trying very hard to do our consumer test properly. Flora already knew exactly what Josie liked to drink.)

'I have a big glass of chardonnay, or I have vodka – posh vodka, Stollythingy – or I have a Smarcardi Bruiser. I like mango flavour best.'

Flora sighed in despair. 'What would you say if we told you there was such a thing as a pink whisky?'

'Cranberry flavour or something?'

'No, just pink. Would you try it?'

She shrugged. 'You can show it to me if you like. How's your decorating getting on, Emily?' she asked. 'Have you done your living room up yet? I know you couldn't stand that flowery wallpaper.'

'Yes, it's better now. What do you think of these bottles, Josie?' I pointed to the row of single malt whiskies.

Josie made a face. 'Looks like my grandad's sideboard.'

'Write that down, Flora. Anything else?'

'They are all brown or green. The labels are kind of yellowy, like they're really old or something. The writing's Victorian or Celtic and the pictures are all of Scottish moors or grouse or stags or stuff like that. They're all pretty much the same, aren't they? Look like they belong in an antique shop – like my grandad's sideboard.'

'But some of them I really love,' said Flora, beginning to crack. 'I mean, I love the Bruichladdich bottle, I love the Lagavulin bottle, I love the Ardbeg and the—'

'You're only allowed to ask questions, Flora,' I interrupted.

'I think you'll find Jack might have a few different opinions to you, Josie.'

'Why don't you go and ring him, then?' asked Josie in a huff. 'Ask if he can come sooner. Go on, and let me drink my Smarcardi Bruiser in peace.'

'Don't let anyone here see you drinking that.'

'It's all right, Flora. Emily has given me a mug.'

'I'll call Jack. Let's carry on when I get back.' Flora disappeared.

Josie smiled at me and settled comfortably in her chair, glad not to talk about whisky. 'How's your mum these days, Emily?' she asked. 'I mean, how's Joanna. She likes you to call her Joanna, doesn't she? I wish I had a cool sort of mum like that.'

'She's very well, still running her business in Marbella. Polly's still at school there. Do you remember my little sister, Polly? She's in her last year now. Polly always calls her Joanna. I sometimes forget and call her Mum.'

'Does she still answer to that, then?'

'Yes, most of the time.'

Our mother had brought us up to call her Joanna. When I was about five, I had rebelled and started calling her Mummy. Unfazed, she had started calling me Daughtie. If I said, 'Hello Joanna', she replied, 'Hello Emily'. If I said, 'Hello Mummy', she replied, 'Hello Daughtie'. She just preferred to be Joanna. 'I think it's nice to be more like sisters,' she would say, 'or really close friends.'

'But you're my mum, Mum.'

'I know, Daught, but I'm your friend too.'

Josie had once been out to visit me in Marbella when I had still officially lived there and she had been very taken with my mother.

'Does she still sing every day?' asked Josie.

'Yes, can't help herself. She loves singing.'

'She doesn't do it professionally any more though, does she?'

'No, she says her voice isn't what it used to be and she couldn't bear to disappoint her old fans.'

'She still does a fantastic karaoke, though.'

'Mum always likes a good party. She could have been a soloist if she hadn't ruined her voice belting out Shirley Bassey hits at parties.'

'I'll never forget it. She's just mad, isn't she? Brilliant fun.'

For a moment, I thought about my mother performing in her usual extravagant style. 'GoldFINGAH!' She could have been a diva and she knew it. 'Diamonds Are ForevAH!' She had the charisma and the necessary emotional projection. I could remember one terrible night when I was ten she had stood out on the balcony of our London flat, clutching my father's forgotten coat and singing out the perfect scream that is the crescendo of 'Un Bel Dia'. She had looked like Madam Butterfly painted by Edvard Munch. Crouched in my hiding place, I had witnessed her despairing solo and realised the world was coming to an end.

'How's Andrew?' asked Josie.

'Busy. It feels like I hardly see him at the moment, but he promised he'd be back by eight tonight so I'll be leaving before then.'

'Me too,' said Josie. 'It's my book club night. I asked Dolores if she wanted to come with me, give it another try, but she said no. She still hasn't recovered from Kate trashing her copy of *Why Women Just Like to Make Things Nice*.'

'Did she make you read the sequel too? It's called *Men Just Can't Help It, You Know*.'

'Yes, we hated both of them.'

'Oh, poor Dolores! She loves her self-help guides.'

'Actually, at the last book club meeting, Kate talked about you and Andrew. She said you were relevant to the theme.'

'Oh really? What was the theme?' (They didn't just do books at the Kelvingrove book club, they did themes.)

'We were reading books about the male mid-life crisis. Kate said your marriage was a useful illustration of the contemporary relevance of a tale by Chaucer about jaded old January marrying pretty young May. She said it was a very old story – older man marries much younger woman. She said Andrew wasn't in the winter of his years yet – he was more like Mr October – but it was still relevant.'

It seemed my marriage had been deconstructed and reinter-preted through the medium of Tesco's Rioja. 'She's just jealous.'

'Don't worry,' said Josie. 'I stuck up for you.'

'You're a true friend.' Privately, I decided not to tell Andrew this news about Kate. Instead, I stored it away.

'I wouldn't mind seeing the pink whisky before I go,' said Josie. 'Is it really pink?'

'Yes, it's really pink.'

Suddenly, Flora was back: 'Look who I've found!' and with her was a man I hadn't seen before. 'This is Jack,' she said, leading him in like a trophy. 'I found him in the basement bar saying he was waiting for us. Jack, meet Josie and Emily.'

He was quite tall and slender with fair hair and a tanned complexion. He looked a little dishevelled, a little tired, but he was smiling to himself when he sat down at the table. An easy, happy smile. 'Jack's just got back from California,' said Flora. 'He's still on West Coast time, aren't you, Jack? Jet-lagged. I caught him having the all-day breakfast down-stairs.'

'What were you doing in California?' asked Josie.

'Just seeing some old friends, but they've changed. Nothing in the house but herbal tea. I'm counting on Flora to help me re-tox.'

She sprang into action. 'Emily, where did you put that bottle? Look at this, Jack. You won't have seen a whisky like this before.' She held the glass up for a reaction.

'It's quite pretty,' said Josie.

'It's only a little bit pink,' said Jack.

'Only a little bit!' Flora was put out. 'It's pale salmon pink. This is a rosé whisky. It's not coloured or anything, it's natu-ral. This is extremely rare and interesting, Jack.'

He laughed. 'I'm fascinated,' he said, humouring her.

'The trouble with you is that you work in all sorts of dif-ferent spirits, whereas Emily and I only work in whisky. You drink all sorts of different things as well, don't you?'

51

'I have no brand loyalty whatsoever.'

'Jack is what is known as a promiscuous consumer.'

'Try some,' I said and offered him a glass. 'Try some, Josie?'

'I'd advise you to add water,' said Flora.

Jack tasted it without. 'It's hot,' he said. 'It just tastes very hot.'

'It's cask strength,' said Flora. 'It's fifty-eight per cent alcohol by volume. Do what I tell you and add water.'

'It's a light, fresh lowland,' I told him. 'Very clean and it will take a good splash of water. If you add the right amount of water, it should feel cooling in the mouth and warming going down.'

'It's nicer than I thought,' said Josie, who had put plenty of water in hers.

'I wonder what Diageo would think of this,' said Jack.

'Who?' asked Josie.

'Diageo, the multi-national drinks company – not to be confused with Dodgio who are even bigger. Dodgio are so big they can do whatever they like. Diageo aren't that big yet. They're still at the stage of making little concessions to the Scottish Whisky Association – things like using a different colour packaging for the new bastardised Cardhu to distinguish it from the old, legitimate single malt.'

'Perhaps "Bastard Cardhu" would have worked as a name for a new blend?' suggested Josie.

'Diageo would never have risked anything like that,' I told her.

'There's Fat Bastard Chardonnay and that's very popular.'

'And isn't there a red wine called Old Git?' asked Flora.

'There is,' I admitted, 'but the wine trade is light-years ahead of whisky in terms of marketing innovation.'

Other people joined us after work. Maisie and Fiona arrived as soon as they had said goodbye to the last courier of the day, and Dolores came when the night-time receptionist arrived for the handover at six o'clock. Ben arrived and Flora rose to kiss him. Seeing how pleased they were to see each other made me feel suddenly alone. I wished that Andrew and my friends could all talk to each other better. One of the sad things about being married to someone who is nowhere near the same age as you is that it's difficult to share the same friends. Andrew liked my friends and they liked him but he rarely came along to things like this because the conversation didn't always work very well and could be a little awkward. Sometimes I didn't think age was the only barrier. He was just different to them.

I checked my watch. Time for me to leave. I put on my coat and picked up my bag. 'Are you going already, Emily?' asked Jack.

'I've got to get home.'

'She always rushes off like this,' said Flora. 'Just when things are getting going. Emily, we should go out properly some time. Just having a quick drink after work doesn't count. We haven't been out properly for ages.'

'I've been really busy stripping wallpaper and finding things in boxes and so on.'

'We never see you any more,' complained Flora.

'We see each other every day at work.'

'I mean outside of work,' said Flora, 'like we used to.' She turned to Jack. 'It's actually romantic, you know, that Emily is rushing home like this. She's on an extended domestic honeymoon, aren't you, Em?'

'Are you really?' he asked.

I laughed, embarrassed. 'Yes, so I'd better go home, hadn't I?'

Jack stood up to say goodbye. He said he had enjoyed coming round to see what we were doing and hoped we could meet again. He was interested to see how the pink whisky idea worked out.

'You could come to our spooky tasting next week,' said Flora. 'It's in the haunted tunnels underneath the Royal Mile. Emily is already scared witless about it.'

'I'm a bit of a wuss when it comes to haunted tunnels.'

'You'll just have to bring garlic and wear a crucifix,' said Flora. 'We've got to do the job. I need you to carry the whisky and the water and the glasses.'

'I really must go home now,' I said.

'See you again, Emily.' Jack smiled. 'And it sounds like next time we get to scare each other.'

I knew they would all stay for a good while longer, and then they would eventually walk home to somebody's flat, somewhere on the north-east side of town. Shared tenement flats with bikes in the hall, stacks of dirty dishes in the sink, rows of empty bottles around the bin and nearly always, at the weekend, friends of friends staying over.

I walked up the hill to George Street and hailed a cab to take me across the city and home to Andrew. I was going in a completely opposite direction to my friends. I was heading south-west, to quiet, tree-lined streets where large houses stood in private gardens behind high hedges.

'No two casks are the same. Even consecutively numbered casks filled with whisky from the same still-run, can produce utterly different whiskies, one fully mature, the other nowhere like it. It is important to understand that maturation is not a simple linear development'

Malt Whisky, Charles MacLean

Chapter Four

'I am forty-five today!' called David, waving from the steps of his house. It was his party and he was celebrating. 'Come in, come in!'

'Happy birthday,' I said, kissing him.

Andrew and his big brother greeted each other with fond insults and pats on the back. 'Happy birthday, you old git.'

'Thanks, little bugger.'

David lived with Jane and their two children and pets in a big old house overlooking the sea at Portobello. ('Welcome to Edinburgh's Seaside,' Andrew would say when we drove past the sign. 'It's so bracing!') Together they made a very happy family of Mum, Dad, son and daughter. They had an old, slow labrador called Sandy and a fast-moving black cat called Sootie and two goldfish called Terminator I and Terminator II.

David and Jane had been together for fifteen years but had never bothered getting married. David kept asking Jane to marry him but Jane always said no. I had asked her why once and she had said she just didn't want to get married. She didn't elaborate and so I didn't press the subject.

My nephew, Tom, rushed past me. 'Hello, Aunty Em,' he called. He was pursued by three much smaller boys with improvised banana guns. Ah yes, the IVF miracle triplets from next door. Their parents would also be here – and there they were, refilling pint glasses from a bottle of gin.

I started trying to name the faces I recognised. Alex, Duncan, Iris, Ella – or was it Ellen? Martin, John, Annie.

When David and Andrew were in their twenties, they shared a flat on Broughton Place and many of the friends at David's party had once been flatmates. They had probably all been at his twenty-first birthday party too. I followed the sound of voices and music. In the living room, a group of people were standing around the television, faces rapt with nostalgia. They were watching a video of children's TV programmes from the 1970s. This, I learned, was a gift that David had been particularly delighted to receive. 'How are you, Emily?' said someone who I think was called Rob. 'Still putting up with Andrew? Is he here?'

'Yes, but I seem to have lost him somewhere on my way in.'

'Ah, that's a shame. Andrew always liked *The Clangers*. He was a big fan.'

'*The Clangers*?'

'Hey, Damian,' Rob said, tapping someone on the shoulder, 'leave off watching the television and come and meet Emily. Remember I told you about Emily? Andrew's much-too-young-and-beautiful wife.'

'Hello,' I said, embarrassed.

'At last!' exclaimed Damian. 'I've heard so much about you.'

'Nothing bad, I hope.'

'No, it was all sensationally good.'

'Enjoying the video?' I asked.

'Loving it. Haven't seen *The Clangers* for years.'

On the screen, three pink creatures that looked like knitted shrimps were walking across a lunar landscape escorted by a metal chicken.

'This sort of thing wasn't on television when I was little.'

'What?' said Damian. 'No Clangers?'

And immediately both men started whistling and hooting at each other in what I knew was Clanger language. Someone else joined in.

'Hey! John!' Whistle, whistle, hoot, hoot.

'What about the soup dragon?' said John. 'Do you remember the soup dragon? Look Emily,' he pointed at the screen, 'the Clangers are going down the soup mine to visit the soup dragon.'

Change of tone. Lots of parping, farting noises, like a tuba underwater. There then followed a classic soup dragon/ Clanger exchange, whistle-parp–hoot, the kind of thing I'd heard before at forty-something parties.

'No one my age saw *The Clangers* on television,' I said. 'When I was little, I used to watch *Bagpuss*.'

'Wasn't he a pink furry cat or something?' asked Damian.

'It was my favourite programme. Bagpuss belonged to a little girl who had the same name as me.' And I recited: '"He was just a saggy old cloth cat, but Emily loved him."'

'Aah, bless!' They both grinned.

'I think I'd better go and see what's happened to Andrew.'

'See, Damian?' said John. 'He was old and saggy, but Emily loved him.'

I escaped to the hallway, where Andrew seemed to have got stuck in a corner. I could see the outline of a tall, blonde woman standing next to him. They were talking. I saw him smile and mouth her name. 'Kate,' he said. 'Kate, it's been good to see you.'

What was she doing here? She never came to anything where there was the slightest chance she might meet us. I watched the two of them together. Another nod from Andrew, a warmer smile. Why was he being so nice to her? I felt a pang of jealousy. And then Kate turned to talk to someone else. The space in the hallway opened up and immediately Andrew saw me standing there, watching.

He came straight across, took my hand and we went out into the garden. I grabbed his coat on the way and put it on. Outside, the night air made me shiver. 'Did you know she was coming?' I asked.

'Yes, David told me he'd invited her.'

'Why didn't you tell me?'

'Because you wouldn't have come and I really wanted you to come and so did David, and it's his party.' Andrew was speaking rapidly as we walked down the garden path. There was no one else about. 'Emily, this is the first time Kate has turned up to anything where she knew she would meet us. You don't need to feel awkward about Kate being here, you really don't. Kate is a part of this circle of old friends. She once went out with David, too, you know.'

'Did she? She gets about, doesn't she?'

'It was twenty years ago.'

'So what did she say to you? What were you saying to her?'

'Just hello.'

'That's all?'

'Yes, that's all.'

'It seemed to take a long time.'

'It was all just on the general theme of hello.'

I buttoned up the heavy overcoat. It reached to my ankles. 'I wish she wasn't here. I know it's all kind of water under the bridge now, but—'

'You look swamped by that coat,' he said suddenly, and he hugged me. 'Emily, you know I love you. You know I'd do anything for you. Let's not allow five minutes' chat with Kate to spoil the evening. I had to meet her again some time. You'll have to say hello to her tonight too.'

'Do I really? Do I have to? I suppose I do.' Looking past Andrew's shoulder, I saw Kate's face in the window behind him. Was she watching us? 'Let's not talk about her right now.'

'Fine by me.'

At that moment David's cat walked down the path towards us, tail in the air. I stroked her and she started to purr. 'Can we get a cat? I've always wanted a cat. Could I have a cat for my birthday? You and David always had pets when you were growing up; I never did.'

'You told me you once had one of those computer game pet things.'

'A Tamogotchi? That doesn't count.'

'Didn't you neglect it or kill it or something?'

'They all die eventually.'

'See – you learned that profound pet-care lesson from technology alone. I had to suffer the trauma of finding a stiff little hamster on the floor of its cage. I still get emotional when I think of Hepzibah.'

'I never had anything.'

'Ah, poor Emily, you were a deprived child, weren't you? Doomed to a life of hotels, planes and computer games. Are you really sure you want a cat?'

'Yes, I want a ginger kitten. You've just said you would do anything for me. I'm prepared to brave Kate for you.'

He sighed and reached for his cigarettes before remembering that he didn't smoke any more. He had been encouraged to quit the previous Sunday when he read in the *Observer* that smoking was responsible for impotence in 120,000 men in the UK aged between thirty and forty-nine. 'I am not a smoker,' he repeated to himself, hands thrust into his pockets. 'I am not a smoker. I do not want to smoke.'

'Do you think the hypnosis is helping?'

He stopped. 'You know what?' he said suddenly, 'I do want to smoke.'

'Are you sure?'

'Yes,' he said, with feeling. 'I really, really want a cigarette.'

'Do you want one or need one?'

'Both.'

'You told me that needing one is what you hated about being a smoker. You said you were sick of needing to smoke.'

'But I enjoyed it,' he said pitifully. 'I loved smoking.'

'If you still want one in twenty minutes' time, have one.'

'All right,' he said through gritted teeth.

I took his hand. 'You know how Flora borrowed this coat when she came over last week? I showed her round the garden, remember? Well, she said that while she was wearing it, she couldn't help but notice your personal aroma.'

'What?' He looked appalled.

'Don't worry. She said it was very nice – very attractive in a masculine sort of way. Don't look like that, Andrew. She's a professional nose. Scent is her job. She was wearing your coat and she couldn't help herself. She said there was still faint tobacco in the background, but it was only a residual scent clinging to the fibres in the coat. She said the key note was a subtle, warm, expensive amber, vaguely musky with a trace of heather honey and some engine oil. There was minty chocolate too, but that was probably just the wrapper in your pocket. She said the overall combination of aromas was undeniably you and it was the first time she had detected your personal scent without the dominating influence of cheap tobacco.'

'It was never particularly cheap.'

'Flora says only expensive cigars have good tobacco – which is true when you think of the difference in smell, isn't it? She also found a ten-pound note in the inside pocket and I told her to use it for a taxi home because you had opened her housewarming present and weren't in a fit state to give her a lift, as promised.'

'Worth it,' he nodded. 'Fantastic single malt. Engine oil.' He shook his head. 'I don't smell of engine oil.'

'It's not real engine oil. It's actually a chemical compound in a number of expensive colognes aimed at the forty-something male market.'

'You're kidding?'

'No. It's very faint. I can pick it up myself on you since she drew my attention to it. Flora says I am a natural good nose, and as far as personal aroma goes, I think she's right about you.'

'Do you?'

'Yes, I'd say so. I'm biased, of course, but Flora isn't. She's a professional. She trained for years.'

He folded his arms. 'Well, I'll take Flora's approval as a compliment.'

'You smell nice, Andrew.'

'I'm starving,' he said suddenly. 'Come on, Emily, let's eat.'

Distraction is what you need for cravings.

We went into the kitchen and Kate was still there. Smart, elegant, super-cool Kate, leaning nonchalantly against the table, chatting to Jane. 'Come on,' said Andrew, taking my hand.

'Emily, there you are!' said Jane brightly, as if she had been looking for me for hours. 'Can I get you both a drink?'

'Hello, Emily,' said Kate. She gave me a long, cool, appraising look. 'How are you?'

'Fine, thanks. How are you?' I was surprised to hear my voice sounding reasonably normal.

'Very well. In good form.'

It occurred to me that these were the first words that Kate and I had exchanged since I stole her fiancé and married him myself. Kate was obviously thinking the same thing. 'I think

61

the last thing I said to you was: "Have a lovely time in New Zealand."'

'Um, yes.'

'But you never went.'

'Er, no.'

I had dreaded this meeting with Kate and, now it was happening, I felt a bit queasy. Andrew stepped in. 'Emily hopes she might still get to New Zealand one day.'

'But only if we go together,' I said quickly.

'I thought Andrew was too old and wrinkly to be allowed in the country,' said Kate. 'Don't you have to be under thirty or something?'

'It would be fine now he's married to me. He'd pass. I'd look after him.'

'Hear that, Andrew? Emily is willing to support you in your old age.'

'Emily is doing some very innovative work in whisky at the moment,' said Jane, keen to steer the conversation somewhere else.

'Yes,' I said, making more of an effort. 'Flora and I are going to show the whisky trade how to talk to girls.'

Kate raised her eyebrows. 'I thought whisky was for old men, or perhaps middle-aged men. Boring old fart golfers and so on.'

'That's because it's marketed to them,' I told her, feeling on surer ground. 'It's traditional, but ask yourself this: Why should we marketing people only address ourselves to middle-aged, boring old fart golfers?'

'I thought they were just your type,' said Kate. 'You've always been very nice to Andrew.'

I tried to think of a light, tension-relieving reply, but all I could manage was: 'Well, Andrew has always been very nice to me.' I remembered how Kate had gossiped about us at the book club she went to. It hurt that she had talked about us like that.

'Drink?' asked Jane, bearing down on us with a bottle.

'Have you got any of that Rosebank left?' I asked.

'You'll be lucky.' She checked the supplies on the table and found some for me. 'You are lucky,' she said, pouring out the last of the bottle.

'Very good with ice,' I said, reaching for the freezer door. I saw Andrew wince at the thought. 'But it is, Andrew,' I told him as I fumbled with the ice tray. It was sticking to my fingers.

'Use a tea towel,' said Jane, handing me one.

'Emily's got a few radical ideas about whisky, haven't you, Emily?' said Andrew.

'Really?' said Kate. 'So it's all right to put ice in your whisky, is it?'

'You can if you want,' I said confidently. 'You can do what-ever you like. You don't have to be all fuddy-duddy and old-fashioned about it.'

'You're having a bit of trouble with that ice tray, though, aren't you?'

'Let me have a go,' said Jane.

'I can manage.'

'Just whack it hard, in the sink.'

'I've nearly got it. It's okay, I can do it.'

'Let me have a go, Emily.'

'No, I've nearly got it; look, it's coming.'

'You're both useless,' said Kate, 'Give it to me.'

She seized the ice tray and slammed it hard on the edge of the sink. Crack! Jane and I both jumped. Ice cubes shattered into the stainless steel.

'There,' said Kate calmly. 'All sorted.'

Andrew folded his arms and watched, silently, as Kate picked up a few cubes and dropped them in my glass. 'Will that do?' she asked.

'Perfect.' I sipped my whisky, cool in the mouth and warm-ing going down. 'If you ever want a bar job, just give me a ring.'

'No ice for me, thanks,' said Andrew.

'Oh, go on,' said Kate. 'You heard what Emily said. Don't be an old fuddy-duddy.'

'Can't help it.'

'You'll have to try harder to keep up, Andrew, or Emily will dump you for a younger model.'

'Kate!' shouted a voice. 'Beautiful Kate!' It was David, the birthday boy, making his way happily towards us. He slapped Andrew on the back, squeezed my shoulders and then threw his arms around Kate, kissing her on both cheeks. 'Thank you,' he said, passionately. 'Thank you from the bottom of my heart for my *Clangers* video.'

'Time for the birthday cake,' said Jane, bustling between us. 'Andrew, would you go and help Tom carry it in? Emily, can you get some plates?'

More people joined us in the kitchen. The lights were turned off and the cake brought in, ablaze with forty-five candles. We all sang 'Happy Birthday'. David blew the candles out and made a wish that Jane would marry him. The miracle triplets instantly screamed for the candles to be lit again, and again, and again. Their parents meekly complied, singing 'Happy Birthday' three more times. The little boys blew spit all over the icing and then everyone got a slice.

The party wore on. I watched Kate talk and laugh with her old friends, moving easily in the crowd, smiling and relaxed. Andrew was sometimes with her again, as part of a little group. I tried to join in but there were too many old stories and in-jokes for me to really follow the conversation. Andrew often seemed to be at the centre of these stories.

Damian, slurring his words by now, was pressing him about something: 'Andrew, shuurrely you're not still convinced Megan did it on purpose?' Everyone started to laugh. I didn't have the faintest idea what they were talking about.

'I think it was deliberate,' Andrew said. 'She meant it to happen.'

'No way,' said someone else.

'Megan Mackenzie was always going to cause me a problem.'

Laughter. 'I don't have any regrets about that night,' said Andrew. More laughter. 'I have absolutely no regrets whatsoever.'

'Still, Megan's all right about it now, isn't she?'

'I think there comes a time when you have to let bygones be bygones.'

'Yes, I would agree with that,' said Kate quietly. 'Just so long as there has been a sincere attempt to make amends. Of course,' she added, speaking up, 'it would have to be a sustained attempt to make amends, not just a flirtation with the idea.' She smiled at Andrew and then walked away to chat to someone else.

'Do you remember at our old flat,' said David, getting his brother's attention, 'the one in Broughton Place – you used to have that absurdly gadgety hi-fi and it was programmed to wake you up with different music for each day of the week?'

'I've still got that. On Mondays it's usually something about resignation and on Fridays it might be an up-tempo kind of jazz.'

Jane arrived. 'I'll never forget that spiral staircase in your penthouse apartment,' she said suddenly. Lethal, it was, completely open at the sides, like a corkscrew going through the floor. Not a child-friendly environment at all, that flat. Even if you were just walking past the staircase it could poke you in the eye.'

'Do you remember that girl whose skirt got caught on the top step and it just lifted, very slowly, as she came down?'

'Oh God, yes!' laughed Jane. 'That was Laura, wasn't it?'

'No, it was Megan again.'

'Megan Mackenzie.'

'No, it wasn't. She was blonde.'

'Incredibly long legs.'

'It was . . . it was . . . '

The sudden guilty looks told me they had all remembered it was Kate. 'It wasn't me, anyway,' I smiled.

'Emily!' called someone from the door. 'You should see the bonfire, it's great.'

'Right!' I said, relieved to have an excuse to get out of the room.

'Here's some sparklers,' Jane said, pressing them into my hand. 'And some matches. Go and light them on the beach. Remember to keep the matches away from your whisky.'

I turned to Andrew. 'Are you coming too?'

'I'll be right out. Won't be a minute.'

Halfway down the garden, I turned to see him and Kate outlined in the kitchen window alone together now. He was trying to explain something to her. I recognised the hand movements: 'Look,' he was saying, 'it's like this.' Kate had her arms folded, head on one side: 'Oh really? Convince me.'

I waited for him to come out and join me but Kate was doing the talking now. She had stretched out an open hand to him and he was listening and thinking about whatever it was she was saying. I saw him look down at the floor and push his hand through his hair; something was bothering him.

I couldn't face it, standing there in the garden, watching my husband absorbed in conversation with this tall blonde woman he used to love. I turned away and walked out the garden gate, across the promenade and on to the beach. There was Damian and the others, faces glowing around the blaze of driftwood. They were all laughing about something, talking about the things they used to get up to when they were my age, happily dropping clangers. I wandered a little further down the beach. Looking out towards the cold North Sea and the dark horizon, I held my sparkler out against the blackness and watched it burn.

Eventually Andrew joined his old friends outside and I waved a sparkler at him. He didn't realise who it was at first, but then he started walking rapidly down the beach towards me. 'What are you doing standing here all by yourself?' he asked. 'Here, give me one of those,' and he started writing my name in sparkling letters, over and over again. EmilyEmilyEmily, he wrote. IloveEmily.

When we turned around the people by the bonfire were calling our names. They all pointed at Damian, who was waving handfuls of sparklers. 'Emily, I love you!' he cried, going down on one knee. 'Emily, leave him for me! I'm old and saggy! Emily, baby, we could be so good together!'

We got back inside to find David and Jane sitting cosily on the sofa, side by side in front of the television, eating a Chinese takeaway, a picture of domestic companionship.

Andrew and I got home at about two a.m. When we were getting ready for bed, I asked him if he knew why David and Jane had never married.

'It's against Jane's principles.'

'Has she got parents with multiple divorces?'

'No, she just doesn't want to marry David. They did once get engaged, years ago, but Jane changed her mind.'

'Was he really upset about it?'

'Yes and no. He was upset they weren't going to get married when she had already said yes, but he understood she had her reasons and so he came to terms with it because that was what was best for Jane. He decided that, under the circumstances, he should put her interests first.'

'What circumstances?'

'Oh, David had a few issues going on back then.' Andrew was quiet for a moment, then he added, 'When we met, I wasn't very good at putting your interests first, was I?'

'What do you mean?'

'Emily, do you ever regret not going to New Zealand?'

This was out of the blue. He had never asked me that question before. 'Of course I don't regret it. Don't be silly.'

'But do you ever find yourself thinking that you're stuck with a boring, middle-aged man?'

'No.'

'Your life changed so much when we got married. You don't see your friends nearly as often as you used to. Do you ever feel left out, Emily? Do you have any regrets? Tonight, I was thinking about a few things and I was . . . concerned about it.'

'No,' I said again, dismayed that he was talking to me like this. 'Andrew,' I told him, firmly, 'I don't want to hear anything like that from you again.' And I kissed him to stop him speaking.

I did think about what he had said, though. I thought about it, lying awake, listening to wind blowing harder through the trees and the sash windows starting to rattle. Andrew slept on, oblivious. I shuffled a little closer to him. He stirred slightly. Then the window made a loud bang and I jumped. Another loud rattle and a bigger bang. He groaned and got out of bed, making his way over to the window to stuff something in the gap. It didn't work. He put the light on, found some socks, wedged them in the window frame and climbed back into bed. 'Come here,' he said.

'Nooo! You're freezing!'

'Warm me up, then.'

'Oh, that's cold! That's cold!'

We huddled together. 'I'm going to put the light off now,' he said, giving me the required warning. I shut my eyes tight and hid under the quilt, but there was no click of the light switch. I peered out to see him watching me. 'Emily,' he said, slowly, 'why are you scared of the dark?'

'I don't know. It's a very common fear. I imagine things.'

'What do you imagine?'

'I don't know. I'm not that bad, really. You can put the light off now.'

The darkness came. We lay down together, quiet and close.

'There,' he whispered, 'it's dark, but everything's okay, isn't it?'

'Yes,' I whispered back. 'But do you know why people always whisper in the dark?'

'Why?'

'Because deep down we know that something could be out there. That's why we whisper. We do it because it's safer.'

'No, we do it because it's intimate.'

'No, it's thousands and thousands of years of human experience. We whisper in the dark because we might be heard by something that could come and get us.'

'Emily, if I whisper to you in the dark it's not because there's something hiding in the wardrobe.' We lay there for a while, listening to the eerie noise of the wind outside, and then eventually he said, 'Do you think you could walk through this house, alone, at night?'

'No.'

'Could you do it if I was with you?'

'Yes.'

'Good.'

We whispered good night and kissed and he turned away from me to sleep. I peered out from under the covers and listened to his breathing deepen and slow. I did two and a half quick breaths to every one of his slow ones. I closed my eyes, curled around him and in his sleep he sighed a little.

taken from Flora's notes

The Second Whisky:
MODERN SPEYSIDE
getting a taste for it

Some notable marketing developments on Speyside

Glenfiddich
led the way in market development for single malt whisky
(useful triangular bottle means it won't roll out of bed)

Cragganmore
rare as a single malt until the late 1980s
when it was selected for promotion as one of the Classic Six Malts
that highly successful marketing device
which introduced many people to single malts

Cardhu
(formerly Cardow)
owned by Diageo, the twelve-year-old is
one of the world's bestselling single malts
so successful, there is not enough of it to satisfy demand

'First impressions suggest a whisky that is cool and sophisticated, but the nose reveals all the warmth of cinnamon and spice. A friendly character, not at all prickly for all its robust strength. With water, there is a hint of polish on the nose and the scent of vanilla and sugar. One Tasting Panel member suggested pouring some over ice cream – and why should she not?'

Cask No. 64·6   *A Friendly Character*
Alcohol: 60.6%   Proof: 106.6°   Outturn: 252 bottles

The Society Bottlings, Winter 2000

Chapter Five

My in-house training at the Whisky Society was coming along well. I could now tell the difference between an ex-bourbon and an ex-sherry single cask malt whisky. I knew a highland from a lowland (most of the time). I knew an Islay from a Jura. I could tell the difference with my eyes shut. I could tell the difference even without tasting it. This, according to Flora, was nothing. Any fool with a good nose could do it. I was to develop my nosing skills still further.

'Come here, Emily,' she said. 'Follow me.' We went into the stationery cupboard, turned the light off and she made me sample whiskies in the dark. 'This is good practice for the spooky tasting,' said Flora.

'Can we put the light on yet?'

'Only if you can identify smoke on the nose. Is this a peated malt or not?'

'Yes.'

'You pass.'

She put the light on. 'See?' she said. 'You can do it. You're not scared of the dark, Emily. You'll be fine at the spooky tasting today. I told Jack we'd meet him on Niddry Street at three o'clock.'

'Is he really going to come?'

'Yes, he rang specially to make sure we were both still doing it. He asked if you would bring along the design you did for the new bottle label. He's genuinely interested in the pink project, Emily. He even persuaded me that we could go for your wildcat idea, and he liked the blue bottle too.'

At my desk, Flora picked up the design that had now been approved by Kitty Gillespie. 'This bottle is completely different to any other whisky bottle out there.'

We had taken inspiration not from whisky but from mineral water. Half a dozen of the mineral water bottles I had found in the supermarket were pear-shaped and softly curving. We opted for blue glass and the words Wild Cat Pink Whisky. Dolores thought the word Pink should be actually in pink. Wild Cat would be written above it in gold and Whisky underneath. There would be a sleek, sinewy Scottish wildcat stalking round the base of the bottle.

My favourite of the bottles from Sainsbury's had been an unpronounceable Welsh mineral water in beautiful blue glass. Unpronounceable names were fairly standard in the whisky trade and didn't seem to do any harm to sales. Bruichladdich, for example, was a wonderful single malt. They also did a quarter-size bottle which they called their 'wee laddie' and which sold phenomenally well. We decided we would put all of our pink whisky into pear-shaped, blue glass, quarter bottles.

This would be horrendously expensive but Kitty wanted to

do it. Her reasons for pursuing the venture were growing more dramatic and exciting all the time. We were now doing it 'for Art's sake' since the budget could not possibly justify the expense.

'For Art's sake,' proclaimed Kitty across the noise of the telephones in the office, 'and in tribute to Elizabeth Cumming.'

Time to take a short break from the office. Time to go downstairs and sit in a corner of the drawing room bar with a newspaper and a cup of coffee. It was quiet; only a few people would be there at this time of the day. In the opposite corner I could see a man and a woman sitting together, also drinking coffee, two friends who were now meeting up more and more often.

She was a mousy-looking woman with soft brown eyes who always wore a navy blue suit. Maybe it was some kind of uniform or maybe she was just a very uniform dresser. He was tall and thin and always wore a charcoal grey suit with a contrasting, very bright tie, as if he wanted to let the world know he wasn't as sombre as his suit. The couple smiled and talked earnestly together. I knew they had met for the first time, in this very room, two months ago. He had arrived with his wife and she had arrived with her husband, and because they had all arrived late and it was very busy, they had decided to share a table. They had all since returned, she with her husband and he with his wife. But this new couple had also returned several times, a hybrid from the original foursome.

It was obvious that they were attracted to each other, but I didn't think their attraction had moved beyond the scope of friendship. Not quite yet. For two months now they had been careful not to sit too close, careful to observe the personal space between them. However, with each meeting they were more attentive of each other, more absorbed and intrigued. At what point does friendship become an affair? I knew I had never been 'just good friends' with Andrew. In the time it had

75

taken the coffee-drinking couple to move their chairs two inches closer together, Andrew and I had gone from flirtation to marriage. I went back to my newspaper but when I looked up again I knew instantly that something important had happened. They were sitting closer than friendship. The space between them had disappeared completely. They were leaning into each other, touching. He whispered something and then she raised her face to his and smiled.

At three o'clock, Flora and I were unloading the car on Niddry Street. It didn't seem at all spooky yet, but I was nervous because I knew where we were going. Subterranean Edinburgh, beneath the Royal Mile, where centuries ago people had actually lived in a labyrinth of dark, stinking tunnels.

Nowadays, only ghost tour parties and Festival Fringe goers and the occasional witches' coven ever spent any length of time in these ghoulishly dank places.

At least we had the whisky to keep our spirits up. And I also had an emergency spare torch in my coat pocket, just in case.

'Still no sign of Jack,' said Flora. 'He's always late. We had better start moving.' She fed the parking meter and we stacked our whisky and water and nosing glasses at the broad, black door that marked the entrance to this, the most commonly visited part of the underground city. People sitting in the hotel bar opposite would be used to the sight of terrified tourists screaming when a man in a skeleton outfit leaped out at them on this part of the tour. The skeletons and ghosts were a normal occurrence after dark. They were known locally as 'jumpers oot'. Even when you weren't part of an official tour, they could still terrify you by 'jumping oot' for free, as you parked your car or visited the cashpoint. This part of Edinburgh always made me uneasy. During the recent renovation of the tea shop at St Giles Cathedral they had discovered a mass grave for victims of the plague. That sort of thing just didn't seem to faze Flora who went there regularly for tea and scones.

'You'll be fine,' said Flora again. 'Just concentrate on the job. Sort out the whiskies and put them in the right order. We'll just take one case since it's only a party of ten.'

We had brought with us five different whiskies: a dry lowland; a rather floral Speyside; a thirty-year-old sherried Speyside; a lightly smoky highland and a powerful Islay malt.

'Let's go,' said Flora.

When we turned around, there was Jack in the doorway, not as dishevelled as the last time I'd seen him but still apparently very relaxed about life. Seeing him outside in the cold winter light reinforced the fact that he looked like he'd spent time somewhere warm and sunny. He had the kind of skin that freckles in the sun. If he stayed in Edinburgh all the time, his face would have been pallid and his hair would have stayed light brown instead of going a few shades blonder. He wore a faded blue shirt, jeans, trainers. Slim, but broad shoulders. Perhaps, I told myself, he was only good-looking in a holidayed, suntanned sort of way. It was easy to find that attractive in a man.

I suddenly felt very pale and dowdy in my work clothes. My skirt was straight, black, neat and tidy and my white blouse was safe enough to be acceptable as part of a school uniform.

'About time,' grumbled Flora, dumping a case of whisky in his arms and walking past him.

He smiled at me. 'Hello, Emily,' he said. 'Ready to be scared?'

As we carried our boxes along the first corridor (which looked like a perfectly normal hall in a normal house) Flora started talking about how we would have to submit our Wild Cat plans for approval by the Whisky Conservative Marketing Board.

'Tricky one,' said Jack. 'You can't sell anything without it getting past them.'

'I know the chairman,' said Flora. 'I'm always nice to him; you'd think he might do us a favour and be nice back.'

Jack laughed and his laughter rang eerily as we went further underground. The tiled floor gave way to packed earth and the corridor got narrower. The electricity power cables came to an end and we stopped to get our torches out. The air was stale, then damp, then sourly dank.

'Who did you say is coming to this whisky tasting?'

'They're already in there. We're their reward for being brave at the end of their tour. We're meeting them in the Final Chamber.'

'I can't hear anybody.'

'It's a bit further yet. Come on, Emily. No flagging.' Flora kept up a running commentary on how she was going to be even nicer than usual to Malcolm McLeod, the chairman of the Whisky Conservative Marketing Board, and how she had listened to him droning on for hours about fishing and golf and his hernia operation and he really owed her a favour. Her loud, bossy voice echoed around the tunnels and for once I was grateful for it. 'This way,' said Flora. 'Keep up. Don't fall behind, Emily.'

'Jack, I don't want to be at the back.'

'Okay,' he said. 'I'll go at the back – let them pick me off first.'

'This way,' called Flora, 'and hurry up, we're already late.'

'We're not late as well, are we?'

'Stop whingeing, Emily.'

Flora made a frightening place seem less intimidating, but we walked on and on for what felt like too long and I began to feel more and more uncomfortable. She stopped. 'What does it say near that arrow on the wall?'

'Wicca this way,' I read. 'It's the Edinburgh Witches' Coven.'

'Ssh!' said Jack. 'I can hear people.' We stood very still. 'Shine your torch over there, Emily.'

From out of the darkness, a figure approached us wearing a long black cloak. It was a woman and her face was chalky white. She didn't smile when I shone my torch into her red-rimmed, ghastly eyes; she just carried on moving towards us, her cloak flowing out around her. The beam of light started to shake and Jack put his hand over mine. 'Hold it still, Emily.'

'I've been looking for you,' the woman said. 'You're late.'

'Wendy, where the hell is the Final Chamber?' demanded Flora.

'Wendy?'

'This is Wendy, the rep,' said Flora. 'You've talked to her loads of times on the phone.'

'We always dress up for this bit,' said Wendy. 'Follow me.'

A few more twists and turns in the dark and the sound of voices got louder. Frightened, giggly, nervous voices. 'This is it,' said Wendy. 'The Final Chamber. Put your boxes down here, turn your torches off, hold hands and follow me.' It was deeply, thickly, pitch black. I couldn't see Flora in front of me, or Jack behind me. I began to feel panic rising slowly from the pit of my stomach into my throat.

'Just stand here,' whispered Wendy, 'while the witch finishes explaining about the plague.' Somewhere in the blackness a voice was talking to the tour party in low, dramatically creepy tones. I clutched Flora's hand and Jack's too. The witch moaned and cried out, 'Feel the agony in here! The terror!'

'Let's get a bit nearer,' said Flora.

'No, Flora, don't let go of my hand. Jack, keep beside me.'

'Wendy, how do we know when it's our turn?' whispered Flora.

'After she's told them how there was a fire and everyone got burned alive.'

'Right.'

'What is it you're going to give them? Are you telling them about the ghosts?'

'No,' said Jack. 'We're doing the whisky tasting.'

'You haven't brought the whisky down here, have you?'

'Why do you think we were staggering under the weight of those boxes?'

'I thought they were props or something. Sorry, but we don't do alcohol or naked flames down here. We don't have insurance. You'll have to take that whisky out of here immediately.'

There was a loud, long, hissing 'Sssh!' from the witch somewhere in the darkness. I made a sort of whimpering noise. Jack stood closer. I could feel his breath on the back of my neck. 'Emileee,' he whispered.

'What?' I squeaked.

'Emileee . . . '

'What?'

'Boo!'

His wicked laughter broke into the witch's performance and echoed spectacularly around the chamber.

'I want to go home,' I gasped, panic-stricken. 'I've had enough. I have to leave. I have to go now.'

'Are you claustrophobic?' asked Wendy.

'I've got to go. I've got to go.'

'I should have known,' said Flora, exasperated. 'What's she like? Come on, then.'

'I'll take you to the Wicca intersection,' said Wendy, 'and you can find your way out from there. There's a red line on the ceiling, just follow that.'

I was already scrambling to get out. Jack and Flora almost had to break into a run to keep up with me.

Outside, I leaned against the car, gulping the air and feeling my heart beating fast and loud in my chest.

'It's all right, Emily,' said Flora, putting her hand on my shoulder. 'It's all right. Try to get a grip?'

Slowly, I got a grip. Jack poured me a drink. 'It's not pink, is that okay?'

'That's absolutely fine.'

'Are you feeling better now?'

'Feeling much better.'

'I'll have to sort something out with Wendy,' said Flora. 'She said I could maybe do the tasting in the hotel across the road – that's where they're all staying, apparently. If only you had a different kind of phobia, Emily. I can't take you anywhere in Edinburgh.'

'What's it like working for Flora?' asked Jack. 'Does she drive you mad and boss you about?'

'Since we were both about six years old.'

'Does she make you keep your desk tidy?'

'I don't have to,' interrupted Flora. 'Emily's desk is as tidy as a Zen rock garden. Emily's very organised and so is her house.'

Between them, Jack and Flora started chatting to me about ordinary things, taking my mind off the panic attack, calming me down.

'Emily has a proper house with furniture in it and everything. I go there when I want to pretend I'm living happily ever after in domestic bliss. Emily even has an Aga.'

'Very exciting,' said Jack.

'It was there when she and Andrew moved in. It can be very slow.'

'Sometimes it's like cooking over a light bulb,' I said.

'The Aga is purely ornamental, isn't it? She doesn't actually know how to use it. Jack, if Emily ever asks you round for dinner, you'll probably find she has to send out for a takeaway before dinner is ready.'

'That's only happened once.'

'And the takeaway will arrive and you will eat it before dinner is ready.'

'I'm not very qualified on the domestic front,' I explained.

'You're just winging it, are you?' said Jack, smiling at me.

'Yes,' I laughed. 'I suppose you could say that.'

'Come on,' said Flora, looking at her watch. 'We've got ten minutes till they come out. Let's take the stuff over to the hotel. I'll do the tasting. Jack, could you make sure Emily gets safely back to Charlotte Square? Take a cab.'

'I'm fine now, honestly.'

We carried the boxes across to the hotel. Standing in the bright, modern lobby made me feel much better after the dungeons I had just experienced.

'Emily, did you know Jack has just come from New Zealand? California was just a short stopover on the way home.'

'Oh, really? How long were you in New Zealand?'

'Three months.' He had come from summer to winter. 'In New Zealand,' he said, 'the summer is just starting.'

'Yes,' I said, remembering it. 'Two years ago, Flora and I were in Dunedin in the South Island. It was just beautiful there.' And quickly, I was asking him all sorts of questions. Did you go to such and such a place? Did you see this? Did you do that?

'Emily travelled a lot from being very small, didn't you, Emily? Her mother was a singer and she was always touring.'

I wanted to ask Flora to be quiet, to let me tell Jack myself, but the trouble with Flora was that she was always quicker off the mark. She sprinted through conversations while I was just warming up. This meant that I usually let her do the talking, even when the question was addressed to me, even when it was about me. It would take an enormous amount of effort to get Flora to slow down, to pause, to be patient, to allow me to say things too. I had tried to tell her how I felt about this but she always got offended and so I had given up.

'So, tell me, Emily,' said Jack, pointedly, 'did you travel around with your mum?'

'Yes, but we mostly stayed in Edinburgh which is how I met Flora and—'

'We lived next door to each other.'

'But then I went to boarding school.'

'She was posh when she came back. You should have heard the accent.'

'I had to adapt to survive.'

'She put on a jolly good show!'

'It wasn't Malory Towers, Flora.'

'And you had a term at an English school in Hong Kong.'

'That was a fluke.'

'And you had a term at a stage school in London.'

'I never wanted to go on the stage. I had stage fright. I only ever wanted to be in the audience.'

And at that point, Flora got a call on her mobile from Wendy. 'I've gotta go,' she told us. 'See you later. Look after her, Jack.'

We found a taxi near the Tron. Sitting beside him, I found myself looking at Jack's face, noticing the colour of his eyes and the laughter lines around his mouth. The other thing about sitting very close to Jack was that I noticed . . . well, obviously I had spent too much time listening to Flora talking about the primitive attraction of the right kind of scent, but I noticed that sitting close to him was very pleasant. That was all. There was something attractive there, something intangible.

It seemed too short a taxi ride. What happened to all the traffic? Very quickly, we were standing on Charlotte Square. Jack and I looked at each other in the clear northern light. 'How are you feeling now, Emily?'

'Better, much better. Thanks. Are you coming inside?'

'You like it here, don't you?' he asked as we walked up the steps. Dolores, on the phone, waved hello to us as we went past and on up the wide spiral staircase. 'It seems like an interesting place to work,' he said. 'Don't let Flora boss you around.'

83

'She only gives that impression.'

He looked at me and smiled. 'I'm sure you're more than a match.'

'Me? I just do what I'm told. Do you not always do what you're told?'

'Tell me what to do,' he teased. 'Find out. By the way, Emily, did you know you stick your little finger in the air when you're drinking? Did they teach you that at your posh school?'

'Day one. They inspect your gym kit and break your little finger.' I showed him my hand. 'See, I can't bend it properly. Lacrosse,' I added. 'Diagonal fracture.'

'I took part in a game of ice lacrosse in Canada once.'

'Ice lacrosse! What a terrifying idea.'

'Yes, I still bear the scars.'

'Where?' I asked, interested.

'They're more mental than physical.'

We looked at each other and laughed.

'When it was my sister Polly's turn to go to boarding school, she did half a term and refused to go back. She said it was a highly privileged orphanage for the abandoned children of rich, dysfunctional families. She goes to the local *colegio* in Marbella now. She's always zipping around on the back of mopeds and playing frisbee on the beach. She does her homework lying by the pool with her headphones on, smoking Marlboro lights. She thinks I'm really boring.'

'You're not boring.'

'I should maybe get out more.'

'I tell you what, Emily, some of us are going to see a film this Saturday,' he said. 'Midnight movie at the Cameo. Why don't you come too?'

'I don't want to go if it's anything violent or upsetting.' He laughed out loud and I cringed at how pathetic I sounded. 'I can't cope with anything more than a fifteen certificate. And fifteens quite often scare me.'

84

He grinned. 'There's one violent, upsetting scene with the death of Bambi's mother, but I still think you should come.'

'You're going to see *Bambi*?'

'Yeah. Why not? Flora will come. I'm going and Ben is going and some other people. We're all meeting for a drink beforehand.'

'*Bambi* is the midnight movie?'

'Well, to be honest, there might be a change of plan in the pub beforehand. I admit, I can't guarantee it's going to be *Bambi*. It might well be something else, but why not just come for a drink anyway?'

'Well, I'll see.'

'Okay,' he smiled. 'In the meantime, get your Wild Cat whisky sorted out. If you get that passed by the Marketing Board this week, I'll be very surprised – and very impressed. Bye, Emily. Hope I see you at the weekend.'

He left. I watched him walk down the hall and disappear out the front door. He walked with a light step. I realised I was smiling. There was something about Jack that made me feel happy.

Before I went back to my desk in the office upstairs, I looked into the drawing room bar. The couple who were seeing each other secretly here had long since gone. The only trace of their meeting was the empty coffee cups on the table and the two chairs inclined together.

'A sweet and pleasant whisky with three complementary dimensions: heather honey, smoke and a hint of liniment which makes it seem very clean indeed. All three elements continue in their exciting ménage. Good for its age, sophisticated, yet feisty at the same time'

Cask No. 4·81   *Ménage à Trois*
Alcohol: 65.4%   Proof: 114.6°   Outturn: 601 bottles

The Society Bottlings, Spring 2002

Chapter Six

When I was finishing work late on Friday, I came downstairs from the office to find Kitty Gillespie admiring her appearance in the mirror at the foot of the grand staircase. She wore a long black dress that made her look even more statuesque than usual. Kitty didn't normally wear black. She always said she preferred the colours of fire and spirit and life.

'Emily, dear,' she said in a low voice, taking my arm, 'I have news about our Wild Cat Pink Whisky and its presentation this morning before the Whisky Conservative Marketing Board. I sincerely hope the chairman approved our design before succumbing to his cardiac arrest—'

'Oh no!'

'—but we shan't find out anything for at least a week. The chairman is currently under sedation. We can only hope for the best and prepare for the worst. Have a lovely evening, Emily, dear.'

She glided past me up the stairs and into the sitting room, long red nails sweeping up the mahogany bannister.

Poor Malcolm! Perhaps his health had been undermined by all the Burns Suppers he had attended – with such dedication on behalf of the Board – and all the shortbread he ate during meetings. I almost changed my mind about taking Andrew some cake at the office.

I sometimes called in to see Andrew on my way home. I would only stay about ten minutes, but I liked to see him and I often took something nice for him to eat to try to make up for the fact he was working so late. Sometimes the chef at the Whisky Society would have some portions of dessert that hadn't been needed at a dinner party. Today I claimed for Andrew a dish of fruity clootie dumpling with marmalade ice cream. It was a bit ambitious taking the ice cream but I thought it might make it round the block in time. It was cold out, after all. I turned the corner of Charlotte Square and then crossed the road at the traffic lights. Andrew will love this, I thought.

It was a bright winter night, the air crisp and cold and refreshing after the stuffy hours in the office. There were two security guards at the reception of the building on George Street where Andrew worked. They recognised me and one of them unlocked the door. 'What have you brought him this time?' he asked. 'He's a lucky bugger.' I signed myself in and took the lift. The ice cream had hardly melted at all. I was looking forward to whipping the lid off in front of Andrew's eyes to reveal the surprise – ta-da! I smiled at the thought.

The lift stopped, the door opened. I stepped out with my ice cream. Down the hall, I could hear voices drifting out of one of the meeting rooms. I turned the corner that would take me to Andrew's office and standing right outside of it was Kate.

I was so surprised to see her that I didn't know how to react. I stared at her stupidly. She was wearing a long white leather coat and smart boots. I stood there in my boring black office suit and white blouse, clutching my dish and feeling like a waitress.

'Hello, Emily,' she said. 'I'm afraid you've just missed him. He's gone into a meeting. I think he might be a while.'

'Can I just put this on his desk, then?' I felt annoyed at hearing myself ask permission. I walked into Andrew's office, cleared a little space in the middle of the mess of papers and put the bowl down.

'What have you brought him?'

'It's a sort of fruity sponge pudding. Clootie dumpling.'

'Do you realise you're famous for this sort of thing? They all joke about it here. I've heard all about your missions of mercy with a hot pudding.'

'This one's cold.'

'It's a shame about the ice cream,' she said, 'considering you've carried it all this way. If I were you I'd eat it myself. I'd help you, but I'm just on my way home.'

'Busy day?' I asked lamely.

'I've just finished a meeting with Andrew – and six other people, but Andrew is my oppo on a case.'

'Your what?'

'Opposite number. We're working on the same case. Didn't he tell you? Obviously not.'

I stared at Kate blankly, trying to take all this in. 'You're working with Andrew,' I repeated.

'Yes, for a couple of weeks now.'

'So are you here every day?'

'No, Andrew and I have had half a dozen meetings first thing in the morning and some over lunch. But today I came over here with a team of people from my firm. It's just work, Emily.' She was enjoying my discomfort. Her smile was all satisfaction. 'Today my team presented our client's case. Now we're going back to Glasgow while Andrew and his team try to work out what on earth they can do to salvage the situation before their meeting with their client next week.'

'I see.'

'I think it's fair to say Andrew will be putting in a late Friday night at his desk.' She made sympathetic noises. 'But don't worry; he won't be here all night. They'll sit up till midnight going round in circles and Andrew will probably be home by one in the morning.'

She picked up her smart leather briefcase from where it lay beside my husband's coat. 'Bye-bye, Emily, and I'd eat that ice cream if I were you.'

She left and walked down the hall. I sat down and stared unhappily at the bowl of melting ice cream. 'Emily . . . '

Kate appeared in the doorway. God, she's back again!

'Emily, you do know that if I've made him late tonight, it's nothing personal, it's just work.'

'I know.'

She hesitated, then came over to where I was sitting. 'I left something on his desk. Excuse me.' She leaned across and started sifting through papers, lifting and moving and searching. 'Did you leave him a note?' I asked.

'Yes, just a suggestion about what he might want to do next, but on second thoughts it would be better if he works it out for himself. He can always phone me. He knows where I am.'

She found what she was looking for on two yellow Post-It notes stuck to the foot of a document. Kate peeled them off, scrunched them up and put them in her bag. 'Right, I must go. Bye, Emily.'

She left. I waited until I could hear her steps retreating

down the hall and the lift doors open and close, then I picked up the yellow Post-It pad and held it up to the desk lamp to see if there was an imprint on the top page.

I could see a faint trace of her handwriting, the strong, spiky hand I had seen on the flyleaf of books she had given as presents to Andrew, and the same hand that had annotated some of the documents on the desk. I could read the last page of her note. It said 'Love, Kate'.

Well, what did I expect? 'Yours sincerely'? I stared at those two ordinary words. 'Love, Kate' didn't really mean much, did it? It didn't sound particularly businesslike but it was the way a woman might sign off a note to a friend. It just meant they were friends again, despite having once been lovers. It meant what it said.

Love, Kate.

I left him a note of my own. 'Dear Andrew, brought you some ice cream but you weren't here. Never mind. See you at home eventually. Love Emily.'

At home, on my own, I moved quickly about the house, closing the curtains, putting things away, tidying up. But when I had finished, when I would normally have flopped down on the sofa in front of the television for some mindless relaxation, I found I couldn't. My mind would not be still. Andrew was working with Kate again and he hadn't told me anything about it. Nothing at all. Never even mentioned it. Love Kate, Love Kate. The words were signalling in my head, unbidden and annoying.

Kate seemed to have had a change of heart about Andrew. After all, the only other written communication I knew about had ended, 'You're a pathetic, self-deluding bastard. Fuck you.' Eighteen months on, it seemed Kate had worked through her anger, processed her pain and was now perhaps even open to the idea of reconciliation. Love Kate. Right now, it seemed Kate wanted to be friends again.

91

And what did Andrew think of that? I wondered.

Nothing that he could tell me, obviously.

I wandered from room to room, and didn't really know what to do with myself. I put the television on, put it off again. I couldn't find any music I wanted to listen to, the radio just annoyed me. I couldn't settle to anything. I felt like I wanted to be outside rather than in.

In the kitchen there were French doors which opened on to the garden. Just outside was a covered area, like an open-sided wooden conservatory, which was part of the original house. The old couple who had lived here before us had called it their verandah. In New Zealand they would have called it the deck. I had been looking forward to sitting out there in the summer. Sitting out there in February didn't look so comfortable, but it was where I wanted to be.

I went upstairs, got changed out of my horrible black skirt and white blouse and pulled on layers of warm clothes. Then I unlocked the French doors. The cold air rushed in, but it was good because it was outside air and it was fresh and reviving. I took a torch and went bravely into the understairs cupboard to find my old rucksack and sleeping bag. They were among the few things I possessed when I met Andrew. Everything else I owned had been packed into boxes in a container ship on its way to New Zealand.

Picking up my hat and scarf and carrying the sleeping bag, I stepped out on to the verandah. There was a wooden bench there. I sat down, stretched my legs out and zipped up the sleeping bag. I pulled the hat down over my ears and folded my arms. Despite being aware that sitting outside on a cold February night might be an odd thing to do, I felt much, much calmer than I had done sitting on the sofa in the central-heated living room. There wasn't a breath of wind and it was a very starry night. You don't see the stars well in the city but I could pick out the constellations, the North Star and the Plough. Lots of times, in lots of places,

I had lain in this sleeping bag and picked out the stars. Flora and I, on our travels, had picked out southern hemisphere stars.

I realised that if I could be anywhere in the world right now, rather than sitting on our verandah, then I would be in Dunedin, because Dunedin is Edinburgh upside down and right now everything would be green and warm and beautiful and lovely.

But I wasn't in New Zealand, was I? I had got married instead.

I began to wonder what my life would have been like now if I had emigrated. I started to imagine myself in New Zealand, in summer.

Out in the garden, I closed my eyes and, despite the winter cold, I was warm in my sleeping bag. I liked staying outside. I would stay outside for a while yet. Andrew wouldn't be home for hours. He wouldn't be home till after midnight, Kate said. And she should know.

'Emily.'

I turned towards the voice and opened my eyes. Andrew's face was level with mine. 'Emily,' he said quietly, 'why are you sleeping out here?'

I sat up stiffly. 'I wasn't sleeping. I just wanted to sit outside for a bit. What time is it?'

'Midnight.'

'You're early. Kate said you'd be home at one.'

He sighed. 'Did she?'

'How are you getting on with her, now you've got to work together?'

'Okay, in a combative sort of way. I got the note you left me. I'm sorry I wasn't there. It was a shame about the ice cream, but it was a very kind thought.'

'That's what Kate said.'

'I wish I'd been there.'

'Never mind. Did you get your work finished?'

'No, I've brought it home. Why did you want to sit outside like this?'

I shuffled about inside the sleeping bag and tried to undo the zip. He helped me. 'I just felt like it.'

'Don't be upset about Kate.'

'I didn't expect to bump into her in your office. Why didn't you tell me you were working with her?'

'I was going to.'

'You didn't though.'

'I didn't want it to be a big issue.'

'It isn't a big issue, but I wish you'd let me know. Imagine how I felt when I turned up at your office with the ice cream and Kate was there and she told me you were working together and it was obvious you hadn't told me and I felt stupid. I felt really stupid, Andrew.'

'I'm very sorry.'

We got into the kitchen and the warmth flooded through me and made my face tingle. I took off my coat and a sweater. He helped me unwind my scarf and I unbuttoned another jacket. 'Emily, how many layers have you got on?'

'I wanted to make sure I didn't get cold.' Standing beside the stove, I could feel the warm floor under my feet.

'You're not worrying about us, are you, Emily?'

'Why did you leave Kate for me?' I said suddenly. 'What exactly was the reason?'

'I fell in love with you,' he said simply. 'I don't think reason came into it. Does there have to be a reason?'

This floored me. It wasn't the kind of answer I had expected of him. I felt he had picked a really bad time to be inarticulate. 'Kate thinks you married me because you were going through a mid-life crisis—'

'Kate's talking rubbish.'

'That's not what they say at her book club.'

'Her what?'

94

'Why didn't you tell me you were working with her?' I felt angry with him now because he didn't seem to think that it mattered.

'Because it's only work,' he said impatiently. 'It's part of my job to work with Kate on this one complicated contract.'

'She says you've been having regular meetings in your office.'

'Yes, it's called work.'

'She said you've had lunch together.'

'Work with sandwiches.'

'Why didn't you tell me? How often do you see her? Andrew, this isn't just any work colleague, this is the woman you were going to marry.'

'But I left her for you.'

'And she was really hurt, wasn't she? She loved you. I don't want her to want you.'

'Emily, for God's sake—'

'She might still love you, deep down.'

'There is no deep down about Kate,' he said sharply. 'People think there is but there isn't. Kate has hidden shallows.'

'Why didn't you tell me about your meetings with her?'

'I didn't want to treat it like it was some big deal. I wanted to be normal about it, as if she were any other person I had to work with. But, okay, now you've put it to me, I accept the fact that Kate isn't just any other work colleague.'

'What do you feel like when you see her now? When you're talking together?'

'This is just ridiculous, Emily.'

For a few moments we said nothing. I stared down at the floor, then watched his feet walk over to the cupboard and his hand reach down to take out a new packet of coffee. When I looked up, he was screwing the percolator together and setting it on the stove. 'She doesn't think you knew what you were doing when you married me,' I mumbled. He didn't reply, so I stared at the floor again and watched him put the coffee away. 'Kate thinks you were just having a mid–life crisis and—'

'Emily!' he cried, banging the door shut. 'I don't give a fuck what Kate thinks and neither should you!'

I stared at him, surprised. 'I just wish you'd told me you were working together, that's all. You don't need to shout.'

He rested his hands on the kitchen workbench, took a few deep breaths. 'Sorry,' he said. I picked up the sleeping bag and pulled it more tightly round my shoulders. 'We've never talked like this before, have we?' he said more quietly. 'This is the very first time and it's just a stupid misunderstanding and we've got to sort it out. It's not hard to sort this out.' He glanced up at the kitchen clock. One a.m. He began to try to explain himself. I realised how tired he looked all of a sudden. The deep lines on his forehead, the shadows under his eyes.

The coffee bubbled in the percolator and he took it off the heat and poured out two thick, dark cupfuls. 'Since I'm forty-two,' he said, 'any major upheaval in my life will be deemed a mid–life crisis. It's just a convenient tag. When we met, I was forty and therefore undeniably mid–life, but the crisis was that you were twenty-one and we got married.'

'Why do I have to be a crisis?'

'Because I love you,' he soothed.

'But what about your two years with Kate? Didn't you love her? What do you feel now about your engagement to Kate?'

He said one word: 'Chagrin.'

'Could you expand on that a bit?'

'Well, chagrin can include things like regret, sadness, embarrassment and even mortification.'

'And that's how you feel about her now?'

'In a muted sort of way, yes.'

'But you started off loving each other, so what made you drift apart?'

96

'We were living fifty miles apart anyway and that was before the drift set in.'

'But when you were actually together, what were the signs that you were beginning to drift apart? Did you have lots of misunderstandings? Did you not see each other long enough to go out together any more?'

He looked at me. 'I should take some time off, shouldn't I?'

'You can't; you've told me you can't. But even when you've got time, you don't come with me when I go out with my friends. It's okay, it's nobody's fault. I know it's difficult. I know you won't be coming to Josie's party next month because you just don't think you'll enjoy it and I understand.'

'I'll try to sort something out.'

'Only if you can manage it.'

He drained his cup of coffee and poured another one. 'Emily,' he said quietly. 'Do you ever wonder what your life would have been like if you had gone to New Zealand? If you hadn't given it up to get married when you were still so young?'

'I don't regret anything,' I said uncomfortably.

'Do your girlfriends ever want you to talk about what it's like being married to a man nearly twice your age?'

'It's a favourite topic of conversation, but don't worry, I always talk it up.'

He laughed, but then added, 'Sometimes I think it hasn't been very fair on you.'

'Don't think that.' I put my arms around him and we held each other close until we felt better. Then we stood up, picked my clothes off the floor and went upstairs to bed. Andrew set the alarm so he could get up early and work.

I woke up at ten the next morning and came downstairs to the living room where Andrew was busy. He was sitting on the edge of the sofa and he was frowning. The floor at his feet was covered in documents. There were five empty coffee cups on the table and enough foil wrappers to prove he had eaten a whole box of Tunnock's tea cakes. I knew he was dying for a cigarette but so far he had resisted. He stared harder at the papers. To see him deep in thought over an intractable problem, his fingers buried in his hair, he looked like primitive man trying to invent the wheel.

I felt sorry for him. 'I'll make you a chocolate cake today if you like.'

'Promises, promises.'

'Okay then, I'll get my clothes on, I'll go to the bakers round the corner and I'll bring you a chocolate cake.'

He turned to look at me. 'Would you really?'

'Yeah, I don't mind.'

But resorting to chocolate was not good. He had put on a few pounds giving up smoking, but he had definitely had too much chocolate recently and I thought I knew why. Flora had once told me that there is a chemical in chocolate that is like an amphetamine. It's called something like funnylithymine and it makes your heart race and your pupils dilate and adrenalin and endorphins rush around your body. It is very similar, said Flora, to the chemical cocktail that rushes around the body during sex. And it always works without fail, unlike sex, which can sometimes be unpredictable. I put my arms around his hunched shoulders and kissed the back of his neck. He breathed out, put his arms over mine, his hands over my hands. 'Are you going to be able to crack this work problem then?'

'No,' he said, sounding very calm. 'No, I'm not.'

'Are you sure?' I asked, surprised.

'Yes.' He stared for a few more moments at the papers on the floor, then shuffled them into a neat pile and put them away. Then he sat back, put his hands behind his head and fixed his eyes at the wall straight ahead. 'I've fucked up,' he said flatly. 'I missed something important. I still can't really believe I missed it, but I did.'

He turned to face me. 'There's one thing that could get me off the hook, but I need Kate's co-operation. This morning, before you got up, I phoned her and we talked it through. She told me she had had the very same idea last night and she had even written me a note to call her at home to discuss it. We've talked it through and we think it's viable. She's doing me a big favour, Emily.'

'She still cares about you.'

'She said that six months ago she would have been very happy to watch me sink in the mire but now she's willing to throw me a lifeline. She's not a bad person, Emily. Kate and I were friends for twenty years before we ever went out together.'

'She wants you back.'

'No, she's just realised she doesn't want to see me dead.'

'Has she said she forgives you?'

He went a little quiet. 'Yes, she has.'

The news of Kate's magnanimity didn't do much to reassure me. I would have preferred it if she had cold-shouldered Andrew for a few more years at least. But he needed her help. I ought to have been grateful she wanted to help him. I was grateful, just not thrilled about it. He knew what I was thinking.

'Is Kate the only person you can ask for help?'

'She is, actually. It's lucky for me that Kate is my opposite number on this, and I hope the plan works because if it doesn't, I'll be resigning. Worry about that instead of worrying about Kate.' He looked at my anxious face. 'But don't worry too much.' He bent to kiss me. 'Honestly, it'll work out and if it doesn't, I am definitely leaving Edinburgh so, Emily, do you fancy a trip to Borneo? You did mention you wanted to travel.'

'But you're good at your job. Everyone says so.'

He shrugged. 'I made a mistake. It's not too late to put things right. After next week I'll be in London quite a lot. I'm going to have to spend some nights away. I think we can safely say I won't be at Josie's party. Go with Flora. See your friends and have some fun.' Then he added, half smiling, half serious, 'I'm going to London with Kate and you mustn't think anything of it. You know I'd rather be here with you.'

I tried to be practical about it but I was still anxious. 'Kate has known you so much longer than I have. She said in her letter that she knows you through and through and now you'll be spending a lot of time together again. When you're in London you'll be having a drink after work and going out for dinner, and talking about things and—'

'Emily,' Andrew said firmly. 'I left her for you.'

'I know, but—'

'I left her for you.'

'In subjective tastings – also termed "hedonic tastings" (as in the pursuit of pleasure) – personal biases are not suppressed and descriptors may be colourful. These are the commonest form of tastings outside a blender's nosing room and are no less valuable than analytical tastings'

Malt Whisky, Charles MacLean

Chapter Seven

I went to see *Bambi*.

I met up with Jack and Flora and Ben at seven-thirty at the Cameo. It wasn't a midnight movie but a seven forty-five movie, and it wasn't *Bambi* either but *The Blair Witch Project*. As soon as I found that out, I knew I couldn't risk it. If I saw it, I wouldn't sleep for weeks. I knew that *The Blair Witch Project* would have to remain one of those movies everyone else had seen but I hadn't, like *The Silence of the Lambs* and *Alien*. I had tried watching *Alien* with Flora once, but I had had to leave before the end because I just couldn't stand the tension.

'I'm sorry,' I told them in the foyer, 'but I think I'll give it a miss.'

Jack looked disappointed. Flora explained that I wasn't being deliberately anti-social, I was just a bit of a wuss. 'She's always been like this,' she said, shaking her head. Jack hadn't realised that I had really meant it when I said I didn't want to see anything scary. I felt embarrassed. Ben tried to persuade me to change my mind. 'Why don't you give it a try, Emily?' he asked. 'It's only a story.'

'I know it's only a story, but I still get scared because I never see the monster coming and I never guess who the murderer is and I can't forget the story for ages afterwards. Then, when I go home, I'm just waiting for the mad axe-murderer to come smashing through the French windows and the aliens to land in the back garden and the crop circles to appear on the lawn. I know it's only a story, but a story can seem very real to me.'

'But it's not real!'

'Being scared is real.'

'That's the point,' said Ben. 'It's the same reason you go on a rollercoaster.'

'I don't do those either.'

'Feel the fear and do it anyway,' said Flora.

'I don't want to feel the fear.'

'You can do it, Emily. I know you can.'

'I can't.'

'Are you really going to wimp out again?'

'Sorry.'

'I think it's about time you got yourself sorted out,' she said. 'I'm going to come round to your place with some videos. We'll start off gently with *Carry on Screaming* and gradually work up to *Carrie*.'

I stood awkwardly in the crowded cinema foyer, packed with people who could feel the fear and eat popcorn anyway, and I knew I was a coward.

'Why don't you and Ben just go and see the film on your own?' Jack told her. 'Me and Emily can do something else instead.'

'Oh, don't worry about me!' I said quickly. 'You go and see the film. I'll be fine, honestly.'

'I'll see it another time. What would you like to do, Emily? Different film? Have another drink then go for food?'

'I'd feel bad if you missed your film. You mustn't miss the movie because I'm too much of a wimp to see it. You go and see it. You've bought your ticket and everything.' I felt more embarrassed than ever. 'Please go and see it,' I pleaded.

But he wouldn't hear of it.

After a lot of huffing and puffing from Flora about how I shouldn't take things too seriously and it was just a film, she and Ben went to see it on their own. We decided to meet them afterwards at Flora's place because that was where I'd already arranged to be picked up by Andrew later on. (On nights when Andrew and I went out separately, carrying on our different social lives, our usual arrangement was to share a taxi home. At around midnight, Andrew would get a cab from wherever he was and I would hop in the back and we would go home together.)

For the next few hours, however, it was just me and Jack.

We set off down Lothian Road, all the way back from the Cameo. It was about a forty-minute walk. On the way, we talked about where we might go and eat. There was this Thai place Jack had heard of that he wanted to try but we couldn't find it. So we just carried on walking. Walking and talking about all sorts of things. I found we could talk to each other really easily. A lot of little coincidences about liking the same books and the same music and things like that. He told me about this new album he'd bought that he loved and I knew it really well – I had been playing it all the time too. It was a debut album by a local band and it was getting brilliant reviews. Andrew thought it was a bit boring, a bit slow. He just didn't get it, but that was only because he didn't want to listen to it more than once and so I never played it when he was home.

We walked along Princes Street, past all the shop windows.

'Have you thought of going back to New Zealand for a holiday?' asked Jack.

'Yes, but we'll have to wait until we can get some time off. It's harder for Andrew than it is for me. I think it's a long way to go for only two weeks. You need three weeks at least. I can save up three weeks, but it's more difficult for him.'

'Would you ever go on your own?'

'Not now, I don't think so. I wouldn't like to go without my husband.'

'I don't see what difference it makes that you're married. Why should that stop you? It's not as if the state of matrimony is a repressive state.'

'Yes, but . . . it's different when you're married. I mean, the idea is that you got married because you wanted to be together.'

'If one of you wants to go to New Zealand for a holiday and the other wants to go to play golf in Spain, where do you go?'

'We haven't really had that question crop up.'

'I bet it will, though.'

'We don't do everything together, you know. We do lead quite independent lives in lots of ways. Andrew's out somewhere in town tonight. I don't know where.' And I waved my hand airily about to indicate that he could be just about anywhere. 'He's with people from his firm, entertaining some clients.'

Jack and I never went to a restaurant. We went to the pub round the corner from Flora's flat and we sat there for an hour. We talked about Barcelona because we both liked the city very much and I told him about Marbella. He'd never been to Marbella.

'Where do you stay when you're in Edinburgh?' I asked him.

'I've got a flat on Broughton Place. I'm away such a lot, though, that I rent out three rooms. I've got flatmates now.'

'Andrew shared a flat on Broughton Place. Top floor flat at number thirty-three.'

'I'm next door. Thirty-four.'

'Really?'

'Yes, and someone called Laura who stays in my flat knows you.'

'Laura? Lots of mad curly hair?'

'That's her.'

'Laura is . . . now, let's get this right: my husband's, brother's, partner's, sister's best friend. What a complicated small world. Yes, I know Laura. She's told me about your flat. She says there's one room on the front with a huge arched window that takes up most of one wall.'

'I kept that room for me.'

'I've never actually been to visit her, but . . . '

'You should come round.'

'Maybe I could come round with Flora one day after work? It's good, working in the same place, because most of the time we just have a lot of fun. I really hope the Wild Cat Pink Whisky comes off. We still haven't heard if Malcolm McLeod passed my design.'

'It may have been his last act on this earth.'

Poor Malcolm had since passed away. The Marketing Board was in mourning at the loss of an outstanding conservative. Kitty Gillespie had taken black tulips tied with barley to lay on the Heart of Midlothian, by St Giles, in his memory.

Not really a good place to lay a wreath, though, is it? I thought suddenly.

By the time Jack and I actually got to Flora's flat, she and Ben had been there for ages. It turned out that *The Blair Witch Project* was quite a short film.

'But that didn't make it any less terrifying,' said Flora. 'And

105

I'd already seen it. I saw it when it first came out,' she added. 'I knew what to expect and I was still scared. It was really scary, Ben, wasn't it?'

Ben grunted. He had just enjoyed a rollercoaster movie ride of screaming terror but it didn't look like it was going to keep him awake at night. He was nestled into the comfy sofa, eyes slowly closing. He got quieter and sleepier until his head started to loll heavily on to his chest.

'Would you like a coffee, Ben?' asked Flora. He nodded, but I don't think it was to indicate yes.

'I'll make you one.'

Poor Ben. He wasn't really a late night person, he was a morning person. He didn't have Flora's nocturnal stamina and she didn't appreciate his rise and shine enthusiasm. Their happiest times were spent in the compromise territory of the afternoon. I knew that, tomorrow, Ben would be clattering happily round the kitchen while Flora sat at the table with a painful frown on her face, eyes closed. She would put a finger to her lips and whisper, 'Shsh . . . Ben, shsh.'

It was midnight. I sent Andrew a text saying I didn't want to go home yet and wouldn't be sharing his taxi and that I hoped he was having a great time too. It took longer to write than my usual message of CM & GT ME.

A text zoomed back saying he'd wait up for me at home.

Flora plonked herself down on the sofa between me and Jack. Jack was unaware, I was sure, that the reason Flora liked him had very little to do with his smile, his good looks or his conversation and everything to do with what she had detected when she impulsively kissed him behind the ear. 'You smell just right,' she told him. 'And you don't use anything, do you? I can tell.'

'What do you mean?' he asked nervously.

'It's a compliment. You're naturally very well balanced.'

Jack admitted to finding the compliment disconcerting,

but rallied by saying she smelled nice too.

Stay up late in Scotland and you'll find people drink the heavier Islay malts. For old friends in the wee small hours and for arguments about sex, politics, religion and money, you need something robust. You need an Islay. And at Flora's at two in the morning that's what I was doing, sitting in the armchair, swirling the peaty dregs and talking.

After discussing the curious sex appeal of Jack's behind-the-ears scent that was actually only Jack, we moved on to even heavier subjects. This was where the Islay came in. At times like this, Flora liked coffee with hers. She had some intensely dark, sticky-looking espresso and Jack produced a packet of Gauloises. Although I didn't smoke, I tried one to see if Flora was right that it went very well with Laphroaig. I was very happy, drinking, talking and smoking like an adolescent, until our conversation geared up a bit more.

'Ask Emily what her middle name is,' said Flora wickedly. 'And ask her why.'

'Oh, Flora!'

'What's your middle name?' Jack grinned.

'It's not that interesting, really.'

'Sorry, but you've got to tell me.'

'Venetia.'

'Venetia? It's a bit odd, but not really impressively mad.'

'Emily Venetia. I was conceived in Venice,' I explained.

He laughed.

'In a palazzo.'

'Of course.'

'My mother was in Venice because she was pursuing her big dream to be in opera and she had a part singing in the chorus of "La Traviata", and my father was there because he was having an affair with my mother.'

'And do you have brothers and sisters named after the place they were conceived?'

'Not as far as I know. I've got half brothers and sisters on

107

my father's side, but I have no idea what their middle names are. It was my mother who wanted to call me Venetia. It was going to be my first name, but she called me Emily instead. I quite like the name Emily. I don't like Venetia much. Polly's middle name is Mercédes—'

'Conceived in a car?'

'I've never liked to ask. Actually, she's called Mercédes because Mum's office in Barcelona is next to the church of St Mercédes, and she used to go in there and pray for profit. Light a candle for cashflow and that kind of thing. It was a hard time for her when she started up the business. She was expecting Polly and Dad had just left her. She's a talent agent. She supplies a lot of the acts for all the big cruise ships operating in the Mediterranean.'

I must shut up, I thought. I don't normally gabble like this. Even Flora can't get a word in edgeways.

'Do you ever see your dad?'

'No, he went back to his wife and family.'

Jack looked surprised. Well, most people are surprised when they hear about my mum and dad. I don't normally tell people. I didn't know why I was telling Jack.

'I suppose you could say that my mother was my father's long-term mistress.'

'It caused a bit of a scandal when it came out in public,' said Flora quickly. 'Very exciting. All over the papers because nobody knew that Sir Douglas Montrose had a secret second family.'

'He came to see us quite often. Mum only went to live in Spain after Dad had left us for good, when I was ten. He left when she got pregnant a second time. She thought that if she had another baby he might leave his wife, but he didn't. He was a businessman, my dad. Still is. He's semi-retired now but he does the lecture circuit in America. He lectures on presence.'

'Presence?'

'Yes. People who have presence have a certain charisma, a kind of charm and magnetism, and he lectures on how to be like that, on how to have presence. He earns a lot of money telling American executives how to walk into a room. He tells them how to walk into a room, fill the space with their presence and then walk out again. It's a three-part lecture. It's made him a mint.'

'When you got married, did you tell him about it?'

'No, course not. But the amazing thing is, Andrew's met him. He met him two years ago at some dinner where my father was the guest speaker. He did a shortened version of his talk on presence with a bit of motivational leadership thrown in and something on the will to win. And the next day there was a golf competition and my father was rubbish in it. And Andrew had a really great game and finished fifteen shots ahead of him. I can't tell you how thrilled that made me when I found out.'

'That counted in his favour when you got married, did it?'

'Well, it didn't count against him.'

'Does he play much?'

'He plays at weekends.'

'And what do you do when he's playing golf?'

'Decorating. Painting and putting up curtains and so on.'

'It's not really weekend tramping in New Zealand, is it?'

'No, but—'

'So you never had any contact with your dad after you were ten?'

'He used to send us a card at Christmas – or his secretary did. He didn't want to see us, but he said he would pay for me and Polly to go to boarding school in Scotland.' I sipped my cold coffee, surprised at myself for going on about it so much. I decided not to talk about myself any more. 'Were you happy when you were little?' I asked.

'I have never been as happy as the day I realised I could ride my bike all by myself.'

109

We laughed, but he was very sincere and went on about how hard it was, as an adult, to recapture that same level of happiness, that discovery of a simple joy. 'You're absolutely right,' I told him. 'It's a kind of freedom.'

'Yes,' he said, 'that's exactly what it felt like. Liberation.'

'It's scary as well, though. I haven't felt completely safe since I took the stabilisers off my bike.'

'Did you fall off?'

'Yes, scar on my left knee – look.'

'She was a wimp,' said Flora. 'Cried her eyes out. I remember because I was there and I rode her bike home because she wouldn't get back on it again. And come to think of it, I really liked that bike, it was a red one and . . . '

Flora started chatting away to Ben and I stopped listening.

'Did it hurt?' asked Jack, pointing at my knee, touching it ever so slightly.

'Yes.'

He bent to examine it. 'It's too late to kiss it better now,' said Flora sharply. 'So don't even think about it, Jack.'

This made me giggle.

'Not even if it would make me happy?' he asked.

'Especially that. Emily, stop giggling. How much have you had to drink?'

Then we got on to the environment, bikes versus cars, which kept us going through a couple more drams each, while Jack defended the right of every American to own a gas-guzzling car and a big refrigerator and to bear arms and even to shoot dead an unarmed nocturnal fridge-raider should the intruder be trespassing on his property. Flora furiously disagreed with him and I just sat back and wondered at the way Jack liked to wind people up, having heard him argue the opposite view passionately in the pub just before. Flora stomped off saying she was going to put the kettle on.

'Why did you do that to her?' I whispered to him.

110

'Couldn't resist. Sorry.'

'She's gone off in a huff.'

'Peace and quiet at last.'

It felt oddly conspiratorial, sitting side by side and whispering about Flora like that. 'You've got to be nice to Flora,' I told him. 'She's my best friend. Be nice to Flora.'

'I am nice to Flora.'

'You could try harder. You're much nicer to me than you are to Flora.'

'Well spotted.'

'Why are you so nice to me then?'

'Why do you think?'

'I don't know.'

'Seriously, why do you think?'

It was almost a relief to get on to money and religion. Here Flora proved herself a fount of useful biblical references, having gone through a Holy phase when she was fourteen. She expounded on the story of the Widow's Mite and how you've got to do your bit for charity and give something, even if it's not very much. I knew Flora gave ten per cent of her salary to charities of her choosing every month. She told me that it was very liberating. She could watch heart-rending appeals on TV and not feel guilty any more. She knew she was doing her bit.

'Ah, yes,' said Jack. 'The mite was small change in first-century Palestine. It's very easy to buy a mite nowadays. Lots of them about. Money as used by Jesus Christ.' I could tell by her round-eyed look that Flora found the idea of God using money slightly shocking. Delighted, Jack homed in. 'Just think, Flora, you could own money that's touched the hand of God. Holy cash. God's small change.'

'Don't be stupid,' she said.

'Or at the very least money that's touched the hand of an apostle. Or maybe somebody who just bought a bit of carpentry from Christ, a nest of tables, say, or a fruit bowl.'

'I'd have bought God's fruit bowl, wouldn't you, Flora?'.

'No, only if God was giving them away. Want another coffee?' she asked cheerfully.

'I ought to be going,' said Jack.

While Flora had her back to us making coffee, and Ben was very nearly asleep, Jack turned to me and said: 'That band we were talking about − if I can get tickets to see them at the Venue, do you want to go? I'll try tomorrow.' And at that precise moment my phone rang. It was Andrew.

'I've been watching an old film on TV,' he said, 'and it's just finished, so I thought I'd give you a ring, see if you were coming home yet.'

'Oh, I forgot the time! I'm sorry. I feel terrible that you've been waiting up for me.'

'No problem, it was *The Great Escape* and I like that.'

'What time is it?' asked Ben suddenly.

'After two o'clock,' said Jack. 'And I really should be going.'

'I'm off to bed,' said Ben. He heaved himself up from the sofa and ambled off in the direction of the bedroom. 'No coffee for you, then?' asked Flora. Ben grunted.

'Andrew, it's so late now that I think I might as well just spend the night at Flora's.' There was a silence while he took this in.

'I'll have Ben's coffee,' said Jack.

I had never stayed out this late before unless Andrew was with me. I had always, always gone home. I had always wanted to go home. 'I'm still enjoying myself,' I said apologetically.

I felt a pang of guilt. I knew exactly what he was thinking: This is the first night we'll spend apart. The same words were going through my own head. This is the first time in almost two years that I will go to sleep without you by my side.

'Will you be okay?' he asked.

'Yes, I'm at Flora's. I'll just sleep in my old room.' I called out to Flora, 'Is that okay, Flora?'

'It'll be nice to have you staying here again,' said Flora. 'It's ages since you did.'

'She says it's okay. I'll see you tomorrow, then.'

'All right, Emily, have a good time. Phone me tomorrow, will you? I'll pick you up if you like.'

'Are you living happily ever after?' Jack asked as I put my phone down.

I thought about his question for a second too long. Looking at Jack reminded me of dreaming in a language I used to know: I understood the language perfectly, but on waking, I knew I couldn't speak it any more. It was lost to me.

Flora could never bear a silence in a conversation. If a silence lasted more than three seconds, it made her nervous and she would leap into the breach with some breezy words. 'Now, Emily, think about this carefully,' she said. 'Take your time when answering this question, because it's important to me. What does marriage mean to you?'

I had no hesitation. 'Being able to have sex with your best friend.'

Flora looked shocked. Possibly because she was my best friend. She shook her head. 'As if he were me?' she said slowly.

'No, not like that, but it's as if he were my best friend. I mean a certain kind of closeness and trust.'

'Surely it's not about being best friends,' said Jack. 'Or it might as well have been Flora you married.'

'Emily and Andrew got married when they had only known each other six weeks.'

'Friendship at first sight?'

'You eloped, didn't you, Emily? Nobody knew anything about it until they came back from honeymoon.'

'You must have barely known each other. Why get married so fast?'

I hesitated. For the very first time, responding to the question I had been asked so many times, I hesitated. 'It was an instinctive thing. But if I try to think about it objectively now – if I question it – then I would say, well, you can only know with hindsight if it was true love or not. You can only hope it is.'

Flora considered me carefully. 'Well, that's new.'

'If you stay together for thirty years or more and you always put the other person first, and you don't try to improve them or make them something they're not, but you love them for what they are—'

'It takes thirty years before you know?' interrupted Flora.

'Do you mean,' began Jack, 'that you can only say you were in love with the benefit of hindsight?'

'Well, if you spend a huge part of your life together and you cherish each other, what you felt at the start must have been love, real love, mustn't it? It wasn't something else in disguise. It wasn't just a phase you were going through—'

'Like a mid–life crisis?'

'People go through lots of phases. You can have very strong feelings, but then they can wear off a bit.'

'How long can that take?'

'Weeks, months, a couple of years. What I mean is, you can think it's love but you can't honestly know it's love. Only time will tell – a very long time. Thirty years or more. A life-time.'

'So you believe you can only know you're truly in love when you've been happily together for thirty years?'

'That's my theory.'

'You're wrong.'

'I don't think so. I've given it a lot of serious thought.'

'Recently or before you got married?'

'I'm conducting a long-term investigation. I'll have my results in thirty years' time. I'll let you know.'

'I'd say it was love at second sight,' said Flora, who had

114

been thinking about it. 'It was when you met him the second time – at Josie's party. I saw the way you looked at him. You got more starry-eyed with every minute you were together.'

'Did I? You've never told me that before. I thought I was pretty cool and normal at Josie's party. I felt fine the whole time.'

'And how are you feeling now?' asked Jack.

'I'm fine, thanks.'

Eventually, at about four o'clock, our little party broke up. Jack kissed me on the cheek when he left, his hand lightly resting on my arm, a second longer of touching.

I went to bed and lay wide awake until it was time to get up again. It was better to be awake than play the anxious bad-sleeper, caught up in her dreams and tangling the sheets.

The following night, I tried a different form of sleeplessness by tangling the sheets with Andrew. Then he slept and I still couldn't. I lay awake for hours. Eventually I forced myself to get up. I actually got my torch out of the bedside drawer, shone a path to the door and walked along it, feeling the hairs standing up on the back of my neck as if I were being stalked. As soon as I got to the hall, I put the lights on. I came downstairs, the fear receding with every light bulb along the way. It was half past three in the morning and the house was winter cold. I got to the kitchen, discovered it was warm there and for the first time realised the point of having an Aga.

An hour later, Andrew woke up, wondered where I was and came downstairs to find me sitting at the kitchen table with my head in my hands. Andrew was my good friend and my husband, and like a lot of men when faced with an anxious woman, he was enormously grateful to be told: 'I'm fine. Don't ask. It's got nothing to do with you. Just give me a hug.'

Andrew knew there could be any number of reasons why his wife might leave the marital bed to go and sit alone in the kitchen in the middle of the night. He asked me what the reasons were. I told him I really didn't know. I honestly didn't know what to think. Bad dream? No. Feeling depressed? No. Why are you sitting here all miserable then? Don't know. Do you want to have a cup of tea and talk about it? No. Do you want to come back to bed? All right then. Come on.

'What have you been worrying about, Emily?' he said to me when we lay down together again. 'What's bothering you so much you got your torch out and walked downstairs on your own?'

'Insomnia. It doesn't matter. I'm just tired. I want to try to get some sleep. I've got to try and sleep. I've got to go to work in a few hours.'

I turned away and shut my eyes but sleep wouldn't come. My mind raced through the plan I had decided on in the kitchen before my husband found me. I turned over and curled up and turned over again. 'Will you keep still?' Andrew said wearily. 'Stop wriggling about. Just try to lie still and think of nothing. Just empty your mind. Stop thinking.'

'It's hard to stop thinking,' I whispered. 'It's hard to be still and not think.'

'Try.'

It was pretty simple, my plan. It was this: You don't think of him, you don't see him, you don't ring him up, you don't talk about him to your friends and especially not to your husband. Talking about him is a dead giveaway and you mustn't give yourself away because that would be a disaster. You just admit quietly, privately to yourself that at some undeniable, basic level you like this man. You really, really like him. And you can't have him, Emily. You can't have him.

So stop now.

Right now, this second.

Stop thinking about him.

Stop.

'Emily,' Andrew whispered. 'You're still thinking.'

If only I could empty my mind. If only I had gone to see *The Blair Witch Project* and not wandered off into the scary woods of my imagination with a very attractive man.

'An unusual if not unique dram – remarkably rich and perfumed. On the nose there is spicy wood, thick-cut orange marmalade, mint. In a corner a girl wearing perfume is doing her nails (it reminded one Tasting Panel member of a French perfume distillery)'

Cask No. 38·11   *Rich and Perfumed*
Alcohol: 53.6%   Proof: 93.6°   Outturn: 141 bottles

The Society Bottlings, Autumn 2002

Chapter Eight

My twenty-third birthday fell on the very day that we were due to hear from the Marketing Board as to whether or not Wild Cat Pink Whisky would be permitted to go on sale. I woke up with more than the usual sense of birthday anticipation.

Andrew surprised me by saying that in honour of my birthday, he had taken the day off work. Without my knowing, he had arranged for me to take the day off work too. He had phoned Kitty Gillespie and fixed it all up and she had agreed to keep it a secret. He didn't tell me I had the day off until the very morning of my birthday. It was a surprise. In the circumstances, I was surprised to notice that I felt slightly irritated. I knew my job was deemed to be lower down the food chain than that of a corporate lawyer, but all the same, it was my job and it was a big day for me at work and I had meetings arranged and things planned and I felt he might have asked me first. I had real deadlines coming up. And what were my new work colleagues going to think of me? They'd have a good gossip about me. 'Emily's off today because her husband wrote her a note. What a skive!' And the other thing was, I knew there was no way I could possibly have rung up Andrew's boss and sorted a day off work for him and I certainly couldn't have said: 'And don't tell him, it's a surprise!'

Of course, this was a churlish reaction to what was simply a birthday treat and it made me feel ungrateful and spoiled, so I didn't let on about it. I just acted delighted. Then I remembered Flora had been going to bring a cake in to work for me, so I phoned and told her I had a surprise day off. 'Lucky you!' she said. 'He always spoils you. I'm so envious. Ben never does anything like that for me.'

Five minutes later she phoned back to say they had all decided to eat my birthday cake because it was basically just a giant strawberry tart and wouldn't keep.

'Flora, will you let me know when you hear if the design has been passed.'

'Course I will.'

'Don't despair, birthday girl!' said Andrew gallantly. 'You shall have your strawberry tart. I'll go to the cake shop this very afternoon.'

I spent my birthday feeling guilty about being spoiled and feeling guilty for not feeling grateful enough for being spoiled.

Just a typical day, then.

Andrew brought me presents in bed, carried in on a tray with champagne and orange juice and toast and marmalade and croissants. And it's a bad, bad thing but I do like being just a little bit drunk on champagne in the morning. 'Happy birthday,' he said. 'Another year older and you're still only twenty-three.' He offered me a croissant. 'Go on,' he said. 'They're very nice. I warmed them up. Do you think you could manage some light present-opening now? Cards first?'

In the envelope from Spain were two cards. One was from Polly with a picture of some bronzed god on a beach. Inside was her present of a pretty beaded bracelet. 'I strung it myself', she had written. 'It took me ages. P.S. Don't you think this guy is just totally, totally gorgeous?' There was a card with sunflowers on it from my mother, saying 'get your present in Marbella'. Enclosed was a plane ticket to go and see her. She had also sent me a cassette. Her method of keeping in touch involved sending me audio diaries of what she was up to, interspersed with whatever favourite music she was listening to at the moment. I put her tape into my Walkman and heard my mother launch into a snappy salsa version of 'Happy Birthday', with what sounded like castanets and trumpet accompaniment. It wasn't a short version either. 'Listen to this, Andrew,' I said and gave him one side of the headphones.

'I didn't know there was more than one verse.'

'Oh yes.'

Eventually the music stopped 'How are you in freezing Edinburgh?' my mother's voice said breathlessly. 'It's quite warm today here in Marbella. I went to a lovely party at Carmen and Steve's yesterday – of course, poor Steve is still detained, but Carmen wanted to go ahead with the party anyway. Montsie and I sang a duet. We did "Stand by Your Man" and José sang Bizet's "Flower Song". It's Carmen's favourite. She's bearing up really well and—'

'Do you want to hear the rest later?' asked Andrew hopefully. 'You do have other envelopes to open.'

I had two cards from Andrew: a silly one with cartoons and a seriously romantic one with soft-focus roses. I had a funny card from David and Jane and a flowery card from Andrew's parents with Marks & Spencer vouchers. There were cards

121

from his three aunts and uncles, his grandma, and the cousin who shared the same birthday as me and at whose wedding we had met. There was nothing from my friend Josie in Glasgow, but she hadn't forgotten, she had just got the wrong date. She had it in her head that I was born in May, not February.

For my birthday, Andrew gave me two books, two CDs, a red stretchy sweater with the receipt so I could take it back in case I didn't like it, perfume (the right kind), a box of chocolates (opened, and with all the hard centres thoughtfully removed and replaced with soft ones). He got me black lacy knickers and white sensible ones, 'to cover all options' as he put it, and he also got me what my mother would call 'a proper present'; in other words, he gave me jewellery. I got earrings – bright, modern, square-cut diamond earrings. They were very smart and I was very pleased.

But there was no kitten.

I didn't say anything because I didn't like to ruin the nice birthday atmosphere, but I was disappointed about there being no kitten. I decided I'd just have to make the best of it. I had another glass of champagne, put my diamond earrings in and played with my knickers.

At midday we got up and went out for lunch.

This was why, he explained, he had booked me a day off, so that we could go out to lunch at this nice restaurant with a view over the city and just have a nice leisurely time together.

It was a very modern restaurant, elegant in that coolly plain sort of way, and the whole place was designed to make the most of the views. 'Can you remember what you did on your twenty-third birthday?' I asked him.

He ate his venison and thought about it. 'Well, I remember it being a pretty good birthday, actually. We had a party. Jane came along and that's how David met her.'

'And who were you with at the party?'

'I was all alone. It was very sad. I had a girlfriend at the time but it was a very on-off relationship. She was kind of moody and neurotic and she dumped me before the exams but kept coming back to me between each paper.'

'Why did you keep taking her back?'

'Because she was a very attractive girl in some ways. She was an erotic neurotic.'

'Did she come to the party?'

'She did. Very, very late.'

'And was she in a good mood?'

'I seem to remember she was.'

'So you weren't alone all night, then, were you?'

'No,' he said, remembering. 'I wasn't.'

I stared out of the big glass windows at the view, right across the rooftops of Edinburgh and the big blustery clouds over the Firth of Forth. 'It's funny to think of you living in that flat when you were my age. You must have been just like Jack and the others who are staying there now.'

'Who's Jack?'

'He lives next door to your old flat.' Don't say much, I thought. Don't give the appearance of having anything more than a passing acquaintance with Jack. 'He's a friend of Ben's – you know, Flora's Ben.'

'If he's got the room at the front, he'll have the big arched window like I had. It was great in summer but freezing in winter. Those big tall windows.' Andrew finished eating and sat back, a look of satisfaction on his face. I wondered about the years of Andrew's life before he had met me. There were quite a few of them, after all.

'How long did you stay in that flat?'

'Well, I was nineteen when I moved in and twenty-five when I moved out, so six years.'

'And it was a happy time, wasn't it? You've always said so. Would you say they were the best years of your life?'

'No, not compared with the time I've spent with you.'

'You're just being nice to me because it's my birthday.'

'I'm always nice to you. You're my lovely young wife.'

'But they were still a very happy six years?'

'Yes, they were. Emily, are you going to eat those prawns or are you just going to push them round your plate?'

'I've had enough, thanks.'

'I'll have a few then.' He stabbed some with his fork. 'Mm, these are good. Don't you like them?'

'Yes, I've just had enough, that's all.' He finished the rest of the food on my plate and drank his wine.

'Andrew, I've been wondering about something.'

He looked at me carefully. 'Wondering or worrying?'

'How many girlfriends did you have before you met me?'

'How many?' he echoed.

'Yes, I was wondering. I know Kate lasted the longest but what about the others? Do you remember Flora's sister, Jenny?'

'Jenny? Yes, she was nice, Jenny.'

'I watched her standing in the garden in the rain, crying over you.'

'Did you?' He looked surprised.

'I've told you before. I was twelve so you must have been thirty-one.'

'God, it's scary, isn't it?'

The pathetic picture of Jenny was still clear in my mind. Flora and I had watched her smoking out on the back green. I could still see her holding one arm tightly round her sobbing, skinny body, while the other hung limply from the elbow, flicking ash. She wore a tight black dress and high heels that sank into the grass. When it started to rain, she wouldn't come in, just stayed there, coming apart like wet tissue paper.

'Jenny wouldn't let us mention your name. Flora and I would whisper it to her and she would chase us out of the room. We thought you must have been really wicked and exciting.'

'I was a pushover – always have been.'

'What about the others? I wonder sometimes. Who's Megan Mackenzie? It's a name that crops up whenever you and your old friends get together.' Andrew looked around the room as if for help. A waiter came, poured some more wine and left again. 'Is Megan another old girlfriend?'

'If you were to ask her, she would deny it.'

'Tell me about her.'

'No.'

'Tell me, Andrew.'

'No, Emily.'

'Why not?'

'Because you'll just brood about it – pointlessly.'

'But I'm the only one who doesn't know. Everyone laughs at things that happened years ago that I know nothing about and you won't tell me.'

'It's really not a big deal, Emily.'

'I could ask Damian. I bet Damian would tell me.'

'Damian is forbidden under pain of death to have any communication with you whatsoever.' Andrew reached across the table for my hand. 'We talked about this happening, remember? We talked this over before we got married and I said I was worried that the time would come when—'

'You never worry about anything.'

'Yes, but we agreed you would inform me when I needed to start.'

I stared down at our hands resting on the table, fingers clasped together.

'Do I need to start?' he asked quietly.

'Of course not.'

'We talked about this,' he repeated, almost to himself.

'I know, but let's not talk about it now,' I said briskly. I had had enough. 'Let's enjoy my birthday.'

He leaned back again. 'A far better idea,' he said, relieved.

'Ask me where I was on my twenty-first birthday.'

'Where were you?'

'I was flying over the Pacific.'

'Not at college, then?'

'I took some time off. My father gave me a cheque for my twenty-first and I went off to see the world. I went with Flora.'

'Not like him to be so thoughtful; not like him to remember.'

'His accountant remembered. There was a fund set up for me and it ended on my twenty-first. It was the last pay-out.' I finished my glass of wine. 'Was it nice, when you were a student, just lying in bed in that room and watching the clouds float by?'

He drained his glass. 'Yes, I liked it. I did just that.'

'Maybe that's why you never wanted to see the world, because you were perfectly happy just lying in bed, playing your old records and watching the sky.'

'I've got a kind of sinking feeling you might be right.'

'Don't you ever feel you missed out?'

'I have done some travelling, Emily.'

'For two or three weeks at the most.'

'Longer than that when I was a student.'

'But do you not feel you'd like to travel for months rather than weeks? I mean a gap year, really see the world?'

'Of course, but who would pay the mortgage?' He smiled at me with that wry, resigned, older smile that was beginning to annoy me slightly. 'We're together,' he said. 'We've chosen to be together and nothing else matters as much as that.'

The waiter arrived and took our empty plates away. 'Have you and Kate sorted out all that complicated work you had to do together?'

He sighed. 'Emily, there is nothing going on between me and Kate apart from some very tedious legal untangling of a very complex mess.'

'Are you any nearer to sorting it out, on your trips to London?'

126

At that moment Flora arrived, just descended on us, crashing through the conversation. 'Andrew, you're so sweet to get Emily a day off, we're all really envious. But I just wanted to tell her – show her something – a real surprise present. Good news, Em! I just had to come and tell you. Look at this!'

She handed me the design I had submitted for Malcolm McLeod's consideration and there, at the foot of the page, was his signature. True, it was very scrawly, but then his signature had always looked like a violent blip on a cardiogram. It trailed away quite dramatically at the edge of the page, but it was still more or less on the line headed: Signature of the Chairman of the Scottish Whisky Conservative Marketing Board.

We had passed. It was possible that Malcolm McLeod's approval of our Wild Cat whisky had been his last act on this earth.

'And here's the bottle we sent him – the mock-up of your design with the Scottish wildcat stalking round the base. We thought we'd let you have it, this first one, since it's your birthday. This means we can open the cask and fill all the other bottles now.'

'It's wonderful stuff, Andrew. Honestly. Wait till you try it, I bet you'll like it. I bet you do.'

'I'll keep an open mind,' he said. 'I'm willing to be persuaded.'

'Well done,' he said when Flora had gone. 'You've worked really hard on this, haven't you?'

'Do you like the look of it?'

'Yes,' he said, surprised. 'I think it's very daring. It's whisky, but not as we know it. It just looks so completely different in a bottle like that.'

We went home in a taxi and, despite the excitement of getting my design passed, I almost fell asleep in the back. Stuck in the early rush hour traffic jam on Lothian Road, I nodded off against Andrew's shoulder. The effects of all the champagne, I suppose. At home, I sat down on the sofa feeling tired and trying to stay awake. 'You're still sleeping badly, aren't you?' Andrew said. 'Why don't you go and have a lie down for a bit? Have a nap.'

'I don't want to. I won't sleep tonight.'

'Go and lie down,' he insisted.

'If I go to bed, you're not going to start working, are you? Promise me you won't.'

'I'm perfectly happy to sit here and read the paper.'

'All right.' I kissed him and went to bed and slept for a couple of hours. I dreamed of lying in a bright room with a tall window full of sky. When I woke up I felt better. I dressed. Sensible new white knickers and old jeans. Clean T-shirt.

On my way downstairs, I stopped in the hall and rang my mother. She was out. Nothing but her answerphone, her voice resonant despite the thin electronic static. I left my message: 'Hello Mum, thank you for the present. I'd love to come to Marbella and see you. Let me know when would be a good time.' And just as I was about to put the phone down, she picked up.

'Emily!' she cried. 'It's Joanna. Happy birthday! Polly says happy birthday too. Are you having a lovely day, Daughtie? What did Andrew get you?'

'He got me the day off work and he's just taken me out to lunch and he bought me earrings, diamond earrings.'

'A girl's best friend. Wonderful.'

'I told you he loved me.'

'How sweet! You really are living happily ever after, aren't you? It's all worked out very well, considering.'

In the hall mirror, I saw myself frown. 'Considering what?'

'Oh, you know what I mean – all those people who said it would never last. I admit, I said myself that only time will tell.'

The cable stretched and twisted in my hand. The old-fashioned, squat black telephone did not always have a reliable connection with my mother's gold-plated mobile. When one of us started to say something regrettable, we were often cut off in the nick of time. We joked about the fault on the line between Edinburgh and Marbella – that regular communication failure.

'We're very happy together.'

'Darling, I'm thrilled to be proved wrong. I am eating my words on toast for breakfast every morning. I have humble pie for lunch with a green judgement salad on the side. You and Andrew are indeed clearly happy together, despite the issues.'

'There aren't any issues.'

The frown deepened and my eyes looked back at me, blue and impatient. I have my mother's eyes, which is good actually – she is famous for her big, blue eyes – but right at that moment they were narrowed with the effort of concentration.

'You enjoy the rest of your birthday, Emily,' she said quickly, moving the subject back on to safer ground. 'Do you think you'll be able to make a trip to Marbella soon?'

'Hope so. Thanks for the tickets, Mum.'

'That's all right, Daughtie.'

We said our goodbyes and I put the phone down, then stared at it for a few moments, half expecting her to ring back. She would often ring back and say she loved me – her usual postscript. I folded my arms. It was cold standing in the hallway. Must do something about the draught from the front door. Was she going to ring back? I waited, shivering. No, I thought, she's not. That's fine, though. That's fine. Things were much, much better between us than they had been eighteen months ago.

'Everything all right?' called Andrew from the living room.

'She sends you her love,' I called back.

'Seriously?'

'She said she wishes she could send us some Spanish sunshine.'

'That'll do.'

As I neared the living room, I could hear the calm clear notes of a Bach cello concerto, one of Andrew's favourite pieces of music. I expected to see him sitting contentedly in the armchair, staring at nothing in particular, but when I turned into the room he was crawling about on the floor. A little blur of orange fur flashed past him in pursuit of a ping-pong ball.

'Oh, a kitten! You got me a kitten!'

'Yes,' he said, getting to his feet. 'The vital kitten surprise arrived when you were asleep.'

'Is it a boy kitten or a girl kitten?'

'It's a ginger boy kitten.'

'He's so small and fluffy!' The ping-pong ball and the kitten came to a stop at my feet. I bent to touch him. 'And he's so soft.' Very carefully, I picked the kitten up. He made a squeaky mewing noise and scrabbled his baby paws in my hand. I could feel his heart pounding very fast. I stroked the kitten and held him close. He allowed himself to rest in the crook of my arm and soon he started to purr, a sound like cream warming up, tiny bubbles of purrs just breaking the surface. 'Oh, I love him!'

Andrew was smiling. 'He's your kitten. He's your own pet to look after.'

'Thank you!'

'And since you've never had a pet before,' he said, coming over all serious, 'I'm going to pass on my dad's advice: All a pet needs is for you to love and care for it, and it's your responsibility to love and care for it properly.'

'I'll love and care for him properly.'

'Good, because he's your proper present.'

Later that night, I stood out in the garden alone, thinking. I looked back at our house, the warmth of my home. I thought of my husband, who was waiting for me, probably asking himself what on earth I was doing standing out in the garden at midnight again. I thought of how much I loved him. I realised I had everything I wanted and yet, looking up at the night sky and the stars, I felt this odd sort of restlessness and it wouldn't leave me alone.

Out there in the zodiac was my own particular little destiny. My birthday stars. Opening my arms, I made a birthday wish. I whispered the words to the night. 'I wish for what I don't know I need.'

My wish was carried on the wind. I listened to its sound in the trees and then I turned and walked back into the house.

'Of course, women are better at whisky nosing'

Mike Nicolson, Whisky Maker at Royal Lochnagar,
on meeting Annabel Meikle of The Scotch Malt
Whisky Society, 4th May 2001

Chapter Nine

At Flora's flat on Thursday night, we were getting ready for
Josie's party in Glasgow. She was having a housewarming party
on behalf of her sister who had moved into the flat upstairs but
didn't want to spoil her new carpet. Josie often gave parties on
behalf of other people. She was the surrogate mother of all parties. Last time I had been to her house, Andrew and Kate had
been there too. Josie had called it Emily's Emigration Party but
it had also turned out to be Kate's Disengagement Party. People
met their fate at Josie's parties. Relationships sparked or fizzled
out. A few hours at Josie's could rearrange people's lives.

I had bought a new dress for the occasion. It was red with
white spots. Andrew had joked it was my Minnie Mouse

dress and I was just a little offended. There was nothing car-toonish about it. The material was very soft and wispy. It was a subtle kind of gipsy-boho look, and Andrew just didn't appreciate that it was very fashionable and kind of expensive. It wasn't the sort of thing I usually bought, but I had gone shopping with Flora and she had egged me on. The decisive moment came when I discovered I fitted the size ten (it was a generous cut, but it was still a size ten). I felt fabulous in it.

'It's very stylish,' said Flora when I put it on. 'And it's very now. You can definitely go out in Glasgow in that.' Flora always felt you should make more of an effort with your clothes when you had a night out in Glasgow, because if you didn't, you could sometimes end up feeling like a cardigan-clad Edinburgh nerdy girl. 'I'm not sure about your footwear though.'

'I know, but—'

'Happy birthday,' she said and she gave me a shoe box with a big pink bow on top.

'Oh Flora, you didn't—'

'Open it,' she said. 'Just open the box.'

Inside were the very beautiful shoes I had tried on in the shop with the red dress. They were scarlet suede, with ele-gantly shaped high heels. I had dreamed of wearing them with the red dress but hadn't dared buy the shoes too. 'Oh, Flora! I can't believe you got me these!' I told her she shouldn't have been so generous.

'Don't feel too guilty about it,' she said. 'I had an ulterior motive because we have the same shoe size . . . but the main reason was that you need some shoes like this. They're what I call "Going Out Shoes". You wear them and you go out. I thought maybe you could do with a pair.'

'Because I've been spending months being such an anti-social stop-in?'

'Yes, but you're getting better now. We're going out again tonight, aren't we? And these shoes match your dress perfectly.'

I tried on the whole outfit, and when I saw myself in the mirror it was one of those rare, wonderful moments when I just knew I looked good. I left Flora to finish getting her own outfit together, knowing she would be some time yet and that if I stayed and talked to her it would take even longer. 'I'll wait for you in the living room,' I said. 'I'll put my feet up on the sofa and admire my red shoes.'

'I'll be five minutes,' she said. 'Promise.'

I had always liked Flora's flat. It was light and airy and seemed much more well-established as a home than other friends' flats I knew. It had grown-up furniture like a dining table and matching chairs, and there were proper curtains, made-to-measure by John Lewis. The sofa was big enough for a tall man to sleep on should Ben ever find himself suddenly out of favour. Ben stayed with Flora whenever he was home from sea (this home leave being his longest ever) but tonight it seemed he wasn't around. 'He's not coming,' Flora called to me from the bedroom. 'It's just me and you.'

'Has he got something else on, then?'

No answer, then I heard the sound of a hairdryer. She would be ages now, painstakingly blow-drying her wavy blonde hair into a smooth bob. I waited until the hairdryer stopped. 'Flora, we're going to miss our train.'

'Then we'll just get the next one. It's not a crisis if we get to Glasgow half an hour later, is it?'

Flora had lived here all her life. When she was eighteen, her mum had married a retired doctor and moved out. (There was a seventeen-year age difference but I don't remember anyone making a big fuss at the time.) Flora stayed on in her old home with its tall windows and comfortable furniture and carefully tended windowboxes. It was a tidy sort of place.

In our house, Andrew tended to scatter a lot of things about – keys, pens, coffee cups, sweet wrappers, and all those little heaps of small change. He seemed to leave traces of himself wherever he went, as if he hoped to be tracked down and rescued. Maybe there was a notice up in his old bachelor haunts, announcing his disappearance:

MISSING
Andrew Drummond, lawyer, golfer & original 80s yuppy
Last seen entering a large family home in Merchiston
with a much younger wife and all her baggage

'I'm nearly ready,' said Flora, bustling into the living room. 'Do you like this?' She posed, pouting in a pink suede skirt.

'Yes, it's lovely. You look wonderful in it.'

'I'm in a pink sort of mood.' I glanced at my watch. 'Don't worry, we're not going to be late. How's your kitten?' asked Flora, putting on her coat.

'He's gorgeous. He's twelve weeks old, but in cat years that means he's nearly five and ready to go to kitten primary school.'

'I must come round and see him. I knew you were getting a kitten, but I was sworn to secrecy. You wouldn't believe the trouble Andrew had finding you a ginger kitten. What have you decided to call him?'

'Jaffa Cat. Andrew thought of it. He was eating a packet of biscuits at the time.'

'Come on,' said Flora happily. 'Let's go out.'

It was freezing as we walked to Waverley Station. I had my long winter coat on – sensible navy blue wool over the red dress – and Flora was wearing her famous pink fur coat. She loved that coat. She only brought it out for special occasions but she had had it for years – since we were both six. Most of that time, the coat had been longer than Flora. It was now Flora's token anti-fashion statement. My mother had worn it on stage in a musical and given it to Flora as a present. It wasn't real fur (obviously), but Mum used to tease me by claiming it was made out of fifty Bagpuss pelts culled on a Bagpuss fur farm.

I followed the pink furry figure through the rush hour crowds at the station and together we got on the train. When the train began to move, we watched Princes Street Gardens slide slowly past the window. We were heading west.

When we were safely under way, Flora started to look troubled. She kept checking her mobile.

'What's the matter?' I asked. 'Is there something wrong?'

'Ben didn't want me to go to Josie's tonight,' said Flora.

'Why not?'

She took a deep breath and said with great seriousness: 'My relationship with Ben is over.'

'Is it?' I was incredulous. I had always thought she and Ben were happy and sorted with not a care in the world. I thought everything was working for them.

'We had a long talk last night and we decided to go our separate ways.' She paused, reconsidered. 'Well, no, what really happened was that we had a long row last night and I've decided to go my separate way.'

I was shocked. I had always really liked Ben; I had always thought Flora loved him. 'But I thought you were really happy together.'

'We were once, but things have been deteriorating for a while.'

'I had no idea. You never said anything. Why didn't you tell me?'

'Because I kept pretending to myself that there wasn't a problem. But last night I had to admit that there was, and I couldn't ignore it any more.'

'What was the problem?'

'Jealousy.'

'Ben? Jealous? I can hardly believe it.'

'Well, to put it briefly, he couldn't come to the party tonight and he never likes me doing anything by myself so he asked me not to go and we had a big row and I decided that was the last straw. The thin end of the wedge-shaped straw that broke the camel's back. But I wish we hadn't had that row. I texted him before we left the flat to say I was sorry and could we talk it over.' She looked at the phone in her hand. 'I'm waiting for his reply.'

'But how did things go so wrong? Was it that he had to keep going away to sea? Dolores thought that would put a real strain on any relationship.'

'Dolores thinks she has a happy relationship with Graeme,' said Flora tetchily, 'but Graeme is a total excuse for a boyfriend. I don't think Dolores is qualified to pass an opinion on what constitutes a happy relationship.'

'But the separation must have been hard at times.'

'It wouldn't suit everybody,' admitted Flora, 'but it suited me. I quite liked the fact that Ben went to sea because I loved all the reunions, but, to be honest, I also liked it when he left again too. Now he's been back for six whole weeks, we've not got on at all well recently. I was just feeling really hemmed in. I always loved being close to him, but not so close that I felt I could never get away. It was claustrophobic.'

Flora's mobile beeped and she read the text that came through. 'Look at that,' she said, showing me the message.

'I don't think he wants to talk it over.'

'No, I don't think he does.'

It was one of those very brief, abusive texts that people like Graeme have programmed in for frequent use. Flora gave an awful little sob. 'This mascara isn't waterproof,' she choked. 'I mustn't cry.' I touched her arm. 'Don't be nice to me! It'll only make it worse.'

'But maybe once you've both had a chance to calm down and talk, then—'

'Change the subject! Change the subject!'

'All right. Er, who do you think is going to be at this party? Who else is going to be there that we know?'

'Dolores and Graeme. Oh God.'

'Who else? Who else? How about Harry? I'm sure Harry will be there because, well, he lives in Glasgow.'

'Yes, he's going. I invited him. I like Harry.'

'And some people we know from Edinburgh will probably be going . . . Maisie? Fiona? I think the usual crowd will be there because they said they were driving over and Jack emailed me to say he was going too.'

'Does he email you very often, Emily?'

'Now and then. He sends me emails saying: This is a test.'

'This is a test?' she echoed. 'Does he not say anything else?'

'A few days ago I got one that said: "This is a test. Will I see you at Josie's party on Thursday?" So I said yes.' I looked out of the window at the suburbs rolling past. 'Flora?'

'Hm?'

'Do you think Jack will be staying long in Edinburgh?'

'Dunno. Six months, maybe. I don't think he really knows himself. I think he's probably just winging it. That's very Jack.'

'How do you mean?'

'Making it up as he goes along, learning the essentials and putting on a good show, as if he's a total expert in everything he says he is.'

'How does he get away with it?'

'Charm, native wit and good intentions – all that and bare-faced cheek.'

'Do you remember Laura, who stays in the same flat as him?'

'Yes, haven't seen her for ages. Maybe she'll be there tonight if Jack is going, Maisie is offering people a lift home afterwards. I wonder if we can get her to give us a lift back too. It's always such a drag having to get the last train.'

'I think it would be good to see Laura again. It's so easy to lose touch. I met her a couple of times about a year ago and I thought she was really nice. I think I might drop by her flat one day and say hello.'

Flora looked at me carefully. 'You mean the flat where Jack lives?'

'Yes.'

'He's nice, Jack, isn't he?'

'He's interesting to talk to, yes.'

'And he's really good-looking and funny and you're always asking me what I know about him. And guess what? Whenever I see Jack, he always asks about you too.'

'Does he?'

'And whenever you meet, you get on really well together and the next day you ring me up and you want to talk about him. Now you tell me you'd like to drop by his flat, but only on the off-chance you might see Laura.'

I shrugged. 'You make it sound like there's something going on between us and there isn't.'

'I think you like Jack more than you care to admit.'

'I just said let's go and see Laura.'

'Jack, I know, can look after number one. But I don't want you and Andrew to get hurt.'

'I haven't done anything!'

'Maybe not yet, but do you know what I think?'

'No, but I'm sure you're going to tell me.'

'You don't just like Laura – you really fancy her, don't you?'

'I do not fancy her!'

'You do too! You fancy her like mad. And you're married, Emily! You're not allowed to fancy anybody any more – only if he's called Andrew Drummond.'

'But I don't fancy Laura. I just like her a lot.'

'Are you sure?'

'Yeah, I like her very much, she's a very nice girl, but I'm not tempted.'

'I think you might be.'

'I'm not, but if I did get tempted, I wouldn't give in to it.'

'In that case, don't drink too much tonight. The last thing

you need is to lose all your inhibitions and end up snogging on the sofa with her.'

'I won't. I'll be good. I promise.'

Josie's flat was a short taxi ride from the station. Even for a studio flat it was very small, and we had to squeeze past people to get in. It occurred to me that this might be one of the reasons why everyone said Josie threw good parties: the space was too small for all the people who were trying to fit inside it. The flat consisted of one main room with a door off to a bathroom and the whole place was kitted out with bright, modern furniture from Ikea, which was where Josie worked (in fitted kitchens). When she wasn't having a party, Josie's tiny studio flat was perfectly neat in the way that only the home of a storage freak can be.

Josie could even store herself neatly away and had a choice of places to sleep: either on a roll-up futon on the floor, on her fold-away sofa-bed or in her hideaway hammock. Interestingly, her mania for neatness sometimes annoyed her, and when this happened she would go and stay with her boyfriend, Angus, who lived next door. She only needed to stay with him for twenty-four hours to make a full recovery. Angus had never knowingly stored anything in his life. He lived at a strictly low, horizontal level, his mattress surrounded by the chaos of his possessions – and that's the way he liked it. There was no way Josie and Angus could ever live together. Not in a million years.

'He must just give her something she needs,' was Flora's comment as we arrived and spotted them, arm in arm across the room. 'Yin and yang and all that. Who knows the secret that makes a relationship work?'

Despite their differences, Josie and Angus loved each other and were committed to living next door to each other for the rest of their lives.

Josie waved to us. She was wearing jeans and a crocheted

lace top, both of which had featured in the latest edition of *Vogue*. She looked as bright and happy as a freshly picked daisy. Angus was smiling at her side. He waved too and beckoned us over. Angus's clothes were, without question, whatever old things he had picked up off the floor that morning. He looked as crumpled and comfy as a pile of beanbags.

We made our way towards them, picking up drinks on the way. 'I love your shirt, Angus,' said Flora.

'It's Prada.'

'New collection?'

'It's not officially available yet, which is why you won't have seen it. This one has been rushed to me from Milan – flown into Glasgow specially for this evening.'

'And the trousers are Armani,' said Josie. 'Can't you tell? Giorgio and Angus are like that.' And she crossed her fingers to indicate just how close they were. 'And I'm so proud of Angus today because he's just been invited to become Armani's brand ambassador in the UK. He's taking over from Lady Helen Windsor.'

'Just keep it very quiet,' said Angus.

'Oh, I love your shoes!' exclaimed Josie, noticing my footwear.

'Thank you,' I said, pleased. 'Flora gave them to me. They're going out shoes and this is their first outing.'

'They're fabulous. I love the shape of the heels. And suede. I love suede.'

'Scarlet suede.'

'Excuse me,' said Angus politely. 'I must go and talk shoes with Paul over there.' He disappeared into the crowd.

'Josie, who are all these people?' I asked. 'How many of them do you know?'

'About half. The rest are friends of my sister upstairs and there's a bunch of lads over there who I've never seen before in my life.'

'Do you not mind?'

142

'God, no! It's a party. And it's very likely they know at least one person here.'

I wondered if Josie's hobby of giving parties for other people stemmed from a deep-seated, subconscious need to trash her perfect flat. I had suggested it to her one Hogmanay party. She had told me I was just being neurotic.

'You must go and talk to Jack,' she told me. 'He was asking about you earlier. I told him you were coming tonight. He's over there, talking to Harry.' She pointed to where they stood, by the window.

'I'll go and say hello.'

I had just turned away when Josie asked: 'So where's Ben?'

'I'm not going to bore you with it,' said Flora. 'I'm going to target Dolores and bore her with it, but the news in brief is that Ben and I have split up.'

'Oh no, Flora, really?'

'Yeah, but let's not talk about it now. I'm here to enjoy the party and forget about Ben – apart from my half-hour moan to Dolores. And Dolores will enjoy that. You know how she likes to savour the collapse of a once-happy relationship.'

Behind us, I could hear a hack-hack of laughter, like a cough. Dolores, I thought. Poor Dolores pretending to get a joke. And sure enough, there she was, thin-faced and brightly lipsticked, smiling eagerly at the man who had told the joke, Graeme, whose humour was casually sarcastic and usually at the expense of Dolores – or Doh, as he called her. 'Doh! Are you still here?'

His friends tried not to smirk. Then she saw me. 'Emily!' she exclaimed. She took a step towards me and the boys gladly got down to discussing football without her.

'It's been such a mad week!' she began. 'I'm exhausted and, honestly, if it weren't for Graeme, nothing would get me out in the evening. But Graeme makes me go out.' She fondly squeezed his arm. 'Don't you, Graeme?' He ignored this. 'If I didn't have Graeme I'd be completely anti-social.' She pulled

143

on his arm. 'I said, Graeme, it's a good job I've got you to take me out.' Graeme made a snorting noise at this.

I spotted Jack watching me from across the room. He smiled and beckoned to me.

'Oh, leave Jack for a moment,' said Dolores. 'I want to ask you something.' Dolores linked her skinny arm into mine, then wrapped her other arm around it and kept me clung to her side. She reminded me of an orang-utan whenever she did that. Orang-utans have the longest arms of all the apes. They're really gentle and affectionate, but they're all arms and they like to cling. Graeme didn't know anything about zoology so he never made an orang-utan joke, but he was a big *Star Trek* fan and sometimes referred to Dolores as the Klingon.

'What is it, Dolores?' I asked.

'Oh, Emily,' she said, 'I'm so worried about Graeme.'

She drew me away to a quiet corner, looking anxious. Dolores always tried hard to understand her man, to see things from his point of view. But as far as I knew, Graeme was not an easy man to love. From what I had heard, Graeme was a sulker. He could sulk professionally once he had finished sulking for Scotland in the Sulking Olympics.

'Graham is in his cave,' said Dolores. 'He won't come out.'

'Yesterday you told me he was like a rubber band and just kept bouncing back.'

'I know, I know, but I can't see him bouncing back this time.'

'Why not?'

'Oh,' she sighed, 'I don't know. Maybe it's just me. Maybe it's because I'm down, down, down in my well today. I try to stay positive and say it's a wishing-well. I keep saying to myself: "Pull yourself up, Dolores, pull yourself up."'

'Are you feeling sad because you're down in your wishing-well, or because Graeme is in his cave and he won't bounce back? Or is it both?'

'Oh, I don't know,' sighed Dolores. 'I do love him though.'

144

I didn't know what to suggest. Perhaps troglodytes and wishing-well dwellers were made for each other.

'How's Andrew?' asked Dolores.

'He's very well.'

'He's quite a bit older than you, isn't he?' she said sympathetically. 'But you know, perhaps that's what I need.' She looked wistful. 'A much older man who dotes on me. And it's not as if he's really old. I mean, forty-five isn't all that old.'

'Forty-two.'

'But he must feel like he's been given a whole new lease of life,' Dolores continued warmly. 'It's easy to see the attraction of marrying someone who's twenty years younger than you.'

'Nineteen years.'

'I mean, all his friends must be so envious!'

'Some of his friends are still very disapproving.'

'Course they're envious!' said Graeme, just materialising out of nowhere. 'Dolores is right.' He turned to her. 'You are absolutely right, Doll.' Dolores glowed with pleasure. 'And I hate to be blunt, Emily, but what you've got to bear in mind is that Andrew's pals will all be stuck with fat-arsed, middle-aged women and have been for years. Then Andrew goes and gets himself a pretty student with a nice bum – and a sense of humour, I hope. Sorry if I put that crudely for you,' he added, 'but that's exactly what they're thinking and of course they're envious. Dolores is spot-on accurate.'

Dolores smiled, uncertainly.

'Anyone would be envious,' grinned Graeme.

'What I meant to say about age difference,' Dolores went on, flustered, 'was that there are good reasons why an older woman might have a toy boy, just like a younger woman might have a sugar daddy.'

'He's not a sugar daddy.'

'Bet he is, though,' said Graeme. 'Bet he gives you anything you like. Wanna drink, Dolores? I'm going to get another. Want one, Emily?'

'No, thanks.'

Dolores trotted off behind him. I watched them go and, despite the fact they had both annoyed me, I couldn't help admitting to myself – very reluctantly – that some of the things they had said had hit the mark. I knew that Andrew certainly did think he was the envy of his friends and quite enjoyed the fact. I had always felt very uncomfortable about it. I didn't like the idea of him finding their envy gratifying.

Flora gave me a little wave from across the room. 'What's wrong?' she signalled. I smiled and shrugged. Nothing's wrong. Flora was making the best of her evening, chatting to friends despite being upset about Ben. I ought to make more of an effort to talk to people too.

I would start with Jack.

Making my way over to the window where Jack stood, I was almost there when a great big wall of Harry appeared right in front of me. 'Emily! How are you?' He gave me a kiss. 'Did you come with Flora?'

'Yes, she's just . . . where's she gone? Oh, she's over there, getting another drink.'

'She's all by herself,' he said, surprised. 'Where's Ben? He's usually glued to her side.'

'They've split up.'

'Have they?'

'Yes. She ended it.'

Harry managed to fight back an expression of joy. 'Oh, what a shame,' he said. 'Is she very upset about it?'

'She's sure she did the right thing in ending it and now she wants to enjoy the party and have a good time. Why don't you go and cheer her up?'

'I'll do my best.' He beamed at me, then cruised on towards Flora, cutting through the crowd like an icebreaker.

At last I got to Jack. He smiled when he saw me – held out his hand to draw me from the dancing crowd. 'Hello, Emily,' he said and he kissed my cheek. An ordinary greeting and yet

146

it felt utterly different to the way Harry had kissed me just moments earlier.

'I'm glad you came,' said Jack.

'Oh, I wouldn't have missed it. I always enjoy Josie's parties.'

'I like the dress.'

'Thank you. Do you like the shoes too?'

'Definitely.'

'Tell me what you've been up to since I last saw you. I always like to hear from you.'

'Do you?'

'Yes, of course. I don't know how long you're going to be around, do I? What's the next travel plan?'

'Not sure. I've got some work I could go and do in France and some in Spain. Do you think I could still get some skiing in? The Pyrenees? That would be good and then maybe I'll go on to Spain for some sunshine.'

'It all sounds great,' I said lamely.

'Does it?' he laughed. 'You don't seem very enthusiastic.'

'I'm probably just envious. We're going to France this year. I think we're going to rent a gîte. A gîte with a pool.'

'You'll enjoy that, won't you?'

'Yes, but it's just for two weeks.'

We talked for quite a while, standing by the window together. We talked mostly about what I would like to do if I got the chance of a long trip. Jack insisted there was nothing to stop me. He said he had met quite a few people on his travels who had left a partner at home while they fulfilled their dream to go canoeing up the Orinoco or whatever. He had met one woman who wanted to sail down the Yangtze River before the Chinese flooded it to make a giant reservoir. 'She left her husband to look after the kids – she had three kids under six – and she made the trip out to China. It was her big dream to make that journey and she did it.'

I listened, and I thought about what he was saying and I

knew that I wanted to go and see some of the places he had seen and do some of the things he had done. But I was also very aware that I liked watching him while he talked. I liked his face and his way of smiling and I liked his eyes which were an interesting sort of hazel–green colour. I realised he was talking and I wasn't actually taking any notice of what he was saying.

'What was that?'

'I said Josie was telling me she had an emigration party for you here – only you never emigrated, of course.'

'It was five weeks before I was to fly out to New Zealand. I had a great time in those few months before I was due to leave. All my stuff had been sent on ahead. I was living out of a rucksack and sleeping in Flora's spare bedroom or on people's floors. I went on an extended tour, visiting all my friends and having a fantastic time and saying goodbye and then . . . and then . . . I met Andrew – that was fantastic too of course.'

'And five weeks later you got married? It's incredible – well, I mean it's very romantic. You must have both been very sure you had met the right person.'

'Yes, we were. That was definitely how we felt when we eloped. We were at the stage of being completely besotted with each other.'

I watched Jack's face. His eyes, questioning. 'And do you know yet,' he asked quietly, 'how long that stage lasts?'

'Well, it doesn't last for ever.'

'Has it ended already?'

'It can't last for ever because you'd never get anything done. You'd never get round to ordinary boring things like paying your bills or going to Sainsbury's. You'd spend all your time in bed or wandering around with a dreamy smile on your face. So, obviously, you can't stay besotted for ever. You enter a different stage. A sort of nice, easy, comfortable stage when things aren't quite so intense.'

Stop talking, I thought. Stop talking, Emily.

'And then you ask yourself if you'll still be in love in a year's time?' said Jack. 'Or two years? Or thirty years? Because you've got to wait thirty years to find out, haven't you? If you use your theory of love with hindsight. What if you wait a long time but you're still not sure? What do you do then?'

'I don't know.' I floundered. 'I'm not sure. I think you just have to rely on the feelings you have for each other every moment. Every moment you're together.'

'Nice, easy, comfortable sort of feelings?'

'Yes.'

'Not head over heels, really intense feelings?'

'No,' I said quietly. 'Just . . . just very deep feelings.' I felt awkward suddenly.

We were saved by Flora, who returned with Harry. Harry must have been doing a good job of cheering her up because she was bright-eyed and beaming. I estimated she was at her third cask strength whisky. Everything would now feel loud and exciting and if she carried on at this speed, it would soon all get blurry. 'Harry says he's going to come along to one of our whisky tastings next week!' she exclaimed. 'He says he wants to hear me do my talk.'

'Yes,' grinned Harry. 'I want to hear Flora's expert chat.'

'You must,' I told him. 'She's very good.'

'I am quite good, aren't I?' she asked. 'On a good day. On a good night.'

'Do I get to heckle you?' asked Harry. 'Can I throw questions at you?'

Flora faced him squarely and put her hands on her hips. 'Anything you like.' She was obviously still feeling robust.

'Can I do it now? Can I have a practice?'

'Course you can. Anything you like.'

'That's a good start.' Harry smiled broadly. He had always had a soft spot for Flora, and it seemed fairly obvious that

Flora now had a soft spot for him. She was flirting, with that kind of full-on Flora flirtation that I hadn't seen for quite a while. Not since before Ben.

'Ask me anything you like!' she repeated. She actually batted her eyelashes. 'Anything, anything at all.'

'What's your favourite whisky?'

Flora took a step back (Harry took her arm to steady her a bit). 'That is actually a very difficult question,' said Flora, pouting. 'I have different favourites for different times and different situations.'

'What about Jack Daniels? I always like JD.'

'Do you?' said Flora. 'I wouldn't have thought you were the type.'

'What type?'

'American whiskey has an e,' said Flora suddenly, 'and Irish whiskey has an e, but Scotch whisky doesn't and neither does Japanese, actually.'

'Does it matter?'

'Not to me, but you'd be surprised how many people get very upset when the spelling is wrong. To me, it's more a matter of taste than spelling. Jack Daniels is American whiskey with an "e" and I actually find it very sweet. To me, it's the Ribena of the whisky world. Did you ever see that photo of Zoë Ball coming out of her wedding holding a bottle of Jack Daniels? I thought: Zoë, you innocent! Get yourself a good blast of Islay malt.'

'I like bourbon,' said Harry.

'Look, Harry, you've got to understand that bourbon is different to Scotch. Bourbon is sticky whiskey. It smells different, it tastes different. I think we should find some and do a scientific test. I'm a fully qualified scientist. I'm a professional nosoligist!'

They disappeared together and the night wore on. I danced, I talked to friends, I made an effort to talk to lots of people and not just to Jack. But I think we felt drawn to each other and we always ended up together again. It was as if we were circling each other, or rather, circling a question.

'Emily, why do you think we're spending so much time together tonight?'

'Are we?'

'It must be companionship at first sight. We should meet up again some time. Do you want to see that band we talked about? I'll get tickets.'

'I'm sure Flora would love to go too.'

'I'd like to go with you.'

'Just me?'

'Just you.'

'Well, I suppose that's okay, isn't it? Going to a gig. Nothing wrong with that.'

'You might even enjoy it.'

'I will enjoy it. It's my favourite album at the moment. I'm playing it all the time.'

'So you'll go?'

'Yes.'

'Wonderful.' He folded his arms and smiled. 'I can't wait.'

'You've got to wait eight days.'

'I'm counting.'

Dolores arrived. 'Have you seen Graeme? He was here before and now he's just gone. He's not answering his phone. I don't know where he is.' There was distress in her dolly blue eyes. Then suddenly, out of the window, she sighted him returning to the party, laden down with lager. 'Oh,' she breathed, 'he walked all the way to the off licence to get my vodkapop. Isn't he wonderful?'

'Heroic,' said Jack.

'Ben's not here, is he? If Flora's not careful, she'll lose him, you know. I don't think she pays him nearly enough attention. It's not surprising he's feeling cross and miserable, is it?'

'They just had a row,' said Jack.

'Flora seems to be recovering rather well, I must say. Look

at her over there.' She pointed to the corner where Flora was almost nose to nose with Harry over the finer points of bourbon differentiation. 'Making a remarkable recovery. She's very robust, Flora, isn't she?'

'Luckily.'

'Jack,' she said, plucking at his sleeve, 'don't you think it's a shame that we never see Emily's husband at anything? It's not really his scene. Andrew's probably sitting all by himself at home.'

'He's in London, actually. He's working, otherwise he would have been here. He wanted to come.' I thought of Andrew and Kate together now in London. They would have probably just finished dinner and might now be relaxing over a final coffee. Talking about things.

'Andrew's four hundred miles away!' exclaimed Dolores. 'Isn't that interesting, Jack?' and she gave an awful little giggle that made me cringe to the very toes of my scarlet suede shoes.

'I think Graeme is looking for you, Dolores. There he is, over there.'

Dolores jumped up and down, waving frantically. 'I'm coming!' she called. 'Bye-bye, sweeties,' she said breathily. 'Don't do anything I wouldn't do!' Off she went through the crowd, smiling and waving, a bouncy little doll. I was so annoyed with her I wanted to throw something at her irritating, bobbing little head.

'Dolores is going to watch us all night now,' I told Jack.

'Just ignore her.'

'I can happily ignore her until she decides to spread some stupid gossip about me.'

'Don't let it upset you. What have you done to feel guilty about?'

'Nothing. Nothing at all. Look, I'm going to go and help Josie move her beanbags down to Angus's flat. There's no room for them up here any more.'

'Okay,' he shrugged.

I fought my way to the door and moved beanbags down the stairs with Josie. It was hard to find a space on Angus's floor. 'Throw them over there,' Josie said, 'then he won't fall over them when he walks in. I don't think I've ever had so many people at a party. Jack's nice, isn't he? Haven't seen him for years. I used to go out with him, you know.'

'Did you?'

'Yes, he was my last boyfriend before I met Angus.'

'What happened?'

'He went off travelling and I didn't see him again. I missed him like mad for ages. But then I met Angus and discovered love.'

'So it wasn't love with Jack?'

'God, no!'

'What was it then?'

Josie threw herself down on the beanbags and laughed. 'Lust!' she cried. 'Lust, lust, lust!'

'Just lust?'

'Mmmmm.'

'Do you still lust after him?'

'Nah.'

'Why not?'

'Because I lust after Angus instead.'

'Do you think it's possible to lust after two people at the same time?'

She giggled. 'Are you kinky, Emily, or what?'

When we got back to the party, Flora was nowhere to be seen and I found myself wandering among the crowd, almost beginning conversations, almost being able to dance.

And inevitably, I came full circle back to Jack and he started talking to me about things I didn't want to think about, things I couldn't think about.

'Emily, you gave up all your plans. Are you sure you don't have any regrets?'

'No.' I wished he would abandon the subject but he wouldn't. 'How can I regret falling in love with my husband?' The woman standing beside me in the crowd suddenly gripped my arm. She was wearing a black cocktail dress with dagger heels. She reminded me of my mother. 'I regretted it,' she said bitterly. 'I still regret it. You think twice about it, darling.'

I moved away slightly. Jack followed me. 'I fell in love and that's why I got married.'

'You said you can only truly know with hindsight.'

'That's the plan.'

'That's not how it should be. I think you're not sure any more. You're having second thoughts.'

'No, I'm not.'

'And if you're not sure, you have to start thinking about all this really seriously, Emily.'

'Forget I said anything.'

'You don't even want to talk about it.'

'That's right. Forget I ever said anything. You don't understand. When I say I believe in love with hindsight, I know what I mean.'

'I think you're worried you've missed out on something important somewhere.'

'I'm fine, Jack. Thank you for your advice and your insight, but I'm fine.'

I don't think we parted very happily. Jack got a lift back to Edinburgh. 'Are you coming too?' he asked.

'I've got to find Flora.'

I realised I hadn't seen her for a couple of hours. I checked my mobile and there was a text from her: At Harrys 4 xxx CU on 7am train. Love Fuh. Oh well, I thought. At least I know where she is. 'Are you seriously going to stay here?' asked Jack. 'Just to meet her at the station in the morning? You don't have to do that.'

'I do!' I groaned. 'I have to make sure she gets the train.'

'Come back to Edinburgh with me,' he said. 'Stay with me.'

He could possibly have meant that as a joke and so I thought I'd better laugh. I managed it after a few seconds of awkwardness, a few seconds of staring into his face and understanding that, no, he really meant it. 'I can't do that.'

'Yes, you can.'

It hit me very hard how much I wanted to be with him. He stood for a moment, waiting, watching me. 'Yes, you can,' he repeated quietly, taking my hand and saying slowly, insistently, 'Emily, please come back with me.'

'I can't,' I said, backing away. He let go of my hand.

'All right,' he said. 'I understand.' That was all he said, and he then turned away, walking quickly to the door. I folded my arms tightly, clamping down on the sickly feeling of desire and confusion. I loved my husband, but I wanted Jack and he knew it, despite everything. He knew I wanted him. Was I really so embarrassingly obvious?

I felt utterly miserable. I didn't want to want Jack. I only wanted to love my husband, who loved me.

By four o'clock, everyone else had left. Eventually, I tried to get some sleep in Josie's hammock above the chaos of the little flat. It made Angus's flat next door look like an oasis of order and neat simplicity.

Travelling back to Edinburgh the next morning was hell. It was dark, cold and windy. I had never had to do this early morning Glasgow–Edinburgh commute before and I couldn't believe how horrendous it was. I thought of the two years that Andrew and Kate had commuted like this, trying to live together while keeping a home in two cities, and I wasn't surprised it had proved to be a serious strain.

Flora arrived on time. If she hadn't, I would have been livid. We stood side by side on the windy platform, bleary-eyed and shivering inside our pink fun fur and sensible navy blue wool.

'I feel terrible,' croaked Flora. 'I'm hungover, I've had three hours' sleep and when I got up this morning, I couldn't find all my things.'

'What have you lost?'

She gave me a sideways look. 'My favourite pair.'

'Oh no, Flora.'

'Oh yes.'

(An Edinburgh woman is all fur coat and no knickers because she's left them in Glasgow.)

'I'm going home to get changed before work.' she said. 'Do you want to come with me and get changed at my flat? Or are you going home for a brief visit to your poor old husband? Don't look at me like that, Emily. When I say "old" I mean old as in poor old anybody – however old poor old anybody might be.'

'I know what you mean. Okay, I'll come round to your place. Andrew is in London, remember.'

'Andrew's not the jealous type, is he?' said Flora. 'Not like Ben. I'm glad I left Ben, even though it was horrible breaking up. Leaving a jealous man is very liberating. Perhaps the rebound potential is greater after a jealous man. It's wonderful to feel so free. I'm not going to let myself get stuck in any restrictive kind of relationship ever again. I'm going to find myself a nice, non-jealous type like Andrew.'

'You can't have him.'

'Well, when you're finished with him.'

'You'll be very old by then – poor old Flora. And anyway I won't be finished with him until he's dead.'

'Scary!'

'Unless I die first. That's marriage, Flora.'

'A fight to the death.'

'We don't fight. It's totally tranquil living with Andrew. And you're right, he isn't jealous and he has absolutely no reason for jealousy.'

'So you've stayed faithful?'

'Yes.'

'Oh, so you obviously didn't share a secret snog with Jack.'

'Of course I didn't.'

'I bet you wanted to.'

'I did not.'

'I bet you did.'

'I did not.'

'Liar, liar, pants on fire.'

'At least I've got pants.'

The Third Whisky:
TRADITIONAL SPEYSIDE
the old sherried influence

Maturation in Spanish sherry casks
can give whisky a dark, rich colour
with sherry on the nose
I call these 'Grandad' whiskies

In the Traditional Speyside Sherried Malt Contest
the winner is:

Macallan
Macallan actually bought a sherry bodega in Spain
to ensure their supplies of sherry casks.
They make sherry, mature it, sell it
and ship the casks back to Scotland
to refill with new make spirit
and to mature into
whisky

'It is difficult to put words to smells, and the language used is hotly debated. Just how effusive or allusive should one be? There are two broad camps: the "Traditionalists" who are tight-lipped and the "Modernists" who are florid. Both styles of notes are justifiable and much depends upon the purposes to which they will be put. Are they for personal use, as an aide memoire, or purely for the pleasure of exploring a whisky?'

Malt Whisky, Charles MacLean

Chapter Ten

It was a big day when we bottled our pink malt. Flora and I visited the bottling hall and we watched them opening up the cask and pouring out the whisky. Walking round in regulation Health and Safety hairnets made us giggle, but it was interesting to watch the process of the bottles being filled on the production line. We talked to the people who worked there and Flora began to sound a bit like the Queen on an official visit: 'And what do you do?'

We returned home with two cases of the blue quarter bottles to distribute in the office and more to send out to journalists for publicity. The outturn was very small – it was only the contents of one single cask – but that was not the point. Kitty Gillespie wanted to do this for fun, to make some kind of a statement, and that was exactly what we were doing. In many ways it was for her the Elizabeth Cumming Tribute Malt.

Over the next few weeks until the official launch, I had to respond to a huge pile of enquiries from journalists. Were the rumours true? Did the whisky actually exist? You'd think they'd never received their free samples. The publicity gathered momentum. Pink whisky and proud. The response was huge among the members of the society, but not all of it was positive.

There were some angry letters. One major industrialist started a campaign to make the promotion of pink whisky illegal in Scotland.

Dolores came on the line from the busy reception. 'Here's another call for you, Emily. I have a Mr McTavish and he's not happy.'

A gruff voice came on the line: 'Is this the woman who's trying to sell us pink whisky?'

'Yes, how can I help you?'

'Do you not understand that whisky is our national drink? Real whisky, proper whisky. What do you think a pink whisky' – he spat the words – 'a pink whisky is going to tell people about Scotland?'

'That we're brave?'

'Are you aware of Scotland's national motto?' said the voice. '*Nemo impune lacessit*. It means "No one dare touch me." If you promote this pink perversion of our national drink then—'

I switched my phone setting from hand receiver to headset and put the earphones loosely around my neck. I listened – or rather half-listened at a safer distance – to his rant while I typed an email to a journalist: We would be delighted for you to run a special feature on the new pink whisky. As you mentioned in your email, the whisky would make a perfect apéritif with ice if only people weren't so shy about putting ice in their malt.

'S'bloodyridiculous,' said the voice in my headphones. 'Absolutedisgrace.'

I look forward very much to meeting you at our launch party on May 24th. I'll send you another wee sample to keep you going in the meantime.

The noise in my headphones seemed to have slowed down. 'Thank you for calling, Mr McTavish. If you'd like to put your concerns in writing—'

'Aw, never mind.' He hung up.

Dolores rang again. 'I've had three nice ones since Mr McTavish, but they didn't want to talk to anyone in particular, they just wanted to order bottles.'

'Good.'

'And Jack rang, but you were busy so we had a little chat and then I put him through to Flora. I think she took a message. It should be on your desk somewhere. He mentioned something about going out.'

I whipped through the notes on my desk. 'Did he? Jack? Really?' I realised I was trying to remember how to react normally to hearing his name. I hadn't seen or heard from Jack for eight days. Not since Josie's party.

'I think he really likes you,' said Dolores coyly.

'I have to call him about work, Dolly. Probably something to do with the press release. He's supposed to be helping us with the pink whisky launch, you know.'

Dolores hung up and I sat reading the note that Flora had taken from Jack. The words 'Call Jack' were circled by pink lovehearts. 'Found it, have you?' I turned to find her looking over my shoulder.

'You didn't need to draw all over it, Flora.'

'Just doodling. He wanted to let you know he'd got some tickets for some band you wanted to see. They're on tonight at the Venue.'

163

'Oh, right. Er, good.'

'Who are you going to see?'

'James and the Athletes.'

'Oh, I like them.'

'There aren't any tickets left,' I said quickly.

'That's a shame.'

'But maybe there'll be some returns on the door,' I said, feeling guilty. 'I mean, do you want to come too? You can if you want. There's no reason why it should just be me and Jack. We got talking about the band and it turned out we've both played their album non-stop for ages and Jack thinks they're great and so do I and so . . . so we're going to go along and see them. And I like the Venue because it's quite small, isn't it? And you can see properly and . . .'

Why am I gabbling like this? It was as if I had to give Flora a whole list of reasons why I should be out on my own with Jack.

'See, those going-out shoes I got you must have done the trick. They look great, by the way.'

'Thanks. You can borrow them for an hour after lunch if you like.'

'No, you wear them.'

'They're not really office shoes, though, are they? I never thought I'd wear them for work, but I just tried them on for a few minutes this morning and when I saw how red high heels can really improve a charcoal grey trouser-suit, I decided to keep them on.'

'And they're obviously doing the trick. You're going out tonight.'

'Just to see a band.'

Flora gave me a wave and went off to the bar to get on with her work. I was longing to sit with my feet up on the desk so I could admire my scarlet footwear, but I didn't dare. Maybe I'd try it when everyone had gone home.

'Oh, I forgot to write it on the note,' she called across the room, 'but Jack said he had emailed you.'

I checked my email and found his message. It was very brief: I still want to go to see this band. Do you? I've got tickets.

Yes, I typed.

I kept it deliberately short. I didn't want to be tempted into an email affair, when your heart leaps every time you open your mail box and his name appears.

Yes is the only word I need to hear from you, he replied.

I deleted it.

Kitty Gillespie had sent me a message which was full of 'quote me' lines in cheerful defiance of the Whisky Conservative Marketing Board. 'Perhaps it is unfair of me to train my fire on such a slow-moving target,' she had written, 'but my sniping skills are highly refined and I enjoy the sport. If the Marketing Board fails to see the potential of our project, then it is simply because our avant-garde approach presents something of a challenge to their stultified imagination.'

She also wanted a full progress report by two o'clock. I looked at my watch. Might just make it.

I had just started typing my reply when Andrew's name flashed up on the screen in front of me: Just got back from London and I fancied having lunch at your place. Can I book your lunch hour? he'd written.

Yes, great, I typed, but I'm v. busy. I can see you for 20 mins at most.

He rang up. 'You can see me for twenty minutes *at the most*?' he laughed.

'But I've got so much to do, Andrew. I don't just sit here drinking whisky all day, you know.'

'Yeah, yeah, yeah . . . '

He arrived early. He'd been sitting in the bar for twenty minutes before anyone told me he was there. I came down from the top floor office five minutes ahead of schedule, distributing function sheets for events that evening – seat arrangements in various rooms, timings and so on – and when I got to the ground floor bar there was Andrew settled very snugly in an old armchair beside the fire. Ensconced in the armchair, in fact. The springs had gone and although he looked very relaxed, the buttons on his shirt were visibly taking the strain. Andrew had put on weight since giving up smoking, but had he really been away so often that I had failed to notice just how much extra weight? He had told me on the phone a few nights ago that, at forty-two, he was much younger than the current James Bond, Pierce Brosnan, who was still looking pretty good at fifty. Yes, I thought, but Andrew Drummond in his crumpled suit was not a man dressed to kill.

He was finishing off a steak sandwich while he read the newspaper. On the table in front of him was an empty wine glass and beside it a dark sherried whisky. It would be one of his favourites, a very fine old Macallan. If he was indulging himself then it would be the Reserva, which is the only sherried whisky I've ever really enjoyed. Very soft and smooth and rich. (Flora said my range was still too limited.) Maybe it was the heat from the fire, maybe it was the whisky, but Andrew was looking quite ruddy of complexion. Maybe it was the broken springs and the slumped posture, but he looked a bit double-chinned, a bit soft around the middle, a bit sagging, a bit . . . old.

'I know what you're thinking,' he said from behind the newspaper.

'Do you?' I said, startled.

'You're thinking: why did he start without me?'

'Oh, why did you then?'

'I always feel a bit bad eating a huge steak sandwich if all you eat is the salad garnish.'

'I was going to have soup. I've ordered it. It's just coming.'

'The soup must be low-fat and healthy today, then. It won't be Cream of Cholesterol with Croutons if you're having it.'

'How was London?' I asked, bending to kiss him.

'All right, I suppose. Missed you, though.'

My soup arrived. 'It's tomato consommé.'

He screwed his face up in disgust. 'It looks like watery tomato juice to me.'

'It's lovely. It tastes really good and it's actually very time-consuming to make. Only a good chef could make this.' Andrew looked unconvinced.

'How are you getting on in the world of whisky today? You and Flora still causing trouble?'

'One man this morning told me I was promoting a pink perversion. He said pink whisky was an insult to the national drink. He quoted Scotland's national motto at me.'

'*Nemo impune lacessit.*'

'He said it meant "no one dare touch me".'

'A more contemporary translation could be: "Did you spill my pint?" Don't let him bother you, Emily. You'll never win over the likes of him. You've had a lot of positive reaction, haven't you? I thought the support outweighed the criticism.'

'It does, but the criticism can still get a bit stressful.'

He looked at me more closely. 'You really are working hard these days, aren't you? I don't suppose insomnia helps matters either. We should go out tonight and forget all about work. We should have a nice quiet meal together and a bottle of wine.'

'I might be working late,' I said quickly. 'Or I might not be. I don't know. I'll see.'

'You don't sound very sure. Well, I'll probably be home before you. I'm not as busy as you, obviously. I appreciate you sparing the time to see me, Mrs Drummond. I understand you are in great demand these days. I realise that this twenty-minute slot could have been allocated to a more deserving case and so I'm grateful.' He laughed good-naturedly.

I ate my soup and listened while Andrew told me about some meetings he was going to go to. While he was talking, I saw the mousy woman in the navy blue suit on the other side of the room, the woman who had been privately meeting her friend or possibly lover for a couple of months now. She wasn't with him today, though. She was with her husband. They didn't say much to each other. He read one section of the paper and she read another. Now and then she kept glancing up towards the door, nervously, as though she thought her grey-suited lover with the bright ties might walk in at any moment and she wouldn't know how to cope with both her husband and her lover in the room at the same time.

'Emily, did you hear what I said?'

He arrived. She saw him as he stood in the doorway looking for her and her face was suddenly agitated. She stood up too quickly and knocked a glass over. The husband swore. Confusion, mess, the barman arrived with a cloth, the lover hovered in the doorway. The woman looked anxiously over to him, shook her head – 'No,' was the message. 'No, don't come in here now' – and she started frantically dabbing at her blouse with a napkin. I thought she might cry.

Right then, I wished I really knew her, I wished I were her friend. I wanted to be able to walk over there and take her to some quiet, private place and let her tell me all about it. I wanted to talk to her and try to say something that might be of help, but what could I say? Use white wine on a red wine stain? Navy blue isn't really your colour? I know you meet your lover here; do you want the use of a private room?

I realised I had been watching her life like a soap opera. But she was real and I felt a bit ashamed of my voyeurism. I wanted to try to make up for it. I could at least help clear the table, get her another drink. I got to my feet.

'Emily, let the barman deal with it.' Andrew put his hand out to try to stop me. 'They're okay, sit down. And look, there's someone here who—'

'I'll just see if everything's all right.'

I walked over to their table, which was now wiped clean. The wine-soaked newspaper had been taken away. 'Are you all right?' I asked. 'Can I get you anything?'

'We're all right, thanks,' said the husband. His wife said nothing. She went bright red and ducked her head.

'Would you like another glass of wine?'

'I think I'd prefer a cup of tea,' said the woman.

'I'll make you a pot.' I went to the kitchen and made tea and brought it in on a tray with some shortbread. Sugar for shock, I thought. The smile of gratitude she gave me made it all worthwhile. The husband ate a chocolate-covered finger and went placidly back to his newspaper. I felt I'd done a good deed.

And then, when I turned around, I saw Jack standing beside Andrew. Jack. Where had he come from? What was he doing here now? The two of them standing there together, side by side. Jack was holding a piece of paper out to me. 'Your ticket,' he said.

I felt as though I were sleep-walking. I had to remember how to speak. 'Thanks,' I heard my voice say. I was looking at them as if from a distance, as if I were seeing them in a dream.

They're the same height, I thought, but Andrew is dark and Jack is fair. One is broad-shouldered and soft-bellied, the other is long-limbed and slender. One is flushed with wine and the other is cool beneath his suntan. Andrew is forty-two and middle age is beginning to spread over his waistband. Jack is twenty-seven and his trousers are a little bit slouchy because that's the look.

Then came the guilty, unkind thought: I'm married to the old fat one. The old fat one is my husband.

The realisation surprised me.

'I hear you're off to see a concert tonight,' said Andrew cheerfully. 'It looks like I'm going to have to start booking space in your diary, Emily, if I want to see you nowadays.'

169

'I was just going to drop this off,' said Jack awkwardly. 'I was just going to say hello and here's your ticket, but then that woman spilled her drink and you had to go and make her tea or whatever. Anyway, here's your ticket for a birthday night out. Happy birthday – kind of late, but I thought you'd still want to go.'

'Thank you.'

I took it in my hand and looked at it. My ticket out. Andrew looked at it over my shoulder. 'James Yorkston and the Athletes,' he read. 'It's their album you're playing all the time, isn't it?'

'Yes. It's their debut album. They're good.'

'Great, you'll enjoy that then. Nice present.'

'I was going to tell you about it,' I began, 'but I wasn't sure if we could get tickets and so—'

'But we have,' said Jack.

'I would have asked you,' I told Andrew, 'but . . . '

'It's okay,' he said. 'You go with your friends. You'll enjoy it.'

'I just forgot to tell you,' I said lamely.

'Memory loss.' He turned to Jack, 'See what it does to you, drinking whisky for a living?'

'I do it too,' said Jack.

'You're kidding?'

'No, I do.'

Andrew made a tutting noise and shook his head. And then, to my complete mortification, he added, 'I don't know . . . young people today.'

'Andrew—'

'It's a disgrace,' he muttered. 'It wasn't like that in my day. We had to work for a living.' He laughed and finished off his whisky. 'I think my twenty minutes are over. Emily, would you say my time was up now?'

'I'll come home before I go out tonight,' I told him.

'Lucky me.' He squeezed my hand and kissed me goodbye. 'Bye Emily. See you later.' He turned to Jack. 'Nice to meet

170

you. Good choice of present. Excellent job.' He made to go and then stopped, 'Emily . . . '

'Yes?'

He paused and turned to look at me. 'Oh, nothing,' he said, 'it doesn't matter.' Then he kissed me goodbye a second time and held my hand a little longer than before.

'A little water is needed to develop the nuances of a gently sherried nose. The mouthfeel is smooth and mellow, but spiced with the intense gingeriness, hot in the way that ginger can be'

Cask No. 24·60   *Sticky Ginger Cake*
Alcohol: 57.1%   Proof: 99.9°   Outturn: 540 bottles

The Society Bottlings, Early Summer 2001

Chapter Eleven

When I got home, Andrew was sitting on the sofa with the kitten asleep on his chest, listening to my Athletes CD. He said he hadn't paid enough attention to the words before and they were quite poignant really.

'It's good, isn't it?' I said.

'Yes,' he said sadly, switching it off. The kitten woke up and stretched. I picked it off Andrew's chest and cuddled it. It mewed and wriggled and started to purr. 'Have you fed him?' I asked.

'No, he's your cat. You have to feed him. I'll feed us, if you like. I'll make us something to eat before you go out.'

'What time do you have to leave?'

'Seven.'

'So what do you want for tea? How about pasta?' Andrew specialised in pasta sauces because he said one of the advantages of being a man was that you could always get the lid off the jar.

'No thanks. Don't bother for me, I'll just have—'

'Emily, a cup of tea is not what I mean by tea.'

'I'll have an apple as well.'

'Still not tea.'

'I'm just not hungry.' I sat down beside him and put the kitten on the floor, who ran off, chasing some imaginary thing. 'Andrew, I think I'll drive there tonight. You don't need the car, do you?'

'You're going to drive? But you hate driving in town.'

'I'll be careful, I promise.'

'You'll look after my car, won't you?'

'You've had more accidents than me.'

He shook his head. 'I didn't crash anything till I was twenty-five. You've got time yet. Are you sure you don't just want a lift?'

'No, I'd rather drive.'

'Then you shouldn't drive on an empty stomach. You might faint at the wheel and be a hazard to traffic.'

'I will eat something. I just don't want very much.'

'You never, ever want very much these days.'

'I had a big sandwich this afternoon.'

'Look me in the eye and say that.'

I felt annoyed at him. 'Andrew, don't talk to me like that . . . '

'Like what?'

'In that irritating way, as if you're talking down to me. If you come out with a line like "look me in the eye and say that", I'm going to feel really irritated, aren't I?'

'Not just over-sensitive, then?'

'No,' I said through gritted teeth.

'So, what did you have in your big sandwich?'

I felt like screaming but I didn't. 'You don't have to cook for me,' I told him in a nice, even voice. 'Stop buying me chocolate and bringing biscuits home and family-size packets of Tunnocks. You're the one who ends up eating them all.'

'You have to eat before you go out.'

'What's the matter with you?' I snapped. 'You never used to be like this. It's like living with a cross-dressing Jewish mother.'

He didn't actually laugh at that. He just looked annoyed. 'Please stop worrying about me,' I told him, more quietly. 'I can look after myself.'

'What if I think you're not right now?'

'But I am. I am! And even if I'm not, it's got nothing to do with you.'

'Don't be ridiculous.'

'I am not being ridiculous!' I shouted. 'I don't want you to fuss about me. I don't want your pasta and I don't want your biscuits. I don't want you looking after me. I don't want your advice and I don't want your—'

'What do you want, princess?'

I was so angry, I was speechless.

He was utterly calm. 'So tell me what you want. If you don't want me to look after you, what do you want me to do?'

'Nothing,' I gasped. 'Nothing.'

I got up and went into the kitchen to be on my own. I stood and stared out of the window at the garden. I didn't think I'd ever shouted at him before. No, I hadn't. Never. That was the first time. Where did that shouting come from? I wasn't a shouter by nature. I believed in containment. I thought you should keep it all in. People who let it all out were just selfish. What gave them the right to vent their anger on somebody else? It wasn't fair on all the people who weren't shouters. It wasn't fair on all the people who just got shouted at. What if you didn't have a huge voice or presence or charisma? What if you weren't a diva belting out your emotions? What were you then? A shock-absorber?

I started to make myself a cup of coffee and when I was waiting for the kettle to boil, I realised my legs had started to tremble. I sat down at the kitchen table.

There was the bread board with the crusts of a new loaf still lying there. Andrew must have made himself a sandwich earlier. Yes, there was cheese too. A huge wedge of solid Parmigiano. The edge he had cut now crumbled on to the plate like scree off a rockface. Why did he buy such a big chunk? It could be because he liked the nice girl in the deli, and he didn't need much persuasion to buy something totally weird from her – some smelly cheese made from yak's milk in Tibet or whatever. We had a fridge full of cheese. If he'd bought something good, he would insist on taking it out of the fridge to let it get to room temperature before eating it. We often had lumps of cheese lying around. At least this one wasn't smelly.

I sat at the table, flicked through a magazine and ate some bread and cheese. I flipped past pictures of girls with long skinny legs and beautiful, huge-eyed faces. I turned page after page of thin beauty and angular celebrity and all that is perfect and posed and elongated and airbrushed and glamorous and theatrical and, in a calm, private act of calculated normality, I ate my tea.

Andrew came into the kitchen and said nothing. He just got himself a coffee, but as he walked past me on his way out he stopped and we looked at each other. 'I'm sorry,' I said. 'I'm really sorry for shouting.'

He bent down beside me. 'My Emily tells me not to worry about her,' he said in my ear. 'She tells me she can look after herself.'

'At least you can be glad she's safely married to a nice man.'

'But how does she put up with him?'

'I don't know how he puts up with her.'

'It must be love.'

'Do you think that's why they put up with each other?'

'I think it can be the only explanation.'

I drove the car very carefully all the way across town to Jack's place. I obeyed the Highway Code and was not a hazard to traffic. I parked Andrew's shiny silver Audi Quattro on the street where twenty years ago he must have parked his old rusty Mini. I parked perfectly. I parked in slow motion so that passers-by could fully appreciate my skill.

It was my first visit to this quiet corner of Broughton Place where Andrew had lived. The place where Jack now lived. I pressed the buzzer for the top floor flat, said my name and the door opened.

As I climbed the stairs to the top floor, I imagined Andrew doing the same years ago, wearing the favourite leather jacket I'd seen in old photographs. I imagined him walking up these worn stone steps carrying law books for the essays he had to write, or the music magazines he now thought might be worth something on eBay. I imagined him carrying his vinyl records under his arm. Records by men who were now rich old rockers with mansions in the country and third marriages and loads of kids. Andrew's old records weren't in good condition any more and he only ever played them late at night. There were times when he liked to hear the scratched vinyl version, even though he had duplicates on CD as well.

I imagined him bringing home a girlfriend.

'Hello, Emily,' said Jack.

I walked inside.

It was a long hallway, curving round like the corner of the building on the end of a street. High ceilings, with three paper lampshades at intervals down the middle. 'I'll just get my coat,' said Jack. I followed him down the hall and when he disappeared into the living room, I hung back. Some people were sitting in the dark watching TV. I could see the light from the screen flickering over the walls. Girls' voices in the room, talking together. I stood in the doorway. Jack picked up a jacket that was lying on the back of the sofa. 'Where are you off to?' one of the girls said.

'The Venue.'

I stepped into the room. 'Hi,' said the girl and waved at me.

'Hello.' I felt shy. I didn't know them.

'This is Emily,' said Jack.

'Hi there, Emily,' said another girl. 'See you later?'

Back down the hall. All those doors. 'Which room is your room?' I asked Jack.

'That one,' he said, pointing.

'Andrew used to have this room, but next door. He had the room with the big arched window. Just like your room. He said it was freezing in winter and good in summer. He said he used to just lie in bed and watch the clouds go by.'

'Yeah, it is good.'

I hesitated. 'Can I see?'

'Take a look.' He opened a door.

The window took up most of one wall. Separate panes of glass with one big fanshaped arch at the top. The room was filled with the dull glow of the streetlight. Jack walked over to a table by the wall and turned on a desk lamp. It lit the space only dimly. The room itself was narrower than I had imagined, with the bed taking up space in the middle and a table pushed up to the opposite wall. It was quite bare. There weren't many signs that Jack actually stayed there. The cupboard door was open and there were some clothes on hangers and some T-shirts on the shelves. A towel was drying on the radiator and there were some books beside the bed. There was a laptop on the desk and some minidiscs and DVDs and a mobile phone recharging on the floor. He unplugged it and put it in his pocket.

'Is this everything?' I asked, surprised.

'Well, pretty much.'

'Where's all your other stuff?'

'Dotted around, I suppose. You don't need much, though, do you? When you're not staying anywhere for very long.'

I felt a little pang that he would be leaving soon and I had hardly got to know him yet. I wouldn't ever really get to know him. 'How long do you think you'll be here? Are you still planning on leaving next month?'

'No, I'm thinking of going sooner than that. I might go to Barcelona. Do you remember I told you that I had a friend there? Well, he wants to come to Edinburgh and so we thought we might do a sort of swap. Except I'll be doing better out of it than him because he'll only get a room in a flat whereas I'll get a whole flat. A small one, but it's a big difference. He's still keen on the idea though.'

'What about your job?'

'I can work in Barcelona.'

'How?'

'Well, it's not that difficult. Emily, if you wanted to travel on your own, you could easily find yourself a job doing something – make enough money to travel and do some interesting things.'

'You mean you could just turn up in a new city, no job, no place to live—'

'I've got a place sorted in Barcelona, but you're right, if I'm not working, just travelling, usually I don't have a place to live. Usually I just turn up.'

'And how do you manage? How do you . . . wing it?'

He shrugged. 'I just do.'

'But how?'

'I haven't really given it a lot of thought, to be honest.'

'Could you just have a quick think now, because I'd really like to know.'

'Why? Are you thinking of giving it a go?'

'Well, I nearly did two years ago but—'

179

'But you got married, you said. Bad timing, Emily.'

'Bad timing? Is that what I said? Did I say that?'

He smiled. 'You'll only know with hindsight.'

I stood up and walked over to the big window and looked out. 'Can you just have a quick think now and tell me what you do when you first arrive in a foreign city. It's not a holiday – which is all I've ever done – it's travelling and working. It's working your way around the world. Say you've just got off the plane and you don't know anyone and you don't speak the language and you don't have a job or a place to stay.'

'I usually do have a job. That's why I go.'

'Well, say it was me, and I didn't have a job.'

'Have you got any money?'

'Money?'

'In this scenario of yours. Can I assume you've got some cash when you arrive in this foreign city?'

'Yes.'

'How much?'

'I don't know. A few thousand?'

He started to laugh. 'Emily, you don't need my advice. That's plenty of money. You wouldn't have to worry about getting a job straightaway.'

'But what if it ran out and I still didn't have a job?'

'You would. You'd have found something. If I'm straight off the plane and short on money, then on day one I find a place to stay and on day two I get a job. Sometimes I do both on day one.'

'What do you do on day three?'

'On day three? Oh, on day three I usually meet a very lovely and unobtainable married woman and wish I'd never got off the plane.'

The butterflies I was feeling all rose together in a dazzling panic and I folded my arms to calm them. He smiled.

'Sometimes I do that on day one,' he added quietly. 'And it throws my whole plan out.'

180

I glanced at the clock beside the bed. 'We'd better go and see this band,' I said quickly, and I walked past him to the door.

'I nearly didn't ring you, you know.'

'There's nothing wrong with asking someone along to see a band.'

'No,' he said slowly, 'but I've never gone out with a married woman before.'

'You're only taking a friend to see a concert.'

'Emily, I think it's kind of difficult that you're married.'

'Difficult?'

'Yes. It's difficult because I'm not really going out with you because I simply want to be your friend.'

I should have said: all right then, that's made it very clear, thank you for telling me and I think I'd better just go home now. But I said nothing. I nodded slightly, just to show that I had heard him, that I understood. And I waited.

'The thing is,' he went on, 'I don't think you would still be here unless you liked me too.'

'But I'm only being friends,' I said, quickly. 'That's all.'

'If that's what you want to say.'

'I mean it.'

He shrugged. 'Let's go,' he said. 'We should be leaving now.'

We drove to the Venue. I parked perfectly again on Calton Road, just where we needed to be, and we went inside. It was a small, dark place and we stood around with plastic glasses on a wet beery floor and I got to see James Yorkston singing songs from his first album, although it turned out he didn't have any Athletes with him. I saw him and his guitar, playing the songs, singing the words. It was good.

I love live music. I love it when it is performed in a small place where you can get close and see the musicians play and it's not a big ego trip for them but a chance to be in the song.

181

I like it when the singer is the songwriter and the songs are something strong and you can lose yourself in them.

We saw James Yorkston in the bar afterwards and I was dying to tell him how great I thought his music was and how much I loved it but I didn't want to go up to him and sound mushy, so I said nothing. I wished I had had the nerve to say something to him but I missed my chance. A live performance is an act of daring which is one of the reasons I felt too intimidated to speak to him. I was not a daring person and it was so much easier in the bar afterwards to try to be cool instead of articulate. I didn't want to admit that listening to the music, I had felt something hard inside me start to crack. No composer ever wrote a decent love song without first admitting a vulnerability. It's a daring thing to do because most of us hide the fact we're vulnerable. We've been through a lot to build our defences and we can't have them broken open.

And because of this, I knew I couldn't tell Jack what I really felt for him. There was too much at risk. I couldn't tell Jack that I had been thinking about him ever since we met – so much so that it frightened me. I couldn't tell him that I had lain awake at night worrying about how I was going to deal with all of this. I couldn't tell him that when I did sleep, he walked through my dreams like he owned them.

All through the concert, I stood with Jack right behind me. We were very close in the dark. If I had leaned back very slightly, I could have touched him. I could have reached out for his hands and wrapped his arms around me.

I got home a long time after midnight. I had forgotten to call Andrew and let him know I was going to be late. It was only when I got my keys out to let myself in that I saw on my mobile he had sent me a text: R U coming home 2nite? He had left the lamp on for me in the hall. I hoped he had gone to bed, but I knew he would still be waiting up for me. I let myself in very quietly.

There was music playing. I followed the sound to the living room. No lights here but the little red and green specks on the stereo. The hiss of the needle in the worn vinyl groove. Cigar smoke hanging in the air. Not cigarettes, then. You have to bend the rules before you break them. He was sitting very low on the sofa, with his back to the door, a whisky in his hand, listening to 'The Dark Side of the Moon'.

'Many women and many young people enjoy a fine malt, despite the fact that the brands are aimed at middle-aged men, and despite the boring, predictable advertising'

Ms Leslie Hills, film producer, writer and founder
member of The Scotch Malt Whisky Society.
It was in her home that the first meetings
of the society took place.

Chapter Twelve

An email flashed up on the screen from Flora:

subject: The Whisky Brand Enforcement Agency

Expect a visit from their representative any minute now. His name is Freddie Fawcett. (Dark glasses, cracks his knuckles.) Will keep you posted.

Moments later I was standing with Flora at the front door on Charlotte Square, looking out for our man. An hour ago he had phoned to say he was caught up in Edinburgh's one-way system. Dolores, at reception with her headphones on, had talked him down as far as Queen Street but then she had lost contact. Five minutes ago, he had phoned again to say he had parked his car and hailed a taxi and would be with us directly.

We knew, however, that Mr Fawcett was delayed because he had confused us with the Scotch Malt Whisky Society and had gone to try to enforce a few points over there first.

'But what does he actually do?' I asked.

'I'm not sure, but his full job title is something long and ridiculous like Whisky Brand Strategic Planning Domination Director. He doesn't really know much about whisky, though.' Flora lowered her voice. 'This is the man who diluted my favourite single malt in order to meet volume targets.'

'I'm surprised he's got the time to come here, then.'

'He was actually very helpful on the phone. Very nice manners, you know, like the kind of gangster who loves his mum.'

And at that moment a taxi drew up and a man climbed out. He was a very big man, well over six feet tall, thick-set and solid. He wasn't actually wearing dark glasses so I was a little disappointed on that score. Flora went down the steps to greet him and he walked towards her with a slow, easy stride like a champion heavyweight boxer taking time off between fights.

I realised, all of a sudden, what very small fry we were to him.

'Freddie Fawcett,' he said in a surprisingly soft voice. He towered above me.

'Would you like to follow us this way, Mr Fawcett?' said Flora with her most polite and winning smile. Off we went to the blue sitting room where a tray of tea and shortbread and a fine single malt awaited us.

'Is Kitty Gillespie not able to grace us with her presence?' asked Freddie.

'She sends her apologies.'

(Actually, Kitty and the Brand Enforcement Agency were embattled in a crossfire of legal writs and challenges. The situation had been like that on and off for years.)

Daintily, Freddie picked up a shortbread petticoat tail and nibbled it. 'I shall come to the point,' he said. 'I think you are aware that the new chairman of the Whisky Conservative

Marketing Board is pushing for an embargo on your so-called Wild Cat Whisky. We are inclined to support him.'

Flora and I nodded. We had been expecting something like this.

'We also feel that you are encroaching on the brand name of Wild Cat Whisky.'

'But I made it up,' I told him.

'We own the distillery, therefore we own all the brand names with any kind of association with the geography of the area. You are cashing in on our brand and abusing our good-will and destroying investment.'

'How?'

'You are asking the consumer to make an association between the highland habitats of the Scottish wildcat and all of our whiskies that begin with the word "Glen". He produced a list from his inside pocket. 'That would encompass Glenlivet, Glen Garioch, Glenglassaugh, Glen Grant, Glen Moray, Glenmorangie, Glenturret, Glenfarclas, Glenfiddich, Glenrothes, Glendronach, Glen Spey . . . ' The names went on and on.

'That's completely ridiculous!'

'You will be hearing from our lawyers. I think you are aware that we have treated Kitty Gillespie with great lenience and toleration over the years, but the agency feels that this pink whisky is the last straw. It will undermine the carefully constructed image of the whisky brand. If you go ahead with your launch then we have it in our power to halt all supplies of casks to this organisation. You won't sell whisky again. You won't have the supplies. Pink whisky must never be offered for sale within the UK market.'

Our Scottish Wild Cat was now truly an endangered species.

At home that evening I told Andrew about our visit from the Domination Director of the Whisky Brand Enforcement Agency.

187

'Sorry, Emily, but you don't stand a chance,' Andrew said. 'You'll just have to go quietly. Perhaps you'll be able to get away with this particular bottling so long as you don't publish or publicise or distribute, but you have to understand that your Wild Cat launch is probably not going to happen. You're just going to have to do what he says. I'm really sorry, Em. I know this mattered a lot to you.'

'Are you sure that's it? It's all over?'

'What would happen if you still had your launch?'

'Everyone would come and word would get out. Then everyone would see what a good thing it is and the Enforcement Agency would look pretty stupid, wouldn't they? And Kitty would be vindicated.'

'That's not really how business works. You don't want to be closed down, do you?'

'Do you really think they would do that?'

'Yes. No doubt about it.'

'But that's not fair.'

'Not particularly, no.'

'But how could they?'

'Emily, it's amazing that place has kept going as long as it has.'

'They wouldn't really shut it down.'

'Believe me, they wouldn't hesitate. You're not really in any position to argue with them. It's up to Kitty Gillespie whether or not she wants to call a halt to all this. She won't want to lose her business, will she?'

'I'll tell Flora tonight what you've said.'

'Are you going round there again?'

'Yes. It's Flora's Scary Movie Season, remember?'

Flora had designed a programme of aversion therapy with the aim of curing me of my fear of horror. Jack thought this was a self-defeating project, but he offered to support me through it. Part of my motivation for going was that Jack was one of the Friends of Flora's Scary Movie Season and a regular on her sofa every Friday night.

'Ah yes,' said Andrew, 'the Friday night special.' He patted the cat who was asleep on the sofa beside him. Jaffa Cat was as round and snug as only a sleeping cat can be. 'Look at him,' said Andrew. 'Not a care in the world.'

'Are you seeing David tonight?'

'Yeah, thought I might.'

'That's good. He left a message on the answerphone saying he was up for a quiet pint and a chat any time you like. Do you think he's worried about something?'

'No, David's like me – he never worries about anything. I'll tell him to come round. Me, David and the cat can have a night in. A few beers in front of the telly. You go to Flora's. Will you be staying over again?'

'It's a double bill with a midnight movie.'

'Are you sure you're up to it? You didn't sleep for a week after the last midnight movie.'

'It was gory sci-fi. *The Thing*. I can't bear to look at gory stuff but Flora reckons I should have built up some immunity by now.'

'What's the scary movie tonight, then?'

'*Alien*, and I've got to sit right through to the end this time.'

'Can I make a suggestion?'

'You can.'

'When they get John Hurt back from the spaceship and he says he's really hungry . . .'

'Yes?'

'And he sits down to dinner . . .'

'Yes?'

'Shut your eyes.'

It was dark in Flora's living room. The light from the television flickered on to the circle of faces. It was like being in a cave, round a fire. The Friends sat, rapt and wracked with tension. Jack was whispering to me. 'This is the scene where—'

'Ssh!' said Flora.

'The alien is going to—'

'Jack, don't tell her!'

'She wants to know.'

I was whimpering with fear. 'Let him tell me, Flora. It won't be as bad if I know what's coming.'

'Don't tell her!'

'Emily, you must be the only person in the world who doesn't know what happens in this scene.'

'Ssh! Ssh!'

'Take your hands away from your eyes.'

'Oh, Emily!' said Flora, exasperated. 'You can't miss this bit. This is the really famous bit.'

But John Hurt was back from the spaceship and I knew to keep my eyes shut. The only way I knew something truly disgusting was happening on the screen was from the groans and gagging noises my Scary Movie Friends were making. Graeme laughed, Dolores squealed.

'That's horrible,' said Flora with satisfaction.

'Is it over yet? Tell me when to look.'

Somehow I made it to the end of the movie. I felt physically exhausted. My legs were stiff from being curled up, tense on the sofa. My hands were clammy.

'You have to realise,' said Jack as the credits rolled up, 'that Emily gets much more scary mileage out of this film than anybody else because she really is terrified.'

'I watched it though,' I said defiantly. 'I watched it, didn't I?'

'You missed the big scene.'

'Oh, that's allowed,' said Jack. 'Loads of people keep their eyes shut for that scene. You'll watch it next time, won't you, Emily?'

'Next time? Do I have to do it again?'

'We've got the sequel now.'

'I don't think I can. I honestly don't think I can. At least, I could, but I'd rather pace myself. I'd rather take a breather at this stage.'

'Okay,' said Flora. 'As your aversion therapist, I think taking a breather is allowed.'

The Friends of Flora's Scary Movie Season said they would join us in the pub. Jack and I started off in the Barony on Broughton Street and then we moved, both of us quietly admitting that if we moved, they couldn't find us.

Back at his place, we sat close. At first people were still around, the girl I had seen there before, some others I hadn't met. It wasn't as if anyone would have known that I was aware of his warmth and his touch all down one side as we sat close together. We touched but only so slightly that no one but ourselves would notice.

As it got later, the room emptied and we were left alone, just him and me. I knew all I needed to say was, 'I'd like to stay here tonight,' and he would have smiled and we would have gone straight to his room.

We joked about it. It was unbelievable how he teased me about it. 'Why are you sitting round at my place, having coffee and whisky late at night, if you're being so faithful to your husband?'

'I'm not doing anything wrong.'

'I know. The tension is unbearable.'

'I'm not committing adultery, am I? We're just friends. Andrew has his friends who just happen to be women, like Kate for example.'

'That's the woman he was going to marry, isn't it? Before he met you?'

'Yes. And now he works with Kate. They're friends and colleagues. Kind of like us. You know perfectly well, Jack, that there's no adultery going on between us.'

'You only have to say, Emily.' There was no pretence at all on his part. 'Just say it.'

'I can't.'

'Then tell me why you're here with me now? I'd like to hear you explain why you bother spending time with me.'

'Because I'd rather be here with you like this than not at all.'

'Would you be jealous if I started seeing someone else?' he asked.

'It's not as if you're really seeing me, though, is it?'

'I'm trying my best.'

'You'll be leaving soon, and travelling again. I'm sure you won't remember me for long.'

'I will. It'll be terrible.'

'You won't remember me. You're one of those people who just pass through and nothing ever bothers them. You know how to wing it. I'm sure once you decide to give up hoping I'll commit adultery, my attractiveness will wear off in a matter of minutes.'

'I'll never forget you.'

I laughed at him and he looked hurt.

Over the next few weeks, I saw Jack often. We met after work for coffee in one of the places on George Street. We saw each other every weekend when we were out with our friends. We met alone and would just sit and talk. Sometimes I told Andrew I'd seen Jack and sometimes I didn't. I reminded myself that I was still a free-thinking, independent woman with a mind of her own. And I was faithful to my husband in those weeks. I told myself I was wonderfully in control of the situation, but slowly, exhilaratingly, I fell for Jack and my feelings started to tangle me up. I fell for him, despite my common sense warning me against it. 'Get out now!' it shouted. 'You've got three seconds to get out! Run! Run!' My sense of alarm was acute. I had a mental picture of us kissing, surrounded by a red warning triangle.

I didn't understand myself except for feeling guilty. But the most consuming emotion of all was that I was longing to touch him; I was longing for him to touch me.

At home, lying awake, thinking about Jack took up all the

space in my brain that I would otherwise have devoted to lying awake thinking about my fear of the dark.

It suddenly occurred to me that my fear of the dark seemed to have gone. I sat up in bed and felt a sense of liberation and excitement that I didn't feel scared any more. It was amazing. I stood up, made my way to the wardrobe, feeling round the furniture, couldn't quite open the door yet, but all the same, I was up. I tiptoed around the room and then went back to bed. Not scared at all. Incredible. I was so excited that there was no way I could get back to sleep. Only someone who has never had an irrational fear could fail to understand how wonderful it is when you know fear is being conquered. It was happening almost by accident. It was something really important and yet it was just on the sidelines of my life. It was the thing in the centre of my life that was overwhelming.

Andrew was under the impression that my recent bout of insomnia and my habit of staying out very late was all Flora's fault. 'I can't believe Flora made you watch *Carrie* this week,' he said after one of my very late nights. 'I told you it would freak you out.'

'I missed most of it. I had my eyes shut and my fingers in my ears.'

'You shouldn't have tried, Emily.'

'I didn't like to let Flora down.'

'I can't think what possessed you,' he said drily.

The next time Flora called round at our house, Andrew joked that her job as an aversion therapist was a breeze compared to his job as a post-traumatic counsellor and would she mind easing up on the programme a bit because his wife couldn't sleep at night. Flora told him she wasn't aware of that and she would, of course, review the schedule, but later she came up to me and said: 'Emily, just tell me to mind my own business, but . . . is there something seriously going on between you and Jack?'

'No. We're just friends.'

'Okay,' she said, nodding slowly. 'That'll do me, for now.'

And later, worrying away at this, I said to my husband: 'Andrew, I know I'm a terrible insomniac most of the time, but do I ever talk in my sleep?'

'No. You wriggle a lot, but you don't talk. Thank God. Why do you ask?'

'Oh, nothing, just wondering.'

I shouldn't have asked that question and I really shouldn't have given such a stupid answer. He came straight back with: 'What do you think you would talk about if you did talk in your sleep?'

'Not sure, really.'

'What do you think about when you're lying awake?'

'I'm just lying awake.' And then, foolishly, I clarified things even further. 'I don't mean lying in the sense of not telling the truth; I mean just being horizontal.'

'Of course,' he said, surprised.

'I mean I'm counting sheep or putting whiskies in alphabetical order or doing something else to empty my mind.'

'Do you spend a lot of time horizontally awake every night?'

'No. Sometimes I get up and go downstairs and sit in the kitchen.'

'And what do you do there?'

'Just think about things.'

There was too long a pause before he said, very slowly, 'I see.'

I curled up and kept very still, eyes closed, method-acting sleep.

The next few nights when I woke up at three o'clock, it felt wrong lying there next to Andrew, thinking of Jack, and so I got up. Before I left our room, I looked at the sleeping figure of my husband and listened to his deep, calm breathing and felt a stab of love and guilt. I willed him to wake up and ask me gently what was wrong, although that was a pointless sort of wish because it wasn't as if I could tell him.

Sometimes I left the house and walked around the garden wearing wellies and a big coat over my nightie. But when I'd done that three nights in a row I decided it was actually mad behaviour, so I stopped. Instead, I got dressed quietly and went out in the car and drove around, which for some reason I decided wasn't mad at all. I would drive all the way across town to the twenty-four-hour garage at the bottom of Dundas Street and I would buy something, as if to prove my journey really was necessary. On the drive out and the drive back, I always went via Broughton Place, past the flat where Jack lived, and sometimes I parked the car and sat there in the dark, thinking about how he was sleeping just behind that tall arched window.

On the occasions that I left the house in the middle of the night, I always left Andrew a note, in case he woke up and wondered where I'd gone. He never found my notes, but if he had he would have discovered that . . . well, it was always a problem, actually, working out what to say. Sometimes I would spend so long writing the note that I didn't go out at all. I would sit at the kitchen table and write my husband pages of mixed up emotions.

Dear Andrew

I have gone out to the twenty-four-hour garage at the bottom of Dundas Street to buy a pint of milk. I'm worried that we got married too quickly. It's hard realising that I hadn't thought everything through properly.

I don't regret marrying you – not for a single moment – because we've been very happy and I suppose I'm just being selfish, wanting to go off on my own for a while. But that is what I want – maybe even more than I want Jack, to be honest.

Sometimes you only realise things with hindsight but then it's too late. I'm going to buy skimmed because I know you're on a diet. Personally, I don't think dieting is the answer; you just need to be moderate in all things and eat in a normal way without actually thinking it out too carefully. I'm glad you're thinking about going to the gym again because it would help you keep fit, wouldn't it? I worry a lot about how, given the age difference, I might be left alone without you and I can't bear to think about it.

love
Emily

I wanted Andrew, but I wanted Jack too.

I thought how great it would be if bigamy was a normal part of social culture and everyone was allowed more than one spouse. Although I wouldn't fancy it much if Andrew had more than one wife. After all, he would have married Kate, then, wouldn't he? He would have thought: might as well, I'll hedge my bets and have them both. And I would be Wife Number Two and Kate would be Head Wife and she would boss me around and tell me what to do. And if he spent more time with her than with me, I would be jealous. No, I didn't fancy the idea of polygamy at all.

However, when a woman has more than one husband, it's not called polygamy, it's called polyandry. A fact I found out at about five in the morning, poring over a guidebook to the Pacific Islands, imagining Jack and I running away together in one of my escapist fantasies, except I didn't want to leave Andrew behind.

Polyandry is rather rare these days, although it flourished most recently in some parts of Micronesia. It existed in matriarchal societies, where people traced their ancestry through the female line – which is just what the ancient Picts used to do in Scotland many centuries ago. It doesn't exist at all in societies which hold to the belief that God is a man. You've got to believe in a Goddess to have a polyandrous society.

We've got a big house, I thought. If Andrew was understanding, I could have Jack as well. We could all live happily ever after. But that sort of thing just isn't encouraged in Scotland today.

The days of Pictish polyandry are over.

Pity.

'What happens inside a copper whisky still is that the copper and the low wines have a conversation. If you're making a light style of whisky, you make sure the still doesn't get too heated and they just have a nice long chat. If you're making a big whisky, the conversation is shorter, cooler and very much to the point'

Mike Nicolson, Whisky Maker at Royal Lochnagar, explaining to the author and Annabel Meikle the influence of copper on the distillation process, 4th May 2001

Chapter Thirteen

At work on Monday morning, Kitty Gillespie summoned Flora and me to her flat for what she called a Crisis Summit.

The Whisky Brand Enforcement Agency had issued their final ultimatum. We had to stop our Wild Cat Whisky or they would stop it for us. They would see to it that no one ever sold us a drop of whisky ever again – and no broker would dare break their embargo.

'They want to kill us off,' said Kitty. 'We've defied them and they don't like it. We now have a choice, albeit a very limited one. We can do as they tell us and survive – lobotomised and humiliated and broken or . . . ' Kitty rose to her feet, her flowing scarlet dress bleeding wisps of chiffon. 'Or, we may choose martyrdom.'

'Oh, God!' said Flora.

'But let's have a little drink and chat about it first,' said Kitty, sitting down, all amiable again. 'Put the kettle on, Flora.'

'We're not nosing any whisky?'

'Not this morning, no. We need tea and sympathy. And we need to make a plan. I think I may be able to squeeze a teeny weeny concession from Mr Fawcett. I think we may be able to launch our whisky, just so long as we never, ever do it again, and as long as I agree to sell the company afterwards.'

'You would sell up to Fawcett?'

'Not to him, no. But there are possibilities, if the price is right. Remember Elizabeth Cumming. We are business-women. We have to make a living.'

We sat and talked for an hour and eventually decided we had to launch our Wild Cat Whisky. If we didn't do it, who would? It had become a matter of principle. Kitty decided we would launch and to hell with the consequences.

Flora and I left her deep in thought over a list of share-holders – all old friends of hers. They were all going to be invited to our launch party. The plan was that they would be so inspired by the magnificence of the occasion they would put their money at her disposal – at least, that was her confi-dent belief.

Back at my desk, I had a call from Kate. It turned out she wasn't ringing for me in particular, she just wanted to make a booking for a lunch meeting with some clients. 'How are you, Emily? Still busy? How's the pink whisky going?'

'Very well. I might be going off to Paris to promote it, especially if we can't sell it in the UK.'

'How wonderful! Good for you. I love Paris. It really is the most romantic city. We used to go there for weekends sometimes. It's a short flight from Edinburgh, isn't it? And when we were both working so hard, it was nice to go away for a short break together.'

The thought of Kate and Andrew having romantic weekends in Paris was almost too much to bear. I hoped they hadn't stayed in the same hotel where we had spent our wedding night. 'Did you stay anywhere nice?'

There was a brief hesitation in her voice and then she said, 'I don't think you need to feel at all jealous, Emily.'

'I'm not jealous. I was just wondering where you'd stayed, that's all.'

'I hope you're getting on all right together.'

'We're very happy, thanks.' I glanced round the office to see if anyone was looking. No one was.

'It was difficult the way things happened,' Kate went on, 'but it's nearly two years ago now and . . . it's all in the past.'

I cupped my hand over the mouthpiece to speak more privately. 'Well,' I said finally. 'Things just sort of happened, didn't they? All in a rush. And . . . and . . . sometimes it takes a while to realise that . . . er . . . ' I didn't know what else to say. What did it take a while to realise? 'Sometimes it takes a while to realise certain things, doesn't it?'

'It does. Look at Jane and David.'

'What do you mean? Jane and David aren't married. He keeps asking her but she keeps saying no.'

'That's because David was unfaithful to her.'

'Was he?' I was amazed. I had always thought David was completely devoted.

'She stayed with him, but she's never going to marry him.'

'I didn't know that was the reason.'

'I'm surprised Andrew hasn't told you. I suppose it all happened about ten years ago, but I used to argue with him about David's infidelity. I thought Jane ought to be told. I wanted to tell her and Andrew said no. He thought David had to tell her himself and ask her forgiveness at the same time.

Jane only found out when he confessed, and she's never really forgiven me for not telling her earlier. She hated being the last to know.'

'Andrew must have thought he was acting for the best. And they are still together, Kate, so perhaps it worked.'

She tutted. 'Andrew always believed there were gradations of goodness, and morality could be a very relative concept. Fidelity, in particular, was a very relative concept. Andrew and David always had a lot in common on that issue.'

I didn't like to think my husband believed fidelity was a relative concept. 'Kate,' I said anxiously, 'was Andrew ever unfaithful to you?'

She burst out laughing. 'You ought to know!'

I felt confused and embarrassed. I didn't know what to say to her. She was still laughing when she said goodbye and hung up.

It was a full twenty minutes later that she rang me back and, not laughing at all, said: 'Emily, I should explain something. Andrew has all these wonderful intellectual arguments about what constitutes fidelity, but the simple truth is that he has no understanding at all of just how deeply it hurts to be betrayed by someone you love.'

After Kate's call, I kept myself very busy with work. I planned the evening's events and sorted out seating plans and typed and emailed and organised whiskies, but I kept thinking about what she had said.

At lunchtime, I met Jack in a café on George Street. He was there first, waiting for me. He looked really pleased when I walked in. 'I'm always so glad when you turn up,' he said. 'I keep thinking one day you'll decide I'm not worth the bother.' We managed to keep things light and easy for about ten minutes and then our conversation began to spiral into its usual frustrating circles. I told him about my call from Kate.

'Emily, you need some time away from Andrew to sort out how you feel.'

202

'I don't think I can just yet.'

'Do you still think you were right to get married when you did?'

'It seemed right at the time.'

'But you're having second thoughts now?'

'I don't know.'

'It's nothing to feel guilty about. Anyone can see you're having second thoughts. You have a lot of doubts about your marriage. I know you do. You married after six weeks.' He reached for my hand and we sat, heads close together, talking. He told me he had decided to leave Edinburgh. 'You could leave and come with me.' I didn't reply. 'I know you want to be with me.'

'I can't sleep with you.'

'Leave him and come with me.'

I suddenly felt annoyed. 'What if I just want to have some time on my own for a change?'

He looked at me, surprised, and then started to smile. 'You choose what you want to do, Emily. Whatever you want to do.'

Back at the office, I told Flora that Jack would be going soon. 'Where to?'

'He's getting a flight to Perpignan and he's going walking in the Pyrenees for a week and after that he doesn't know.'

'And when does he leave?'

'Day after tomorrow.'

I tried to keep my mind on my work – Kitty had insisted we carry on as normal, despite the threats from Freddie Fawcett. The launch date was set and invitations were being printed. Although I was very busy, I found it hard to concentrate. If Flora noticed, she didn't say. By the time I was getting ready to go home at the end of the day, I knew that I needed to talk to Andrew. I couldn't put it off any longer and, at last, I knew exactly what I had to say. I wanted to do those things

I had planned to do, only I had got married instead. I wanted to see places and travel around the world. I had my own money and I would give up my job and have time, just as I had planned. I would broaden my mind and my experience of the world.

Whisky has many uses, hedonism and drunkenness among them, but in my experience whisky is the perfect stimulant for an exchange of confidences. Some things can be discussed over any kind of drink and some are best shared over wine, but when you're nervous about owning up to something and uncertain about your husband's reaction, then only a whisky will do.

However, I had reckoned without Andrew having a pre-planned agenda of his own. When he reached for the bottle and poured us a dram each, I didn't know that he had already rehearsed a whole lot of questions he wanted to ask me. A whole lot of difficult, leading questions, with an intricate pre-amble and a lot of agonising.

A smoky highland malt can be as dark and heavy as a late night conversation. It can take on any subject. Infidelity, for instance.

One sip and I was shockingly alert. I wasn't sure yet if he was talking about infidelity in practice or just in theory. It was hard to tell. Andrew sometimes talked in theory only. He had once told me that he always liked to have an exit strategy from an argument should he need to get out of it fast. So I wasn't sure now if he really meant what he was saying or if he was just exploring a difficult area while keeping an eye on the emergency exit.

He started by talking about independence.

I listened and felt nervous, but I was hopeful that a talk about independence would give me a chance to explain my feelings to him. But he was soon two drams ahead of me and that wasn't a good sign.

'What I'm saying, Emily, is that the most important thing to realise about marriage is that when you love someone, you sacrifice your independence – your absolute independence – in order to live together with the person you love. We talked about it before we got married, didn't we? You surrender your independence because you hope and trust that it will be worth it, that you will be happy in your shared life together. It's as if you've made a pact. You've made a pact with your partner and the first clause is: I will be faithful.'

'Yes,' I said. 'I know. I understand.'

'Well . . . ' He put his glass down. 'I think it's probably true that for some people, under certain circumstances, perfect fidelity –' he held out the idea to me in the palm of his hand – 'is something of a superhuman virtue.'

'Superhuman?'

'I mean, if you were to ask me for the best exemplars of fidelity, I'd say angels and dogs. And angels aren't as good at it as dogs. Some angels didn't keep the faith, did they? Lucifer and his gang attempted a kind of angelic putsch and got cast out of heaven into hell – so that just leaves dogs with an unblemished fidelity record. Do you remember how Jane's dog pined when she went on holiday? Dogs are better than angels at fidelity. Fido is Latin for "I am faithful".'

'Fido?'

'It's a name for a poodle, maybe. But the thing is, Emily, compared with dogs, human beings can find fidelity a bit of a challenge, despite good intentions and superior intelligence. Even very good, very devoted, saint-like human beings have been known to succumb to temptation. But the thing about marriage is that you've got to take a long-term view. After all, that's why we married. We took the long-term view and I understand that fidelity can still be tested and what if . . . I mean, what if, when it came to the test . . . perhaps you were unfaithful to me – well, I want you to know that I would be very hurt and—'

I felt anxious. Had someone told him something? Who? And what could they have said anyway? I hadn't been unfaithful to him. 'Andrew,' I interrupted. 'Please don't talk like this.'

He poured me another drink. 'Have you ever heard that saying about "virtue never tested is no virtue at all"?'

'Why are you asking me that?'

'All I'm saying is that I understand that you're still very young and—'

'Please don't use that approach. It's not a useful argument.'

'Look,' he said, 'it's part of the whole fidelity thing to be tested. It happens to everybody. It's what I was saying before: fidelity is only simple when it isn't being tested.'

'I've not been unfaithful.'

'I'm glad to hear it.' Then he reached for my hand and said intensely, 'I love you, Emily.'

'I know,' I said, wanting to cry.

'Do you still love me?'

I nodded, unable to speak.

We sat very close and he went on, 'You've been thinking of all the big plans you had before we got married – all the things you wanted to do. Isn't that what's been on your mind?'

'Sometimes,' I said in a low voice. I ached for hurting him.

'It's okay, I understand. If you want to go away for a short while then why not use that plane ticket your mother gave you for your birthday? Take a few days in Marbella.'

'That's not the kind of travel I mean. Andrew, I wish we could go together. Can you not take some time off – a sabbatical? You know lawyers who have done that. There's no reason why you couldn't. We could rent the house out and . . .'

He was shaking his head. 'I can't. You know I can't. I couldn't possibly take a sabbatical.'

'What about next year?'

'I'm not just starting out in my career like you. There's no way I can take a year off.'

'Not even six months?'

'I can't, Emily.'

'At least tell me you'll think about it.'

'I'll fantasise about it. Try to understand. I'd love to, but I can't. It's out of the question.'

'But it would be good for us,' I said, getting upset. 'I think we should be together more, so we can talk about things.'

'I'm here now.'

I wondered if he had put it in his personal organiser: must talk to Emily about our marriage, allow 1 hour, priority B.

'What would you think if I took a gap year on my own?' I asked. 'What would you say? Would you mind?' I felt guilty just suggesting it. 'Of course, I wouldn't go unless you were happy with the idea.'

He leaned back and looked at me. 'If you want to go, why bother even asking? Why not just go? I think what you really want from me is my approval, my support for the idea. You'd like me to say: Off you go, Emily, and do whatever you like, for as long as you feel like it, and I'll be waiting for you when you get back. Is that what you want?'

The silence that followed lasted a very long time. 'Is that what you want?' he repeated.

'I'd come back,' I whispered.

He shook his head. 'No, it wouldn't happen like that. You might come back, but not to me. I don't want to lose you. In any relationship, you've got to be together or it doesn't work. Emily, you're my wife and I love you more than anything. I want you to be happy, but it's completely unrealistic to think you can take a gap year from marriage.'

'Visky . . . and don't be stingy, baby'

Greta Garbo in *Anna Christie*

Chapter Fourteen

It was now three months since Flora and Ben had parted and Flora was still adamant she was never going to tie herself down in any relationship ever again. She was commitment-free, seeing Harry now and then, 'but we're not really involved'. She had told me that Ben had also been spending a bit of time with Maisie – 'but only on a very casual basis'. However, Flora found she still missed Ben very much. 'You can't just turn off your feelings for someone.' He had since apologised for the things he had said in their parting row and Flora had said sorry too. They had started seeing each other again – just as friends.

'Did you see him this weekend?'

'Yes. We had another good talk and we've decided that we're going to have a trial reconciliation.'

'Really? Are you sure?'

'It's worth a try. We were very happy together, remember.'

'But you said you felt so suffocated in that relationship. How do you know you'll still be able to breathe?'

'It's a trial reconciliation on the understanding that it's an open relationship.'

I was astonished. 'Are you serious?'

'We've talked it all through very carefully.'

'So you're still going to carry on seeing Harry?'

'Yes, and anyone else I want to see.'

I stared at her and she smiled, kind of gleefully. I had to admit, I was impressed. 'And Ben didn't mind?'

'He agreed, so long as he can see Maisie and anyone else he wants to see. It cuts both ways.'

'And you won't be jealous?'

'I know that's a danger. We're going to see how it goes.'

'Do you really think it could work?'

'I don't honestly know,' said Flora, looking me in the eye, 'but it's better than lying to him and having an affair, isn't it?'

After work that day I went to say goodbye to Jack. I climbed the steps to his flat feeling sick at heart. I couldn't really believe he was going. We stood in his room with the tall windows and I tried to take it all in and remember everything in detail because I knew I would never be doing this again. When I told him this really was goodbye, he looked so unhappy about it that I felt terrible. I had to remember to stand back, to try to keep myself somehow detached from all this, otherwise it was too much. 'I'll miss you,' he said.

'You won't,' I said firmly. 'And I don't think we should try to stay in touch.'

'How is it you're so good at being an ice queen?' he asked.

He put his arms around me and it was such a good thing to have that warm physical contact that I wished I had done it earlier. The sense of detachment just dissolved. I wanted to hold on to him for ever. And then we kissed. We kissed one tentative kiss that became a second, more confident kind of kiss and then a third, more passionate one. And then we stopped. I felt panic-stricken.

'I have to go.'

I left. I ran down the stairs in tears. Not because I'd kissed him but because I knew it was all over now and I couldn't do it again.

When I got home, Andrew was there and I didn't know what to do, how to behave. I couldn't face him so I spent ages in the bath. I locked the bathroom door and ran the taps loud so he wouldn't hear me crying.

Considering he knew something was wrong, Andrew was very good at leaving me to myself over the next few days. At home, I spent a lot of time being in a different room to him, keeping a sort of parallel existence. He didn't intrude, but I was aware of him being around, like a benign presence. When I eventually joined him in the living room one night, I found him reading a book. He had got into the habit of reading a lot more than he used to and I realised all of a sudden that he had more time. Less work, somehow. How did that happen? There was music playing very quietly in the background. It was the sort of music you should guard yourself against late at night – something achingly tender in a minor key.

I sat down in the armchair opposite him and tried to still myself. He looked up. 'Hello, Emily.' Glancing around, I could see the acquired comforts of my life. The room was warm and soft. Lamps in pools of gentle light; the pleasant, civilised trappings of home.

'I'll go and clear away in the kitchen,' I said.

'There's nothing to clear away.'

'Well, I'll just go and check.'

In the kitchen, I put the radio on, a phone-in about nothing in particular. Vapid voices punctuated by noisy commercials. I moved about the room, aimlessly wiping the bench and feeling useless. Andrew appeared in the doorway. 'I think I'll go out for a bit,' I told him.

'It's raining. It's nearly midnight.'

'Well, I'll just take an umbrella and walk around the garden.'

He took my hand. 'Emily,' he said quietly. 'Do you want to talk to me?'

'No,' I said, turning away. 'Please, not now.' I was too upset now for any kind of talk. I sat down at the kitchen table and reached for the newspaper, turning the pages mechanically. He bent to kiss me. I didn't raise my face so he kissed me apologetically on the head and left the room.

I was alone again. I thought about what he had said about my wanting to go away for a while, and how our marriage would never be the same. Staring at the wall, I asked myself: Do I want it to stay the same? I knew that I would have given anything – anything – to have felt as happy as I had been when we first got married. Our marriage had already changed.

A few minutes later, I was aware that Andrew had returned. He stood beside me for a few moments before bending down to speak. The words came slowly and carefully. 'Jack left a few days ago, didn't he?'

I nodded.

'Have you heard from him?'

'No.'

'You miss him, don't you?'

'He was a friend. I miss him like you'd miss any friend.' I felt completely exhausted. I wanted to curl up in a corner and close my eyes very tight.

'I'm sure he'll get in touch.'

'When we said goodbye, I told him I didn't want him to get in touch.'

Andrew was silent for a moment. 'That's the end, then?'

'Yes, that's the end of a friendship.'

'Did you give him a kiss goodbye?'

'What do you mean?'

'Did you kiss goodbye?'

'Yes,' I said weakly.

'What kind of kiss?'

'What do you mean – what kind?'

Andrew kissed me on the mouth. A warm, tender kiss. 'Like that?' He kissed me again and I reached up to draw him towards me. Another kiss. I didn't know what I was doing any more. I felt he'd caught me out. I gave in and let myself disappear. I lost myself. I was a long way out, a long way from land. I was drowning in all this.

I had to get out.

The Fourth Whisky:
HIGHLAND & ISLAND
exposure to the elements

now things get a little smoky
a warm, sweet finish
often fudgy flavours

Some Highland & Island Malts:
Highland Park
(from Orkney, the northernmost distillery)
Glenmorangie
(pronounced with emphasis on MOR, not ange. Who is this
Angie anyway?)
Clynelish
(explosively sweet and fruity with a smoky kind of whisky kick
makes a Smarcardi Bruiser look like a cup of tea)
Talisker
(from the Isle of Skye, over the sea)
Jura
(one to catch you out; it's near the island of Islay, but hardly
peaty at all)
Glen Garioch
(pronounced Glen Geerie, now sadly closed
full-bodied, pungent, rich, spicy with a thread of gentle, sweet
smoke)

'Founded by a well-known smuggler and ne'er-do-well, this distinguished distillery's malt has always had a great reputation and this well-matured cask is a good example ... trampled orange-blossom, peardrops and honey with light smoky notes'

Cask No. 4·67   *Trampled Orange Blossom and Bonfires*
Alcohol: 61.8%   Proof: 108.1°   Outturn: 624 bottles

The Society Bottlings, Early Summer 2001

Chapter Fifteen

Getting on a plane to go and see my mother always reminded me of school holidays. Even now, when I was worrying about things and getting used to feeling that tight knot of anxiety in my stomach, I was smiling when I checked my bag in at Edinburgh Airport. It was as if I had just broken up for the holidays and was running for the sun. I always looked forward to seeing my mother. She was associated in my mind with breaking free.

On the plane, I listened to the latest tape she had sent me. I heard about her collection of lilies ('I've been considering the lilies again and I'm going to get new ceramic pots for the patio – with a blue glaze, I think . . . ') I heard about her drinks parties and her trips to Barcelona for the opera. I listened to an aria from Turandot, a bit of Burt Bacharach and a really happy country and western song. At the end, she signed herself off with, 'I'm so much looking forward to seeing you. I've been thinking of you a lot recently. All my love and kisses, Joanna.'

I stared out of the window of the plane as the Spanish coast appeared thousands of feet below. She would be there to meet me at the airport. She would be wearing elegantly casual clothes with high heels and sunglasses, like a film star on vacation who knows the paparazzi are out there. Her hair would be styled into youthful, short blonde waves. Her make-up would be both subtle and immaculate, with a sun-kissed glow over high cheekbones. She would look ten years younger than forty-four. She would stand out in the crowd and people would wonder if they ought to know who she was. Right now, she would be stalking impatiently up and down the Arrivals area of Marbella Airport like a haughty catwalk model intent on making a comeback.

My mother could seem terribly aloof, until she smiled her big, goofy smile and laughed her big, fruity laugh – which she detested, although these were the flaws that made people love her. I loved her dearly. I admired her beauty and her daring and her determination and her style. I had never wished her to be any different to the way she was.

Joanna was always pointing out that we were very different. Although she had spent the past seven years being a talent agent and not a singer, she still saw herself as an artistic diva driven by passion and song, whereas she thought of me as a sensible girl, mature for my age and never driven by anything more exciting than her Jaguar coupé the night she lost her licence. The talent agency was successful but Joanna missed the stage, she missed performing. It had been hard for her to adjust to being a back-seat diva.

When I got married, Joanna had admitted (on the record) that eloping with a man you've only known for six weeks showed a far more reckless nature than anything she had expected of me. She had been shaken to the core. I had replayed that tape over and over again until every syllable was singing joyfully in my head.

'I just feel shaken to the core, Emily. You've always been so sensible and level-headed, I just can't believe you would do something like this. Maybe it's my fault for spending years telling you how mature you are. To be perfectly honest, I'm worried about you – and I've never had to say that before, have I?'

She had been dying to meet Andrew. 'I'm not sure I'm too happy about the fact he's only a few years younger than me. I'd say he was old enough to be your father if it weren't for the fact that your father is sixty-four.'

When I came out of Arrivals, I spotted her straightaway. A slim, elegant woman dressed in cool blue, standing confidently at the front of the crowd. She was holding up a card saying 'Daughtie'. She saw me and a huge smile broke across her face. She waved and I waved back. We walked quickly towards each other, my sandals flip-flopping and her heels click-clacking across the floor. When we embraced, I recognised her perfume and it was so much my mother, so much the very essence of her, that for a second all my memories overwhelmed me and the tight feeling in my throat made me want to cry. 'Hello, Mum.'

'Hello, Daught. I've missed you such a lot.'

We held on to each other tightly. I gulped back my tears and she wiped her eyes behind her cool designer shades and blew her nose.

'Come on,' she said. 'I've left us a bottle of champagne in the freezer and we have to get back quickly before it explodes.'

Out on the terrace of my mother's villa, we sat among the lilies. The white flowers were pearlescent and glowing in the twilight and their scent was sweetly heady. 'I do love madonna lilies,' she said. 'I'm not really into gardening, but I do like my lilies. I like the way they lie very still for months, then shoot forth and dazzle you. They're the kind of flowers that put on a really good show.'

She opened the champagne with a bit of a struggle. 'Polly won't be home till tomorrow. Carmen is looking after her. They're doing a few cabaret numbers on the *Mediterranean Star*. Polly has been rehearsing for weeks. She's so excited about it. It's her first official cruise ship engagement. I didn't want to be a stage mother and push her into it, but she's thrilled to be earning the money.'

'Is she well? I'm really looking forward to seeing her again. Polly always has such energy for going out and doing exciting things.'

'Yes, she's a treasure. She's still trying so hard to be discovered. She's even started busking in that new twenty-four-hour shopping mall. I took her down there myself at midnight, just for an experiment – the acoustics are marvellous. I told her to sing 'Memory'. She sounded lovely. We made two euros in twenty minutes. It's not actually much of a turnover, but it was just so she could say she had done it.'

'How is she getting on at school? Is she doing any work?'

'I think she wants to focus on her singing career.'

'Do you still let her skive off school?'

'Actually, she's left school.'

'You let her leave?'

'She's got quite a bit of work lined up, you see. She's doing rather well. She's been so much more confident since she found her image.'

'Her image?'

'She's calling herself Polka Dot. It's going down a storm. It suits her. Polka Dot is fun and confident and kind of sexy in a girlpower way. Polly's happy being Polka Dot.'

'I can't believe you let her leave school.'

'She just wanted to get on with her career. Polly is very ambitious.'

'She gets away with more than I ever did.'

'But Emily, you were always so much more biddable than Polly. I can shout at Polly till I'm blue in the face but it doesn't make her do anything I ask. If I tell her to tidy her room she just shrugs and says Maria can do it. She even goes outside and shouts for her. "Maria! Maria!" God knows what people must think. And now she's started giving Maria the day off. She takes her to the beach. "Maria! Maria! *Vamous a la playa!*" What can I do? She's worse than me.'

Some people have imaginary friends, but for as long as I can remember, my mother has had an imaginary servant. When it's time to clear away after dinner, Mum says: 'Leave it for Maria' and whenever the house is looking a tip, Mum complains that she will have to sack her. Maria once stole my mother's car and drove it at 150 kph while under the influence of sangria, but she was caught and exposed by the Guardia.

'Let's drink a toast!' said Joanna. 'You know I don't normally need any reason to drink champagne but this is a little celebration.'

'What are we celebrating?'

She raised her glass to mine. 'My success,' she beamed.

'What have you done?'

'The business is doing well. Just finished the year-end with a decent profit and we've got a full order book. Cheers!'

'Well done, Joanna, that's great. That's all your hard work.'

'Thank you.'

She leaned back in her chair and gave me an appraising look. 'You've lost weight, Daught,' she said. 'You're looking more like your old self.'

'I'm a slim size twelve now,' I said, pleased. 'I'm nearly a ten.'

'Well done. You can really tell the difference.'

221

'Thanks. You look good yourself, Mum.'

'I'm a size ten,' she said. 'Always have been.' (Competitive Mum.)

'I thought you were a twelve in jeans.'

'Okay, I'm a slightly pear-shaped size ten. The only time I was really curvy in the proper places was when I was sixteen weeks' pregnant with you. I didn't look pregnant, but I had this amazing hourglass shape. I felt like Marilyn Monroe. Of course, it was all downhill after that. But you, Emily, have got a proper, feminine, curvy kind of shape and I envy you for it.'

'I'd rather have the tall, skinny look.'

'Don't waste your time thinking like that! The Frenchwomen I know have the best attitude – they don't wish for what they can never be, they just make what they've got look fantastic.'

'But you've always looked so great, Joanna.'

'Oh, everything has begun to sag. It's a bit depressing. I'm going to the gym more often – doing more weights. Got to stay toned. You know I used to be able to eat whatever I wanted, but let me tell you, after the age of forty you can't. I'm going to stay a size ten if it kills me.'

'Andrew thinks I'm getting thin.'

'He should have seen you when you were a size eight.'

'He says he would have wept.'

'Emily, you're lovely just the way you are. You suit a twelve. It's more you than a fourteen. You looked good when you were a ten as well. I'm always telling you how good you look. Drink your champagne before it goes flat. You've just been staring at it.'

I leaned back in my seat and rubbed my eyes. Since arriving, I had felt a great tiredness come over me. I wanted to sleep. 'I like your lilies,' I said. 'I've planted snowdrops in the garden at home. Andrew's mum gave us the bulbs as a present. They should come up next year.'

'I think it's lovely that you've got someone to advise you on things like snowdrop-planting and how to use an Aga. I think it's good that you now have the chance to experience what it's like to have a more ordinary mother figure in your life. She made you a birthday cake, didn't she? I'm sorry I never managed to be a cake-baking kind of mother. I did buy you beautiful cakes, though, didn't I?'

'You did.'

'We've always been very close, haven't we? Think of all the times we've borrowed each other's clothes and gone out together and had fun.'

'You've still got my favourite jeans, Mum.'

'Sorry, Daught. You can have them back.'

My mother loved to borrow my clothes. The only times she hadn't been able to wear my jeans was the summer I did my A levels when I had been an anxious, black coffee-drinking size eight, and the year following my marriage when I had been a blissed out, ice cream-spooning size fourteen.

Joanna reached for her cigarettes. 'Sorry, Emily. I know you hate it when I smoke, but I usually have one or two in the evening on the terrace. It's very relaxing and it helps keep the mozzies away.' She lit her cigarette with her thin silver lighter and I watched it flame up in the dark. She inhaled deeply and sat back. 'How's Flora? Tell me what you've been getting up to.'

'Busy at work. I really like my job.'

'I'm delighted! It's amazing to think of you flogging bottles of whisky for a living. I'm sure that's not what your father had in mind when he paid for your education. Well done, Emily.'

'Thank you.'

'You know, it's taken me a long time to make the business work but it's growing really well now, and that does give me a lot of satisfaction. It's very important for a woman to have her own money and make her own way in the world. Never rely on anyone for anything, Emily.'

'I know.'

'So long as you're earning your own money, you'll have your independence – and that's especially important because if your relationship fails, you'll be able to support yourself.'

'Money is probably very low down on my list of priorities. I need Andrew for lots of reasons but money isn't one of them.'

'You only say that because you've always been privileged enough never to have to worry about money. If you had lived without it, you would find money becomes a much bigger priority.'

'I was prepared to go all the way to New Zealand to start a new life with nothing but a backpack.'

'Travelling on the ticket I paid for.'

'I didn't ask you to pay for it. You offered. As soon as I told you I was going to emigrate to the other side of the world, you offered to buy me the one-way ticket.'

'I thought you'd be pleased! I have always said I will support you in whatever you want to do. I was just showing my support.'

'It's not how most mothers would have reacted.'

'Well, I'm sorry, Emily, if I got it wrong, I didn't mean to. Anyway, you were still happy to let me pay for your ticket, weren't you? Tell me a bit more about this friend of yours, Jack. You did mention him a few times in your emails.'

'Oh, he's Flora's friend really.'

'He sounds very interesting.'

'Yes, he is. He's gone now, though. He's off on his travels again.'

'And you said he had been in New Zealand.'

'Yes, and he was in Canada and lots of other places. Always on the move.'

'I was so restless in my twenties,' Joanna said. 'I always needed to feel free to move about and move on.'

We watched the sky darken until all the stars came out. We talked more quietly and I wanted to tell her, talk to her, but I

224

couldn't get started and she sensed it. 'Is everything all right between you and Andrew?'

'Sometimes,' I began, 'sometimes I wish I had gone to New Zealand, only I don't really because Andrew wouldn't have been able to go with me, except now I think there's a bit of regret building up and it's getting difficult to sort it out.'

'Ah, yes,' said my mother, 'but if you hadn't met Andrew would you still have emigrated? Because –' and she dropped her voice – 'because sometimes, I wonder if you just suffered massive stage fright and couldn't go on and then Andrew came along and asked you to marry him and you did because you knew you could just stay backstage then.'

'I fell in love with him!' I protested. 'And I don't know what you mean about not wanting to emigrate. I was all set to go. I had my stuff sent ahead on a container ship.'

'I was proud of you wanting to go. I thought you were very brave'

'Of course I would have gone.'

'But you got married instead, didn't you? And you didn't even tell me until afterwards.'

There was a hard silence. I shivered in the night air. We both counted the seconds. 'Don't you think marriage is a brave decision too?'

My mother sighed heavily and stubbed her cigarette out. 'Emily, you know it's troubled me that . . . that, now don't be annoyed when I say this, but—'

'Don't say it then.'

'Maybe you married Andrew because you were looking for a father figure and—'

'Oh, Mum, please don't!'

'All right, but you've got to consider it.'

'I have considered it. I don't think of him as a father figure. A father figure was not what I was looking for.'

'Are you happy together?' she asked quietly.

'Yes. Although it's a different kind of happiness to before.'

'Not still on honeymoon, then?'

'I think we came back from honeymoon a while ago.'

'So you've spent the past few months coming back down to earth, have you?'

'We're very close,' I said, rubbing my tired eyes, 'and we love each other . . . '

'But?' she suggested.

'But . . . I don't know.'

Silence. 'But what?'

'Oh, I don't know, Mum!'

And I started to cry. I couldn't remember the last time I had cried in front of my mother. She put her arms around me and hugged me. 'Just cry,' she said. 'It's all right.'

'No, it's not all right!' I shouted. 'I don't want to cry about it!' I stood up, agitated, and breathed in deeply. She let me stand there, on my own. 'I don't know what I want any more. I do still love him, although . . . he knows something is wrong and he asks me what it is and I can't tell him, and he just keeps on being patient and telling me I'm wonderful and telling me how much he loves me and I just feel . . . so . . . guilty.'

'Don't feel guilty.'

'But I do.'

I turned to my mother and saw that she was watching me closely. 'What have you done to feel guilty about?'

I folded my arms. 'There's somebody else.'

'Jack.'

'Yes.'

'Have you been having an affair with him?'

'No. We kissed once and that's it. End of story. And it's not a matter of being in love with him, but I do feel very attracted to him and sometimes I feel overwhelmed by it all. And he's said things to me that made sense, like I should still be able to do the things I wanted to do but didn't because I got married. He says I married too young. I've never let anyone else tell me

226

that but when he said it I realised he might be right. He said I should still travel if I wanted to. He asked if I wanted to go away with him, just travel around and be together for a while. I wanted to go. It was exactly what I wanted. I did the right thing in saying no, didn't I?'

'Where is he now?'

'I don't know. France, Spain or Italy.'

'Can you still get in touch with him?'

'I've got an email address.'

'Send him a message to meet you.' I looked up. She was intent. 'Send him a message,' she repeated.

'I can't do that. It's all over. It never really got going. It was just a—'

'Just what? You're never going to get the chance to find out.'

'It can't be a serious, long-term thing. It's a difficult kind of longing, that's all. It's just a very testing time because I want him. I really want him.'

'Then get him out of your system.'

'What?'

'Emily, you're only twenty-three years old. You have your whole life ahead of you. Your independence was very short-lived. It's not surprising that you're having regrets.'

'But I still love Andrew.'

'What if Jack is the man you should really be with? You have to find out.'

'What if he isn't?'

'It sounds to me like you've still got to find out. The trouble with a big age gap in any marriage is all the inequality of experience. Andrew had a good twenty years of being single before he finally decided to settle down and then he was lucky enough to find a nice girl like you. You married very young and very quickly. No one would blame you if it didn't work out. They'd blame him.'

'It wouldn't be his fault, though.'

My mother lit another cigarette. 'I don't think you've had that many partners, Emily, have you?'

'How many should I have had?' I asked, embarrassed.

'You won't have had that many compared to Andrew. I'm not asking for a figure but I don't suppose it's been many, has it? You're a late developer,' she said briskly. 'And that's no bad thing, that's no bad thing at all. It just means you've got more to look forward to and now you've started developing, you've got to go back a few steps and find out whether you should have married. You can't in all conscience go back to Andrew feeling like you do now. Have you tried talking to him about this . . . longing?'

'About Jack? God, no!'

'I meant this idea of going away for a while – taking time on your own.'

'I tried.'

'And what did he say?'

'He says it wouldn't work.'

'You've got free will. So long as you take responsibility, you can do whatever you want.'

'I can't do whatever I want!'

'Listen to me,' she said intensely. 'Most people, including you, Emily, never dare do anything without first getting approval from someone else, but that's rather a limiting way to live your life, don't you think? You don't need his permission. You simply have to decide for yourself what you want to do.'

'I don't want to hurt him. If I just try to carry on as normal then everything might sort itself out.'

'Emily, don't sit around for ever waiting for your problems to solve themselves.' She was angry now. I could see two bright spots of colour appearing in her cheeks. 'If there was just one thing I could say to the female population of this planet it's that patience is a very overrated virtue. Oh, Emily,' she cried, suddenly, 'you're so very young!'

'I'm tired of being told how young I am. I feel ninety-six.' I drained my flat champagne and stood up. 'I'm so tired, Mum. I'm really tired.'

'Yes, it's late. You're right. It's gone one o'clock. We've been out here ages, haven't we?'

'I'd like to go to bed. I need to get some sleep.'

'Of course,' she said. 'Of course. Time for bed.'

I bent to kiss her and we hugged and held each other tightly. 'Emily, you know I just want you to be happy.'

'I know.'

'We'll go out tomorrow, shall we? Have a little stroll along the beach.'

'Yes, okay, I'd like that. I'm off to bed now. Night-night, Mum.'

I walked away across the terrace, through the warm, still night air, and the scent of the lilies seemed to cling to me. 'Emily,' Joanna called. 'The computer's still on in the study if you want to send an email.'

'I don't think so.'

'Just ask him how he is. Say you're in Spain. Leave him a message and see if he replies. You're here a week, aren't you? This whole thing might be settled if he simply doesn't bother to reply.'

I thought of Jack sitting in some internet café, maybe in Paris or Rome or Madrid, wide awake and drinking espresso. I imagined him seeing my name appearing on the screen. I imagined him smiling.

'I don't know, Mum.'

'All right. I won't interfere. See you in the morning. Night-night, Emily.'

I went to bed but I didn't sleep. By two o'clock I was sitting at my mother's computer, typing a few short words: I'm going to Barcelona on Friday, 4th July. I'll be at the Café Catalana in the Plaça Reial at six p.m. in case you're going to be there too.

I stared at it, then pressed Send.

It was not a romantic kind of note but it said all he needed to know, even if it wasn't all I needed to say.

Maybe he would reply.

The next morning, Polly arrived back from her cabaret on the cruise ship, she was smiling her dazzlingly bleached pop star-let smile. She had a light, buoyant step that always made her look as if she was about to start dancing. We said hello and hugged and I thought again how she was very, very like my mother. 'How's your old man?' she asked. 'I do love him, the sweet thing! I hear he's given up smoking. How long has he lasted now?'

'Four months.'

'Four months! What a hero! I've never lasted longer than four hours and that was absolute hell.'

'How was the cabaret?'

'They loved me! It was brilliant. I can't wait to do it again.'

'Oh, Polly, I'm really pleased for you.'

In the last email I had had from my sister, she seemed to have been going through a period of the most profound lan-guor, telling me she hadn't been able to summon the energy to do anything more strenuous than sunbathe. But here she was, bobbing up and down and full of energy.

'Let's go out,' said Polly. 'Shall we go out for lunch? There's this great new bar opened. They have the best, thinnest pizza and they play salsa. Oh, and tonight I must take you to Bellitzo – you know, down by the harbour? It's just totally amazing!'

'I thought that place had a really bad reputation.'

Polly looked scornful. 'Don't worry, Emily, we'll be fine. I'll look after you. Never, never leave your drink unattended and always buy your own. And I really think we should go out because you were here with Joanna all last night. Of course, if you don't want to go, if you'd rather stay home and

230

have a dull and boring life, then that's fine. I'll do Bellitzo on my own.'

'No, don't go on your own, Poll.'

'No, really don't go on your own, darling. Can't you go with her, Emily? Just to keep an eye on her?'

'It's not such a big deal,' said Polly, amazed.

'I usually let her go,' said Mum. 'So long as she's with someone and not on her own.'

'Don't call me "she" as if I'm not here. I hate that.'

'Sorry, darling.'

'I'm not a child.'

'You're an artist, darling. You're Polka Dot.'

'I am a professional.'

'Okay,' I sighed. 'I'll go with her – sorry, I mean I'll go with the artist formerly known as Polly.'

Later, when Polly and I were alone, we talked about Joanna. 'Is she still going out with that guy she met in Marseilles?'

'No, it's all over, ended two weeks ago.'

'Oh, that's a shame. I quite liked him.'

'They had a terrific argument and he walked out. Then she went through her defiant stage – you know, when she goes round the house singing "Je Ne Regrette Rien", but last week she entered the maudlin phase, playing a little cheesy country and western.'

'What was the argument about? She didn't talk to him about Dad, did she?'

'You guessed it.'

'Why does she do it? Why does she go running whenever he calls?'

Polly shrugged. 'I don't know. I don't get as worked up about it as you, but then I've never met Dad, have I? You saw him practically every day.'

'No, I never saw him that often.'

'I thought he lived with you and Joanna?'

'No, he lived with his wife and kids. He only visited us.'

'I can never understand how his wife didn't find out.'

'She didn't know until Joanna told her.'

In Spain, the sun was warm and beautiful. I spent the week doing holiday things. I even hired a car so we could drive up into the mountains. Joanna wasn't a good passenger but she said she was getting more used to it. We played tennis and had picnics and I went swimming in the next door neighbour's pool. I visited some of Mum's old friends, people who had known Polly since she was a baby and me since I was ten. With Mum, I drank cocktails at the chic little bars she liked to go to near the marina. Whisky sours made with scotch, not bourbon.

Mum pointed out a yacht that had once been owned by my father. 'Do you ever hear from him?' she asked.

'No, does Polly?'

'No.'

'Do you – still?'

'Yes, sometimes. We had a few days in Paris last month.' I groaned and made to walk away. 'I know, Emily,' she said, taking my arm, 'I know what you're going to say and I didn't tell you because I knew you'd get annoyed.'

'He couldn't care less about me and Polly. How can you go on seeing him?'

'Because despite everything – and I don't expect you to understand this – he is still the love of my life and the father of my children. I want to see him. I want us to be together and it was strange the way we could preserve a little bubble of happiness as long as I didn't mention any sensitive sub-jects.'

'Like me and Polly?'

'He does think about you, you know.'

'Polly hasn't even met him.'

'He has offered to meet her but she won't.'

'I'm not surprised.'

'I wish she knew him. You at least remember how he was. You were ten when he left. You were there for ten years of his life – the ten best years, he says so himself. He still talks about you when we remember those times.'

Despite myself, I wanted to know. 'What does he say?'

'He talks about how he had never had a little girl until you were born, only boys and they were grown up by then. He adored you, Emily. You were such a dainty thing and I always dressed you beautifully. Your wardrobe was entirely made up of party dresses. All those glamorous parties we used to have. When you were small, he used to carry you into parties on his shoulders. Do you remember? You loved it. You would clap your little hands. And he always gave you lots of lovely presents. Every birthday, something extravagant. He even gave you Sleeping Beauty's tiara. Do you remember? After the ballet?'

'Yes. I was seven.'

'I don't think Sleeping Beauty was very pleased. She'd had her eye on that tiara herself, but then your daddy pointed out that she was not a true princess. She was only a ballet dancer, an actress, but his little Emily was a true princess. That's what he used to call you. You were his princess.'

'And what does he call me now?'

She sighed. 'He calls you a very sensitive subject.'

I turned away and carried on walking down the promenade. Mum hurried along behind me. 'He does talk about you, Emily. He does ask after you.'

I wasn't surprised Mum had met him again. He was like a bad habit she could never quite break.

The week passed. I phoned home and told Andrew that I missed him. He said he missed me too. I went on a few long, contemplative walks on my own.

'Do you think you'll have a baby?' asked Polly. 'Because I suppose that's the next thing, isn't it?'

'I'm not planning on it – not for a long time yet.'

'Oh, but babies are so sweet!'

'There are other things I want to do first.'

'That's a sensible thought. You're so right. Sensible Emily. *Muchos prudente*.'

'I'm not that sensible.'

'Oh but you are. You always do the sensible thing.'

'Do I?'

I didn't tell Polly about my longing for Jack.

'I believe in free will,' said my mother again over her morning session with the tarot cards. 'I never make a choice blind if I can make it with my eyes open.'

My mother's belief in practical decision-making was undiminished by her fondness for signs and portents. She didn't really believe all that tarot stuff and neither did I, but every morning she liked to shuffle the cards and spread them out, face up, and choose one for the day. It was very important they were face up. She didn't believe in luck, my mother, she believed in judgement. Choosing a card for the day helped her focus. She liked to do it after her yoga practice when her mind was clear.

It was a modern deck with bold colours, and all the pictures were very contemporary. 'Which one would you choose?' Joanna asked me. 'Which one is you?'

I chose a nice picture of a young girl pouring rainbows from one jug to another. This, it turned out, was The Fool.

'Don't worry, Emily,' said Joanna. 'You can change your mind. You've got free will, remember? Now, who do you want to be?'

I chose a picture of a woman draped in silk robes, reclining on a couch. The Empress. 'You've got a long way to go from Fool to Empress. Choose the Chariot that'll help you.'

'I can't see a chariot.'

'In this deck, the Chariot is portrayed as a bicycle.'

'You mean I've got to get on my bike?'

'Spiritually speaking, yes.'

I looked at all the cards spread out on the table. 'On my birthday, I made a wish. I said: "I wish for what I don't know I need."'

'That's a blind wish. You wouldn't catch me wishing for anything like that.'

'But if there was a card for the thing I don't know I need, I wouldn't know what it looked like, would I?'

'Suppose not.'

'I want to pick a card blind. Turn them over.'

'There's The Fool talking.'

'Turn them over, Joanna.'

'You know I don't agree with that,' she said, lighting a cigarette.

'I wish you didn't smoke, Mum.'

'But I love smoking, Daught. I didn't smoke for years because I had to protect my voice. It's up to me what I do, you see. All right then. You take over with the cards. Up to you. Your responsibility.'

I shuffled the deck and laid them out in a fan on the table. As I reached out to choose, she stopped my hand.

'You want it to be The Lovers, don't you?'

'Yes and no. I'm not sure. If you ask me what I want right now, more than anything in the world it's to feel as happy as I did when I got married.'

I turned the card over and I didn't know what it meant, but it didn't look good. It wasn't The Lovers. It showed a wooden hut in a dark forest, with a fox just outside the door, a knife between its teeth. Inside was a young woman, sitting with her eyes shut, holding a flaming torch.

'Ah, yes,' said my mother, taking a look at it. She exhaled long and slowly. 'Yesss . . . '

235

'What do you think it means?'
'If you don't know, Emily, I'm not telling you.'
'Is it bad luck?'
'It's –' she hesitated – 'It's entirely up to you.'

' . . . the flavour, for those bold enough to taste it at full strength, is very hot and sweet, the spirit evaporating on the tongue'

Cask No 30·28   *Hot and Sweet*
Alcohol: 60.5%   Proof: 105.8°   Outturn: 306 bottles

The Society Bottlings, Summer 2001

Chapter Sixteen

He never replied to my email, but I got the train down the coast to Barcelona anyway. My mother saw me off at the station. She knew he hadn't replied. She'd been checking her in-box on the hour. 'If he's not there, don't worry about it. It wasn't meant to be. You can put it down to experience. But if he is there then—'

'I'm not expecting to see him.'

'If you see him, then spend the time you've got left there together. I'll meet you here at the station tomorrow and take you to the airport for your flight home. Just give me a ring.' She kissed me goodbye. 'And Emily, please try to suspend the guilt trip. All of life's difficult decisions happen in tricky moral areas. That's what makes them difficult. Now, we've talked this through and you've made a decision. I think you've made a carefully judged decision, so try to lay off the guilt for the next twenty-four hours.' She looked at me anxiously. 'Save it for later,' she added.

On the train, I thought about Andrew. I had spoken to him regularly on the phone and told him where I'd been and what I'd done. We never mentioned the things we had talked about at home and I never mentioned the thoughts that still kept me awake. Andrew had encouraged me to take this holiday – change of scene and all that – but on the phone I was acutely aware of the things I didn't tell him. After all, when he had dropped me off at the airport he had said: 'It'll cheer you up to see your mum in Marbella,' and not, 'It'll cheer you up to see your boyfriend in Barcelona.'

Just that morning he had told me he was glad I was having a nice break. He said that he missed me and Jaffa Cat missed me and they were both looking forward to me coming home. He said the cat hated him now because he had taken him to the vet's for his big appointment.

Jaffa wasn't a kitten any more and we both knew we couldn't have a swaggering tom cat in the house, boldly marking out his territory on the sitting room curtains. 'The poor thing has had his ginger nuts cut off,' Andrew said. 'If he wants to live in shared domestic bliss, he has to surrender the right to rove. He's under my desk now, washing the sore spot where his balls used to be.'

'Oh, poor Jaffa.'

'I feel like a traitor,' said Andrew.

It was pleasantly warm walking down Las Ramblas in Barcelona. I could feel the Mediterranean sun on my skin. It was five o'clock in the afternoon and very quiet. Only the tourists were about. None of the locals would think of meeting up to go out until at least nine or ten o'clock. Dinner might be at eleven, and at midnight the nightlife of the city would just be getting under way. Some clubs didn't even bother opening until three a.m. Anyone who is an insomniac should really move to Spain. You feel that, at last, your bio-rhythms are in tune with your environment. An insomniac from Edinburgh would be thrilled to discover there are many more exciting places to go than the twenty-four-hour garage at the bottom of Dundas Street.

The time for bed is the afternoon.

I turned down the empty lanes that led toward the Plaça Reial. I didn't expect Jack to come and so it didn't really matter that I was very early. A whole hour early. This was one of my favourite places and my favourite time to sit here, when the afternoon light was soft and golden and the pavement cafés were quiet. Only a few people drinking *café tallat* and reading the papers.

The colonnaded square of the Plaça Reial was surrounded by elegant buildings, all with ochre-painted plaster and white marble pillars. Tall palm trees reached to the third-floor windows and there were flowers trailing from balconies, bright geraniums and roses and lilies in pots. In the centre of the square was a fountain with a bronze statue of three beautiful young women holding aloft an overflowing basin of water. They were the Three Graces and they represented the three phases of love: Generosity, Desire and Fulfilment.

There was, I noted, no Guilt.

And I did feel guilty. I was sure that much of that tight knot I felt in my stomach was my guilt and not just the excitement of desire. I knew I would wait for a long time just in case Jack came. I knew exactly what I would do if he did arrive. I certainly wouldn't run away as I had done when I'd kissed him goodbye.

I knew what I would do and, oddly enough, this decision had a calming effect on my sense of guilt. The decision had been made.

239

I walked down one side of the square, through the stone colonnade, turned the corner and on towards the café where I'd said I would be. There were the little round tables and wickerwork chairs. A waiter in a long apron stood beside a stone pillar and served a coffee to his only customer. The waiter moved away and there, sitting alone at a table, with a new cup of espresso, was Jack.

I stood still and looked at him. I saw him before he saw me and in that brief, private moment I felt such elation. I had wanted to see him so much and here he was. A whole hour early, like me. A whole extra hour stolen from the rest of our lives and added to the hours of our one night together.

He raised his eyes and saw me, and I watched his face light up. He stood and walked towards me. We met halfway and waited a second, taking it all in, neither of us speaking yet. Here we were, this very first minute, and already we were pressing out the moment to make it last. I reached out my hand and he took it and we kissed. 'You're here,' I said. 'You're really here.' I was overjoyed to be with him again. I could think of nothing else. I would not think of anything else. I had only one night.

'Hello, Emily,' he smiled. I put my arms around him. We were alone together in Barcelona, two thousand miles from home. I felt so far removed from my life in Edinburgh I could have been on another planet.

At first we hardly talked at all. It was as if words would only complicate things, which they would. We were quiet together, but with a low, gathering excitement that was bubbling away like happiness, like desire. We kissed; urgent kisses. We held hands. This is what it's like being a couple, I thought. Being a couple, openly together.

'I'm so glad that you're here,' he said. 'How long can you stay?'

'Just tonight. I'm going back tomorrow.'

He didn't make any comment and I was glad, because I couldn't bear to talk about it. I just wanted him to know how long we had. And because he knew me, he understood. Just like he'd understood everything all along.

After a little while, we walked, still holding hands, through the lanes and little streets of Barcelona. The Barri Gòtic and the old town. We walked back to the flat where he was staying, the place that belonged to his friend who was now, presumably, visiting Planet Edinburgh.

The place was just off the Carrer d'Avinyo, on the last corner of the street before it meets the Carrer Gignas. It was a nineteenth-century building, originally built as grand tenement flats, now subdivided many times.

'It's on the top floor,' said Jack. 'And you can get out on to the roof and see across the city. Great views.'

The entrance to the building was through tall double doors made of dark Spanish oak. There was a small, gloomy hallway, not the kind of wide open space you would expect behind such big doors. Up a few steps and there was an antique cage lift, its black wrought iron running up the centre of the stairwell, circled by worn stone steps. I could hear the clank and whirr as the winding machinery dragged the cage up the lift shaft. When it reached the top there was a thin, squealing noise as the brakes came on and it lurched to a halt.

We stood in the gloom of the hall a hundred feet below. The air was cool after the warm summer streets outside and I shivered. Jack pressed the button to summon the lift back down. I heard the noise of clanking metal as it started its descent. 'Is it safe?' I asked.

Jack shrugged. I stared up at the criss-cross of scaffolding and then the lift itself came into view, a wooden box bearing down on us. The winding stopped and Jack hauled the cage doors apart. The box was dark oak carved with swirling leaves and, inside it, polished wooden panelling with mirrors at head height etched with flowers and birds. I saw my face in the mirrors, myself as an odd mix of excitement and fear.

'Well, Emily,' said Jack, looking at me, looking at the lift. 'Are you going to risk it? I'm sure it'll be all right.' Then he stepped inside and jumped a few times on the spot, making the whole thing shudder.

'Don't!'

He grinned at me. 'I'm not leaving you to take the stairs in case you change your mind, and anyway, I think you should take the lift.'

'Why?'

'Because you're scared of it.'

'Why is that a good reason?'

'Because you'll get there, whether you're scared of it or not.' I stared upwards, a hundred feet of antique lift shaft. 'Come on,' he laughed. He stood and waited, watching me hesitate. 'Come on,' he repeated softly. He held out his hand to me and I took it.

I was inside. We started to move slowly, falteringly to the top floor. Jack put his arms round me and started to kiss my cheek and my neck. I kissed him too. That good smell of sun-warmed skin. I rested my head on his shoulder and saw in the mirror his fingers stroking the back of my neck and I thought of all the people who must have been here before us, carried along like this.

The lift came to the top floor, juddered and stopped. I opened the sliding doors as quickly as I could and pulled at the cage. He helped me. I just wanted to get out. There was a real sense of urgency about everything now. He dropped his keys twice before managing to open the door of the flat. We stepped inside.

It was warm and shady. The hallway opened on to a living room. I got the briefest possible description from him: 'Living room, kitchen, bathroom, bedroom,' he said, pointing quickly round the hall. Straight ahead of us there were tall shutters leading out on to a little balcony. The light filtered through, making stripes along the floor. We kissed again, and some more, and we made our way, stumblingly, towards the sofa in the living room which was the nearest comfortable horizontal surface. Fell on the sofa. A lot more kissing. I looked up and thought (bizarrely) what incredibly high ceilings there were in this room. Much higher than the ceilings at home; much taller windows even than the tall windows at Jack's other flat.

I pulled my T-shirt over my head, reached behind me to unfasten my bra. We kept kissing. Bra on the floor with T-shirt and now joined by my trousers. And his. No guilt at that point but powerful desire, and at the back of my mind a detached kind of awareness: I am doing this, I want to and I am. I had decided of my own free will to do this, this adultery, because I had very serious feelings for Jack. Very serious feelings of overwhelming physical attraction and then the major realisation that sex was just a brilliant piece of mechanical biology. And what Jack and I had together in that room was, in fact, all we had together: simple, effortless, urgent, needy, very exciting sex.

Later, when we were lying, breathless and clammy, together on the sofa, I looked up at the very high ceiling and the tall windows and the light falling in through the shutters and found that I started remembering my husband and how he loved me and how I loved him. Yet, I felt surprised at how easily I was able to put Andrew to the back of my mind. He was still there somewhere in my head, but not close, not near.

We sat out on the little balcony above the street. We rested on cushions, with our feet pressed up against the warm, stone balustrade.

It was noisy outside. There was music from the bars further down the street and the faint sound of a television in the house opposite, with bursts of Spanish indignation and canned laughter. Far below us we could hear people's voices, talking and laughing, friends calling to each other and going out together. Looking through the balcony rail, I could see quiet lovers walking arm in arm.

'Have you decided what you're going to do?' said Jack in a low voice. 'Are you going back to him?'

I said nothing.

'How can you even think about going back to him?'

'I love him.'

'If you love him, what are you doing here with me?'

'Finding out.'

'Finding out what?'

'This.'

He gave me a sideways look. Some annoyance on his face. I watched his expression change as he decided not to tell me I was being a pain. He drew his legs towards his chest, curling up, resting his head on his arms. 'And what do you think "this" is?' he asked eventually.

'Just being with you, just being together.' He raised his head and I leaned towards him and kissed him again.

'You can't go back to him, Emily,' he said. 'How can you possibly go back? Things are different now.'

'I know and I feel guilty.'

He lay down, his body across the threshold to the flat. He shut his eyes and put his hands behind his head and let go of a long, slow breath. I lay down beside him, propped up on one elbow, and touched his cheek. I felt sad looking at him because I knew I wouldn't be able to do this ever again. I knew that we would never be alone like this again.

And knowing that this was the way it had to be, I turned to him for the last hours of our shared time together. I tried to quieten my conscience about my infidelities. I clung to Jack and felt the touch of his lips on my neck, on my ear, and the warmth of his breath.

244

'I think you're wrong, Emily,' he said. 'I think we will be together like this again.'

The next day I sat on the bed, fully dressed, and waited while Jack got showered and ready. I noticed I felt differently about myself. I felt a strange mixture of sadness and elation and a low hum of anxiety. My old worries, like my fear of the dark, didn't seem to matter any more. I was more concerned about Andrew and what he would think of me if he knew what I had done. The thought was lodged there in my mind and my heart. He wouldn't love me any more, would he? Would he hate me? The thought came and went, a moment of fluttering panic.

But I didn't want to *unknow* anything. There was no way I would have turned back the clock and never met Jack. However, I also knew for certain that I couldn't meet Jack again. I would have to crush my feelings for him because if I had to choose – and I did, polyandry being forbidden outside of Micronesia – then I would choose Andrew. I would give up Jack. Was this, then, love with hindsight?

When I got home, I knew I would have to act as if nothing had happened. I would have to try to be as normal as possible.

To practise being deliberately normal, I stood up and walked into the living room where I passed the time looking through the bookshelves while I waited for the cab to take me to the station. I wondered what sort of books Jack's close friend liked to read. The friend who was now staying in that room with the arched window in the flat in Edinburgh.

There were a lot of CDs and DVDs, computer games and minidiscs. The music and computer games took up twice as much space as the books. The books were mostly non-fiction – biographies of sports stars in particular. There were a few well-thumbed guidebooks and a paperback full of newspaper cartoons. There was a pile of glossy men's magazines

245

with pictures of glossy women on the front. In a special display area, there was a small collection of vintage comics, neatly stored in plastic covers, some arranged face-out so you could admire them. Almost everything was in Spanish and some things were probably in Catalan, but there were also a few English books in translation, which I recognised. He had the complete scripts from every series of Blackadder, or *L'Escurço Negre* as it was in Spanish. He had J.R.R. Tolkien's *El Senyor dels Anells – La Trilogia Completa* and he had Nick Hornby's *Alta Fidelidad* which was described as '*una novela de humor, amor y musica*'. A boy's bookshelf, then. A nice boy, I reckoned.

There were certainly no nice girls' self-help books like *Hombres are from Mars and Señoritas are from Venus* or even *Porqué Hombres Don't Listen and Señoritas Can't Read Maps*.

A few weeks ago, Dolores had lent me her books about these subjects. She thought they might be useful to me in my relationship with my husband. She said she had noticed I was getting out and about more, and seeing a lot of Jack and she had heard from Maisie who was friends with Laura who lived in the same flat as Jack that I had been round there quite often. She thought I needed some advice, some guidance about relationships. I had taken Dolores' books and read them, but I hadn't recognised myself. I had only recognised Dolly.

This week in Marbella, I had read one of my mother's old self-help books. It was called *Women Are Divas and All Men Are Bastards*. I had only recognised Joanna and my father.

I thought of Flora. Flora didn't have a manual. Flora reckoned you had to make up your own book as you went along.

'From the "capital" of Islay, where there is a round church (so the Devil can't hide in the corners), this whisky presents us with an unreduced nose of Love Heart sweeties and air freshener'

Cask No. 3·83 *Love Hearts and Perfume*
Alcohol: 63.2%   Proof: 110.6°   Outturn: 177 bottles

The Society Bottlings, Winter 2003

Chapter Seventeen

Andrew was there to meet me at the airport when I flew home. 'It's so good to see you again,' he said, hugging me.

I must live with this guilt, I thought. I have said goodbye to my lover and I must put him out of my mind. I love my husband and I can never tell him what I've done.

'You've caught the sun,' he smiled. 'You've got freckles.'

'Mum says they'll fade quicker if I dab them with lemon juice.'

'Don't listen to a word she says. How is Joanna, the Demon Diva?'

'She's very well. She's asking after you.'

'In a good way or a bad way?'

'Just in a way.'

'Oh God, she's cursed me again, hasn't she?'

'She was only being theatrical when she did that. It's part of her repertoire.'

'Why couldn't she have just said, "hello, come in," like a normal person? I'd never been cursed before.'

'You're a lawyer, you must have been.'

'I'd never been cursed in song.'

'It was just her little joke. You know she collects folk songs. Anyway, this time she says she's suspending her judgement. She says time will tell.'

We walked out to the car park. 'Did you talk to her?' Andrew asked when we got in the car. 'I mean, did you talk to your mum about . . . anything?'

'I just had a nice holiday, that's all.'

'Okay,' he nodded.

We drove out of the car park. 'While you were away, I got fit and lost weight.'

'In a week?'

'I've lost half a stone,' he said proudly, 'just pining for you. And I went to the gym and started running again.'

'Good for you. Was it really hard after not going for so long?'

'Nah – I'm ultra fit.'

'You must have had to take it slowly at first, though.'

'No, no, not particularly.'

'You must have done.'

'I was fitter than a lot of other people there.'

We drove home. He was happy and pleased. 'I've missed you,' he said. 'Me and the cat have been through hell without you – well, obviously the cat's been through more than me, but—'

'How is poor Jaffa?'

'His miaow is a bit castrato, but I think that's just the shock. He's recovering. I've given him loads of his favourite fishy cat treats but he still hates me. Not surprising, really.'

Jaffa Cat looked a bit sorry for himself when I saw him again, curled up in the basket I had bought for him. His fur seemed a little less well groomed than normal, and when he climbed out of his basket to greet me, he walked – well, gingerly.

I stroked his head and made a fuss of him and he purred. He certainly made it clear that he liked me better than Andrew.

I walked around the house, remembering my home. It looked so comfortable, so settled. I had a look at the garden and took a cup of coffee outside to drink it on the verandah. Andrew joined me, bringing a sweater and a tartan rug. The house and garden seemed very peaceful, and if I ignored the jumping in my heart, everything seemed gentle and good.

'Guess what?' he said. 'David and Jane are getting married. Jane has said yes. David's ecstatic about it. I think he'd just about given up.'

'They're getting married? Really? I thought Jane wouldn't because . . . well, Kate told me why.'

'Kate? When were you speaking to Kate about it?'

'At work. She's been there a few times with clients and she was telling me that David was unfaithful and Jane was so hurt she couldn't forgive him and . . . ' My voice got thin and trailed off into nothing. 'But she stayed with him,' I rallied. 'Gave him another chance.'

'Yes, luckily for David. He had one regrettable fall from grace, one drunken one-night stand at some office party, and it's taken ten years of good behaviour for him to make up the distance.'

'It was only one night?'

'It still counts, though, doesn't it? Jane certainly thought so. And everybody got to hear about it and it was humiliating for her.'

'But she didn't leave him.'

'She did for a bit. Then they got back together again. They had been going to get married, but that was very much off the cards after that. I thought they might have got married before they had the kids, but they didn't. Jane was clear about what she wanted and what she didn't want.'

'She must have been very hurt by what he did.'

'Yes, she was.'

'But she's forgiven him now.'

'Yes.'

'Do you think something happened for her to forgive him now?'

'No, she just said that enough time had gone past. It took a long time, that's all, and she could see he loved her and he had been faithful to her and . . . well, she could see it was working and so she decided she wanted to get married now, ten years later than originally planned.'

'So it was love with hindsight?'

'I suppose so, yes. That's one way of putting it. With the benefit of hindsight, they're getting married. It's going to be quite a big wedding, I think. They want to celebrate on a grand scale. They feel they've earned it. Tom is going to be his dad's best man and Sarah is going to be bridesmaid. We both get to be witnesses. It'll be good. A nice family occasion. And it will be in English, not French, so we'll know what they're saying. We can be reliable witnesses.'

'Are you still glad we got married?' I asked him suddenly.

'Yes. Are you?'

'Yes, but it all happened so quickly, didn't it? We hardly knew each other. I mean, we thought we did, but . . . you know, I think getting married is like emigrating to another country. The State of Matrimony. And it looks very settled in all the brochures, and you think you know what it's going to be like because you've read about it and seen it in films and you know people who've done it, but you don't really know what it's going to be like until you actually live there.'

'And what's your opinion?' Andrew asked. 'Now that you're actually living there.'

'I think there's more uncharted territory than I would ever have thought possible. I think that perhaps . . . ' I stopped, couldn't speak any more.

'Tell me,' he said gently. 'Tell me what you think.'

'I think that you can have second thoughts sometimes and you shouldn't feel guilty about that because it's just natural homesickness for what you had before you emigrated, when you were more of a free spirit. And I think you've got to find your own way around all this new uncharted territory. I think you have to make your own map.'

'To find your way home.'

'Yes.'

There was a long silence and then Andrew got up from his chair and came across to where I was sitting and bent right down beside me. 'I know you've been feeling a bit lost recently. When I see you sad it just breaks my heart because I know I can't really do anything, I just have to stand and wait.'

'Patience is supposed to be an overrated virtue, you know.'

'It depends on what you're waiting for.'

'I'm not worth waiting for.'

'Oh Emily,' he laughed. 'Modesty is an even more over-rated virtue.' He kissed my forehead. 'I'm glad you didn't wander off too far. I'm glad you didn't do anything silly.' I ducked my head. 'You worry too much, that's all. I'm so glad you came home.' He kissed me again, put his arms around me. 'You're the only really lovely thing in my life.'

I found it impossible trying to live with this kind of duplicity. I knew that there were plenty of people who had managed their infidelities with far greater competence than I had. I knew there were some people who could just keep on being unfaithful over and over again. Serial infidelities, where each one becomes easier than the last because the taboo has been broken with the first. I had always felt such contempt for men who were unfaithful to their wives, especially the ones

251

who did it again and again, like some free-wheeling psycho-adulterer who gets a taste for it. Each new infidelity, another little murder of his wife and even another little agony for his mistress too. And yet the women stay. Why? They choose to put up with it because that's just the way he is and they still love him, still need him – need his money or his mere Presence. Each infidelity, a little murder. The half-dead wife who stays, and the despairing mistress who loves him too, and has his daughter. The mistress who sings out a perfect scream at his killer line in goodbyes. His highly acclaimed, unsurpassable Walking Out.

And his daughter? A nice girl like me?

Only the first taboo broken. And I didn't want to go any further. I wanted to step back. Even though I ached with longing for my lover, I had married a man I loved more, and I couldn't betray him again.

Jane and David called in to see us the following weekend. I wondered if Jane would be quite serious and philosophical about her big decision, but she was all radiant cheerfulness. 'I just decided to step off the cliff,' she said, smiling serenely.

'Drop off the cliff?'

'I said step off the cliff. It was a considered step, not a drop.'

It was a beautiful day and we were sitting outside drinking champagne to celebrate their announcement. They held hands and were very affectionate.

'We're going to have a proper wedding – a real ceilidh,' Jane added.

'What do Sarah and Tom think about all this?'

'Sarah wants a bridesmaid's dress that won't embarrass her in front of her friends and Tom thinks his mum and dad have been a bit yukky together recently, but he has offered us his formal congratulations.'

'He's asked us not to do the "you may kiss the bride" moment,' said David. They laughed together and were happy.

Before they left, Jane and I had a stroll around the garden and she told me the names of some of the plants that had appeared.

'Those are peony roses,' she said, pointing to the full, round flowers that were my favourite of all the plants that had come up in the garden since the spring. 'Peony roses take time to establish themselves. When we first moved to our house in Portobello, I planted peonies. They need time to put down roots. You plant peonies when you know you want to stay a long time. Emily,' she said suddenly, 'I'm really glad you and Andrew are going to be there at the wedding. We want all our family and friends there, but we want you to witness our vows and sign the register with us.'

'Do you think you'll feel different about each other when you're married?' I asked.

'Possibly,' she said. 'I'm looking forward to being able to use the words "husband and wife" instead of "partner". I want the solemn, scary bit of saying the vows. I want the public declaration. I want the frightening moment of courage about something joyful and good. Normally you only get moments of courage when you have to face something difficult or bad. I know I want to spend the rest of my life with him. It's as serious and as simple as that. If the world was going to end tomorrow, I'd want to be with David and our children. We're together – till death parts us,' said Jane confidently. 'We're good together.'

I couldn't rid myself of the feeling that the world was about to end and I developed a fixation that Andrew was going to die. I didn't tell him about it, I was just careful to keep in touch with him and know where he was, and I made sure the tyres on the car were always the right pressure and the head-lights were working and the seatbelts were lying nicely flat in the runners and not twisted. Once, for no particular reason, I got the idea into my head that he really was dead. In my mind's eye I saw him lying in the road somewhere near Glasgow, blood on his face. I knew this was irrational but my panic was real, so I left a desperate message on his voicemail saying I'd had a premonition he was dead and could he please, please get in touch immediately and let me know he was still alive. And he hadn't been able to get in touch with me. He had tried and there was something wrong with my phone and he couldn't get through, so he had driven dangerously fast along the M8 to be with me. I had been so grateful to see him, so overwhelmed and relieved after all my ridiculous anxiety, I had clung to him and told him I couldn't bear to live without him.

He had been very relaxed about it, saying he had been ready to come home anyway. 'Emily,' he said, extricating himself, 'for a free spirit, you can be very clingy at times.'

Was I turning into Dolores? The ape with the longest arms? Me? Clingy? I told him I didn't know what he was on about.

'Do you remember the first time you told me you loved me?'

'Of course I do.' I admitted that I had clung to him on that occasion.

'That was fine, that was nice – that was clinginess in context. But you can be very inconsistent about your clinginess, Emily.'

I tried to get back to normal, to a normal level of clinging on, and as the time passed, as one week succeeded another, I sought comfort in routine, in the things that had only seemed to frustrate me before, the things that had made me bored. Now I wanted to feel bored. I longed for Sunday afternoons of gentle tedium.

I still thought of Jack. I still had the tenderest feelings for him and a lot of simply lascivious ones as well. Every time I thought of him, I had to force myself to think of something else. I had to teach myself not to think of him at all,

254

because if I did, I knew it was very likely that I might unravel completely. I could hardly hold myself together as it was.

Just keep running.

'The ideal temperature at which whisky should be drunk varies according to the climate of the country in which you are drinking it. Chilled whisky does not readily yield up its aromas and the addition of ice will close them down altogether . . . warming the glass in the hand – as one does with brandy – helps to release the volatiles in the spirit'

Malt Whisky, Charles MacLean

Chapter Eighteen

At the end of July, just a week before our Pink Whisky launch, Andrew had to work in London again for a few days. On the first night he was away I called Flora to ask if she would like to come and stay, keep me company. 'We could sit in the garden and have a drink and a chat,' I told her. 'It would be nice.'

'Yes, I'll come round,' she said, 'but I'm not sure about sitting in the garden. That depends on my hay fever.'

Flora had never suffered from hay fever before and she was taking it badly. She had always worried about losing her sense of smell and made a point of avoiding people with colds and sore throats and sniffs and sneezes. Losing your sense of smell counts as a medical emergency for a professional nose.

She arrived an hour later, smiling and not sniffling at all. 'I took an extra dose of antihistamine,' she said. We sat out in the garden. The air was warm and muggy and there was a heaviness about it that promised rain. The garden smelled of earth and grass. I opened my last bottle of Rosebank.

'I love this Rosebank,' Flora said. 'It's such a summery kind of whisky. I tried a pink Bruichladdich last night as well and it was excellent. Just think, Emily, if I had lost my sense of smell, I wouldn't have been able to nose this. I wouldn't have been able to do my job.'

'So you've got the hay fever under control now, have you?'

'Yes, thank God. Last week the doctor gave me this new nasal spray. I have to squirt it up my nose three times a day. I asked him what it smelled like and he said he didn't know. He said no one had ever asked that before. I was amazed.'

'You'd think people would want to know.'

'That's what I said to him: If you've got to put it up your nose three times a day, surely people want to know what it's going to smell like? "Does it matter?" asked the doctor. I couldn't believe it! So I told him: Doctor, my nose is my fortune. My sense of smell is very important to me. What if squirting this stuff up my nose damages my sense of smell? He said he was pretty sure it wouldn't, but he would try to find out since my job depended on it. Anyway, he was really nice and he checked and got back to me and said there was nothing to suggest it would do any long-term damage to my sense of smell. I've been taking it ever since.'

'So what does it smell of?'

'Roses, and not a bad rose perfume either. I was pleasantly surprised. A gentle mono-scent, not a mixed bouquet or anything like that. It's a bit odd, though, squirting perfume up your nose every morning – wake up and smell the roses. It's like Prozac for your nostrils.'

'Did the doctor know why you got hay fever this year when you've never had it before?'

'He said all sorts of things could trigger it. Maybe my immune system was running a bit low. Stress or something.'

'And are you stressed, Flora?'

'The most stressful thing that's happened to me has been breaking up with Ben. I know it was the right thing to do, but that doesn't stop me feeling a bit depressed about it at times. I did love him, you see.'

I felt the first specks of rain. Flora held her hand out for the drops. 'I hope it passes,' she said. 'I don't really want to have to go inside because I think we both fancy a cigarette. Well, I do.'

'There aren't any in the house because Andrew's still being really good about giving up.'

'I've brought some.'

'Oh, excellent. Well done. And you've got matches and everything. You're such a good friend, Flora. If the rain gets any heavier, we could always go and sit in the shed. It's a very nice shed. Andrew's mum even calls it a gazebo; a sort of wendyhut. There are deckchairs in there and I think it's probably time we started on the whisky.'

'What have you got?' asked Flora, perking up a bit.

'I've got Highland Park. We should pour our fourth dram because, as you know, the fourth dram always tends to be the most revealing.'

When I returned with the bottle, the rain suddenly became a downpour and we had to run to the garden shed. I propped the door open and we sat inside on stripy deckchairs, the bottle between us. We poured our fourth dram and for a long time I listened and sympathised while Flora talked about Ben and how she loved him and how the open relationship wasn't working because they both got jealous. 'I hate Maisie now,' she said. 'And Maisie used to be my friend.'

'What are you going to do?'

'I don't know,' she said, bewildered. 'What can you do?' she asked. 'What on earth are you supposed to do?'

We smoked and watched the rain tipping down outside. We talked for hours about all sorts of things. I talked about my father. I confessed I had dreams where I killed him and the violence of my anger frightened me. We talked about Joanna and how she still liked to do her tarot cards and how I had picked an unlucky card but I didn't know what it meant exactly.

It got cold. The thermometer on the wall said fifteen degrees centigrade, which by coincidence was the perfect serving temperature for whisky – traditional Scottish room temperature. At our feet was a nearly empty bottle and a completely empty packet of cigarettes.

'It's very late,' I said. 'We should go in.'

'It's still raining. We'll have one more, then go back inside.'

I stared out at the darkness. Everything in the garden was turning to mud. 'I'm feeling cold,' I said.

'Come on then. We'll go in.' Flora turned to look at me. 'What is it?'

'Flora, I've done something really wrong.'

Flora was used to me being over-anxious. 'You're human,' she said. 'Stop worrying. Only God's perfect.'

'I've made a big mistake.'

'Only one?' she said breezily. 'Well, Emily, that's almost divine. Come on, let's go in.'

'I've had an affair.'

'Jack,' she said.

'Yes.'

Flora nodded to herself. 'Have you told Andrew?'

'No. I don't want to tell him. I've decided it wouldn't help matters, it would only be me offloading my guilt. I don't want to hurt him and I don't think I need to tell him because I've already decided that I'm not seeing Jack any more.'

260

'Oh Emily, why didn't you let me know earlier? When did it start?'

I told Flora what I had done. I told her I'd only done the whole adultery thing once. I told her how much I thought of Jack and how difficult it was to give him up, but I had made my decision. 'If I tell Andrew, he'll leave me, and I couldn't bear the thought of living without him.'

'You lived without him in Barcelona.'

'I was just finding out. I just wanted to know. I just wanted to—'

'Just checking?'

'I had to know. And it's difficult because I still have all these feelings for Jack. They don't just go away. But I'm not going to see him again.'

'Are you sure?'

'Yes. I don't want that one mistake to ruin everything and I want to hold things together. You mustn't tell anyone, Flora. You mustn't say anything. I don't want anyone to know.'

'I won't. Will Jack say anything?'

'Do you think he might? Why should he?'

'I don't know. Things just tend to get out, that's all.'

'I couldn't bear it if Andrew found out.'

I felt as if I could hear all of Andrew and Kate's friends joining together in singing the mighty 'I Told You So' chorus.

'Andrew's been away a lot, hasn't he?' said Flora.

'Yes, he's been working with Kate quite a bit, and he didn't want to take time off – I mean, he couldn't take time off, and I know it doesn't excuse this . . . affair I've had, but—'

'What will you do if he finds out?'

'I don't know.'

'Does he honestly not suspect anything? He knew you were seeing a lot of Jack, didn't he?'

'But usually as part of a crowd of people, and he's just not a jealous sort of person. Andrew was kind of . . . giving me time, I think, and—'

'Giving you time?'

'To get through it. To work it through. He was just being very patient about it, I suppose because he knows I love him and —' my throat felt tight — 'because he trusts me.'

I started to cry. Flora gathered me up, along with the bottle and the glasses, and we walked unsteadily through the rain together to the house.

taken from Flora's notes

The Fifth Whisky:
ISLAY
strong medicine

keep it for last
because once you've tasted this
you won't be able to taste anything else all night
powerful & robust
there's something passionate about an Islay
that can be overwhelming

Some Islay Malts:
Lagavulin
(Kitty Gillespie's favourite proprietary bottling
'justifiable scarcity is a price worth paying')
Laphroaig
(chewier than Lagavulin)
Ardbeg
(the one we drank on the beach at Kintra on Islay. Remember?)
Bruichladdich
(a lighter Islay from an independent, re-opened distillery)

'This whisky has been re-racked into a port pipe for the final months of its maturation. The result is sensational! Deep rose in colour, with a fresh grape-like nose, light vanilla and raspberry jam behind, the flavour hot and berry-fruity, with some spice and a bitter finish . . . It will take lots of water and we think it will make a perfect summer's drink, drunk long, even with soda, and with lots of ice, possibly accompanied by strawberries'

Cask No. 25·32   *Deep Rose and Raspberry Jam*
Alcohol: 54.3%   Proof: 95.0°   Outturn: 235 bottles

The Society Bottlings, Summer 2003

Chapter Nineteen

'This is it,' said Flora. 'Wild Cat Pink Whisky Day.'

All the blue quarter bottles were lined up. Our rare Wild Cat brand had been saved from extinction.

The morning of the launch, we came to work early to finalise preparations. Many of the ordinary members at Charlotte Square were keen to attend, as well as journalists who had enjoyed promotional samples and were ready for more. The guest list included all of Kitty Gillespie's great and good friends from a lifetime in the whisky industry, as well as her other friends, the infamous and the peculiar. There were blenders and distillers and whisky makers, and even Piers and some wine boys up from Knightsbridge. Very few people had said no to our invitation. The alcopop team from Vodkapopsi couldn't come, but only because they weren't allowed out on a school night; everyone else from Vodka Inc was going to be there.

Jack had told Flora he was coming back for the party. He hadn't contacted me, but then I had told him I thought it would be best if we didn't stay in touch.

The launch didn't start until six o'clock, but nevertheless the whole house was busy from first thing in the morning with other events and private functions. All the rooms were in use for meetings, and what was more, Kate was going to be there all day. She and a team of lawyers would be in the blue sitting room on the third floor from nine to five-thirty. I checked the function sheet: coffee on arrival, flipcharts and mid-morning coffee, two-course lunch, house wine, projector screen, afternoon tea, video, and coffee, coffee, coffee.

Dolores rang from downstairs at reception. 'Are you the only one up in the office?' she asked. 'Can I put early callers through to you?' Between calls and orders and bookings, I started working on my text for the Festival Fringe Whisky List.

Kitty always liked to put together a special whisky list for the Edinburgh festival. It was all quite expensive stuff, with big names and special bottles. Part of my job was to put together a separate list of Fringe whiskies, with rather more unusual, quirky bottles and some interesting special offers. I had struck up some promotional deals with a number of the venues and theatre companies and I had to get the text finished before all the phones started ringing at nine o'clock.

Kitty appeared by my desk. 'The word about Wild Cat whisky is out,' she said. 'A demand has been created and I would be very surprised if this doesn't cause a little stir. If the idea proves popular, as seems likely, Dodgio will probably launch something similar themselves in a few years' time. Just you wait and see. It'll take them a while, but they'll get there eventually.'

'But we thought of it first,' I replied.

'We didn't think of it. It's always been there. We just opened it up. And Dodgio won't sell pink whisky as a true single cask single malt like ours, they'll sell it as a blend. I hope it'll be a good blend. No reason why it shouldn't be. Have you got everything organised, Emily?'

'Yes, I think so.'

I had been promoted. My new role at Charlotte Square was a very interesting one, with more money and a whole lot of extra responsibilities. The first thing I did when I got the job was go out and buy new shoes. I also bought a smartly tailored, assertive jacket. It was charcoal grey, so it could deal with any kind of serious situation, as well as matching all of my office skirts and trousers and my red suede shoes. It was fitted and shapely and cinched at the waist so I didn't feel as if I had been fobbed off with something from Menswear. I kept it on a hanger in the office for the growing number of times I had to go out and be a professional businesswoman. I needed the clothes to help me feel the part. The shoes made me walk with purpose. I just put my feet in them and became instantly taller. I got further faster.

'Have you written your copy for the Festival Bottlings List yet?' asked Flora as she passed my desk.

'No, still working on it.'

'Kitty asked me how you were getting on with it yesterday.'

'It's nearly finished.'

I checked over what I had written so far: Cask strength whisky is essential for the appreciation of conceptual art. Avant-garde and extraordinary, this stunning pink malt will draw gasps of surprise. It's the perfect apéritif before you head off to see The Maori Tap Dancers at St Vincent's Presbyterian Church, or watch the acclaimed Snorkelling with Shakespeare at Drumsheugh Baths. Your Charlotte Square membership card will get you two shock-absorbing measures of this fabulous single malt, as well as a more robust attitude to stage nudity . . .

I chewed the end of my pencil. I wasn't really sure where I wanted to take it from there.

Dolores called me on the phone again. 'Can you come to reception, please?' I put my notes away and walked downstairs. On my way, I had a quick look in the rooms that had been booked for the day. The lawyers' blue sitting room on the third floor was prepared. Good. I passed the drawing room, opened the door and sitting there alone was the mousy woman in the navy suit – no husband, no lover. By herself. She looked pale.

'Can I help you?'

'No,' she said shortly. 'I'm waiting for someone. I'll be leaving soon.'

I hesitated. 'Coffee?' She was silent. Well, she had answered the question. On the next floor down I checked the dining room and there was the husband, sitting alone at a table, grim-faced, staring at a piece of paper. He looked up when I opened the door. 'Can I get you anything?' I asked.

'No thanks.' He looked tired and miserable.

I walked on to the ground floor. If I see the lover now, I thought, I'll know something has gone seriously awry here. I turned the corner and there he was, standing at reception, agitated and red-faced, tapping his keys on the desk. 'This gentleman is very unhappy,' said Dolores. 'He has lost something important.'

He started to explain. He had lost an envelope containing a letter and a ticket for a flight that very morning. It was addressed to a Mrs Meriel Hampton.

I thought of the husband upstairs. 'I'll check for you,' I said. 'Dolores, I need to take your flower arrangement to the dining room.' I went back upstairs with the vase of pink gerberas. The husband moved the piece of paper off the table so

I could put the vase down. I read over his shoulder: Amsterdam. Easy Jet. Only seventeen pounds fifty return from Edinburgh. Special Offer. I went back to the drawing room but I didn't open the door. I could hear her crying. She was going to miss her flight. Back downstairs again. The careless boyfriend, waiting hopefully.

I wanted to say: Flee now! All is discovered!, but instead I said, 'I'm sorry, no luck this time.'

'Shit. I'm going to have to go on my own. Can I leave her a message?'

He scribbled something down, signed it 'Sorry' and stuffed it into an envelope that Dolores had passed him (thick, cream, self-sealing – she was nice, Dolores). Then he left.

'I'll keep it for her till she gets here,' said Dolores. 'Poor soul, having to go on his own.'

'He'll be fine.'

I went back upstairs. Peeped through the dining room door. The husband was leaning over the table, his shoulders heaving, awful sounds escaping from him. I shut the door silently. Does he know she's still here? I wondered. In the drawing room, she was standing at the window, staring out. 'Mrs Hampton?' She looked up. 'There's a letter just been delivered for you at reception.'

Then I shut the door and walked back upstairs to the office. Don't worry about them, I thought. I handled that all right. 'Detachment is my default mode,' I recited under my breath, remembering my father's lecture. My father on the stage last year at the Edinburgh International Conference Centre. 'Presence on any stage is an expression of power. Presence is projected by a sure and steadfast belief in self; by confidence, courage and charisma; but most of all by detachment. Presence is a gift, not an obligation.'

My father, grandiloquent.

Out of curiosity I had wanted to go and hear him speak. I had wanted to see him because I hadn't seen him since I was ten. Andrew had come with me. We had sat at the back of the auditorium and ten minutes into the lecture my husband had taken my hand and whispered, 'Emily, I know he's your father, I know he's been knighted for his services to industry, but quite frankly he's talking a load of bollocks.'

I sat down at my desk. What was the last thing I had written? Ah yes, stage nudity. I finished my piece: We suggest you invest in a large hipflask for the Festival. One dedicated festival-goer confessed he could not have remained in his seat during last year's special lecture by Sir Douglas Montrose, 'Presence of Mind Over Matter', had he not had his society hipflask to sustain him throughout the performance.

I couldn't resist going back downstairs again to see if the husband and wife had gone. They had. Separately. 'She got her message,' said Dolores. 'She took it and ran. But she gets what she deserves, you know, because I've checked the bookings and she stayed in one of the flats here last night. But I tell you what, it wasn't with the poor man she was supposed to go on holiday with! Oh no, it was with somebody else.' Dolores tapped the side of her nose. 'I know. I saw him. He left via the back door. He looked furtive if you ask me.' Dolores settled herself back on to her receptionist's chair, surveying the hallway, ready for further action.

The front door opened and a woman entered and filled the space with her presence. Tall, blonde, smiling and confident. Really, really good shoes. She was carrying a chic leather briefcase and a laptop and she wore a smart suit that was way, way beyond me. It wasn't grey or navy or black or brown. It was pink bouclé tweed. A pink suit for work? How did she have the nerve to wear it? I knew I couldn't wear anything that daring – but, I realised, I would like to. It didn't look silly on her, she could carry it off. She looked cool and together and stylish. She looked like a professional business-woman who was writing her own self-success book. It was Kate.

'Oh,' breathed Dolores. 'If you don't mind my saying, I think I know you from somewhere . . . '

'Yes,' she smiled. 'I remember. Dolores. It's Dolores, isn't it? I remember you from the Kelvingrove book club. You had us read *Why Women Just Like To Make Things Nice* and I wasn't very nice about it.'

'It's okay. I don't mind.'

'Morning, Emily,' she said, turning to me. 'How are you?'

'Fine, thanks.'

'How's Andrew?'

'Oh!' said Dolores, checking her notepad. 'He rang earlier, Emily, but I couldn't put him through because you were on the phone. He says he's booked a table at your favourite restaurant for after the party. Just the two of you.'

'Well,' said Kate. 'I'd better be going. Must make a start. It's the blue sitting room, isn't it? I know the way.' And she walked off briskly, heading upstairs.

When she had gone, Dolores turned to me with round eyes and said, 'Did you see that ring she was wearing? What a rock!'

'What rock?'

'It was as big as . . . ' Dolores searched around her desk for something to compare it with. 'It was as big as that pencil sharpener,' she said, holding it over her middle finger. 'I thought it looked quite common, actually,' she sniffed. 'I tell you what, a diamond like that – Kate has got to be seeing either a footballer, a movie star or a gangster.'

We heard laughter. 'None of the above,' she called. 'I bought it myself.'

'Oh God,' cringed Dolores. 'She heard me.'

I went back to work. An email from my mother. 'Go for it!' she'd written. 'You go out there and do it. Break a leg'. It read as though it should have gone to one of the acts she represented.

An email from Andrew. 'See you for the launch at six and then we can have dinner at nine. Is that okay? If you're still busy at nine, I could always go to the restaurant and wait for you. I can have a starter and you can practise being late. Perfect. See what harmony we have together?'

Thanks, I typed back. Looking forward to it. Love Emily.

Love Emily, I thought. It's not the simple kind of love it used to be.

By the time six o'clock came around it was time to change into the right shoes and go out and complete the pink project. People were arriving for the party. Flora was already rushing up and down stairs, organising people, arranging bottles and pouring pink drams.

'Where's Jack?' she asked. 'He said he would be here.'

'Maybe he's changed his mind.'

It was now a month since I'd said goodbye to him. I had told him not to send me anything and he had obviously taken me at my word. I ought to have been grateful. I was grateful, but sometimes . . .

I shut my eyes for a moment. I still thought about him, allowed myself to think about him. You can't just stop. It has to fade. It goes gradually. A slow, deliberate forgetting. I was realising that it would take a long time.

I got my smart shoes out of my bottom drawer and put them on, along with my new jacket, and then I went downstairs.

The first person I saw was Andrew and I was pleased that he was there. He had made sure not to miss it. He admired the pink whisky, and the label and lettering, and the wildcat slinking round the base of the bottle. 'It's all going very well, Emily,' he said. He looked proud of me and that made me feel guiltier than ever.

The launch party was soon in full swing. Kitty Gillespie, looking fabulously glamorous in her favourite red dress, disappeared up to her flat and returned with the stuffed Scottish wildcat, which she stood on the bar (poor thing). All her

272

friends gathered round to share jokes and tell stories of defiance of the Enforcement Agency. Kitty was organising her Resistance.

Flora, I noticed, was looking flustered. Freddie Fawcett, the Domination Director himself, had arrived and had had a quiet word with her. He had explained that although he would have to take very serious action against us, he couldn't help admiring our nerve and it was quite an interesting idea, pink whisky. He said the Brand Enforcement Agency had long been intrigued by the potential of the female market. It was worth millions if only they knew how to talk to girls.

Flora had heard a rumour that Dodgio were going to track our pink whisky experiment very carefully. Together we tackled the man from Dodgio about it. 'We're interested,' he admitted. 'Let's just say, you've alerted us to its potential. We at Dodgio have been thinking about making a pink whisky as a blend and selling it in Spain.'

'But it's very rare,' said Flora. 'There wouldn't be enough to go round. It's not a whisky for mass distribution.'

However, the man from Dodgio didn't seem to have heard her. He had turned to talk to Freddie Fawcett and they were already deep in discussion. 'It would be a very simple thing to blend a pink whisky,' said Freddie.

'It's time to break away from the old restrictive standards,' said the man from Dodgio, smiling into his glass of fine old single malt. 'We should do away with the practice of branding whisky according to age. We all know that age is simply a marketing device anyway. Why not brand a pink-coloured whisky instead?'

'Our whisky isn't coloured,' interrupted Flora, 'it's naturally pale pink.'

'We'd have to have a strategy to address that, obviously,' he replied.

Flora looked aghast. 'You're not thinking of selling an artificially coloured whisky?'

The man from Dodgio smiled a little smile. 'I can guarantee it will be completely pure. Pure malt whisky with natural pink colouring.' He smiled, turned his back on us and moved on through the crowd, a juggernaut cutting up all the other guests at the whisky party.

For the next three hours, I worked hard. I circulated and smiled and shared jokes and made conversation. I introduced whisky makers to whisky blenders, and gin distillers to other gin distillers, and wine boys to whisky brokers. I offered drinks to journalists and canapés and pink cocktails to the vodka people. I tried to cheer up Flora who was dismayed about Dodgio's plan for pink colouring in blended whisky.

'I don't know what Jack would say about that,' she said. 'Where is Jack? He's always late.'

Privately I hoped he would stay away. I didn't think my conscience could cope with seeing him and Andrew in the same room together again. There was only an hour left before the guests were due to leave. The press had been busy all night and, having got their free samples, they were ready to go. I remembered faces and names and did my job until Kitty asked me to go upstairs to fetch emergency supplies. I went up to the office and stood on the top landing holding my list of things to do. I still had a few things to sort out. Walking down to the floor below, I saw, just out of the corner of my eye, a movement – someone going into the room on the right. Must be one of the lawyers. As I drew level, I heard the word 'sorry', and then the door opened again quickly, like an ambush, and a man ran straight into me, almost pushing me down the stairs. I reached out and grabbed his arm and steadied myself. 'Emily!'

It was Jack. Exactly as I remembered him. Tall and slender and smiling and holding on to me. And right there, on the landing, right in that moment of surprise and sudden joy at seeing each other, we reached out and we kissed.

It's very, very difficult to kiss someone you desire and then just stop, like you never meant to do it in the first place. Your body won't let you. It shuts down your notions of common sense because it deems them unnecessary, and all the lights go out. I could feel myself crumbling, all that hard-won edge of common sense sinking and softening. Then we pulled away and looked at each other at arm's length. I wondered if I looked as stunned as he did. I didn't know what to say to him.

'I wanted to talk to you,' he said. 'I haven't contacted you at all because you asked me not to, but I've come back because I think you should—'

'Oh, Jack, I just can't do this, I can't—'

'You left your husband, Emily, and came to see me. You wrote to me. You asked me. We were together and it was what you wanted.'

'But you have to understand that—'

'I just want to talk to you. When can we meet and talk properly?'

'I don't think we should.'

'I'm not leaving without agreeing a time and place for us to meet.'

I had to give in. 'All right. Tomorrow at six o'clock. I'll meet you at that place we used to go to for coffee after work.'

'Okay. And we'll talk.' He hesitated, as if unsure whether or not to kiss me goodbye.

'Bye, Jack,' I said. 'I'll see you tomorrow.'

He kissed me on the lips, a little kiss, and then turned and left. He walked down the stairs and I heard him say a cheery goodbye to Dolores as he walked past her on reception.

I sat down heavily on the stairs and put my head in my hands. Detachment is my default mode, I told myself. Don't cry, don't cry, don't cry. I've got to meet Andrew soon. I've got to be able to make happy conversation like nothing's happened. Oh God! I can't put on this act. I can't do this.

I heard steps behind me. Someone sat down at my side. I didn't look up. I could smell her perfume. It was cool and confident, with cypress and vetivert and as clear as a sea breeze.

'Well, well, well,' said Kate. 'What on earth are you going to do now?'

'Clean and rich for its age, with whispers of barley sugar, but at reduced strength this whisky dries out substantially and finishes bitter, like black instant coffee or liquorice. Be careful'

Cask No. 107·4   *Bitter Sweet*
Alcohol: 62.2%   Proof: 108.85°   Outturn: 330 bottles

The Society Bottlings, Spring 2001

Chapter Twenty

'Shall we talk?' she asked. 'I've got five minutes to spare.'

'Kate, it's private. It's my problem.'

'I know about it now, though, don't I?' She stood up and waited. 'Let's go somewhere to talk.'

We went into a tiny room off the landing which was really just a box room, a walk-in cupboard that had one small, high-up window above the door to let in borrowed light from the stairwell.

I wiped my eyes and took a few deep breaths. 'Jack coming here today was totally out of the blue. I didn't even know he was in the country. I ended it with Jack a while ago.'

'It didn't look like it was over.'

'It is over.'

'What would Andrew think if he knew?'

'I've ended it, Kate. I mean it. It never really got started, not much anyway, and I love Andrew and I want to stay with him. I'll tell Jack all that again when I see him tomorrow. I've already told him but it's just all so complicated and difficult.'

'But you still want to be with Jack, don't you?'

'It's over,' I repeated dully. 'I want to stay with Andrew.'

Kate appeared to consider my dilemma with the same detachment a lawyer might reserve for a particularly emotive case – just the kind of cool detachment a lawyer needs to do the job. It's a serious issue, breach of trust.

'You have to tell Andrew the truth,' she said. 'You have to talk to him.'

'But what good would it do to tell him now? It's better that he doesn't know. He would be devastated.'

'You'd rather just keep on deceiving him?'

'I'm not deceiving him if I don't see Jack, am I? I don't want Andrew to know.'

'I bet you don't.'

'I'd rather bear the guilt, and that's hard enough. It wouldn't be fair to tell him.'

She looked at me intently. 'It's wrong to lie to him. I think you should tell him the truth.'

'I can't.'

Long, cool pause. 'I can.'

I stared at her and saw she meant it. 'Don't, Kate. Please. I know what I did was wrong and I'm sorry. I regret it now very much. I won't do it again. Please don't tell Andrew. I love him, Kate. I don't want to hurt him.'

'I know it's difficult,' she said, her voice very even, 'but you have to take responsibility for this. How would you feel if it was the other way around? How would you feel if Andrew had been unfaithful to you? It would hurt, wouldn't it? It would hurt very much to be told the truth.'

278

I felt cold and scared. 'Don't tell him,' I pleaded.

She looked at her watch. 'I have to get back. Look, Emily, I understand that you're nervous about telling him straight-away. You should think it through and then decide what you're going to say. Why don't we talk about this again tomorrow evening after you've seen Jack? Why don't you ring me up and we'll talk it through then?'

'Right,' I breathed. 'We'll do that. We'll talk again.'

I knew now that I was in Kate's hands and the idea appalled me. Telling Andrew the truth was too awful to contemplate and I had only a brief period of grace.

I went back downstairs to the main party in the drawing room. And there was Jack, circulating and chatting to all his old friends and contacts in the industry.

Kate was talking to Andrew. My stomach turned over as I watched them. Was she telling him? But Andrew was smiling and seemed happy. Kate seemed happy too: she was making him laugh. I ran back upstairs, terrified I might have to talk to them both with Kate knowing what I had done. I turned around to see that she had followed me out of the room as far as the hall. She was looking for me. Why? What did she want to say to me now?

I escaped to the office and the phone rang at my desk. It was Dolores. 'Isn't it great that Jack's come back?' she cooed. 'You and Jack got very close when he was here, didn't you? I've just been talking to him and, oh, hang on a sec—' I heard her speak to someone else. 'Sorry, Kate.' The words were muffled. She must have put her hand over the phone. 'I didn't see you there. Yes, thanks, if you wouldn't mind just signing for that . . . thank you. Emily,' she came back, 'Jack was telling me he'd seen you in Barcelona and I said wasn't that an amazing coincidence? Seeing him on holiday like that, what with you being on holiday in Spain at the same time?' And she went on and on and on.

'I have to go.' My voice sounded hoarse. 'I have to go, Dolores.'

'Oh, wait a minute! Andrew's here.'

'Hi, Emily.' He still sounded perfectly cheerful. It didn't seem as though he had heard a word Dolores had said. 'I'm going across to the restaurant now. It's ten past nine. Are you going to be much longer? Everyone's just about gone. It's really only Kitty and her friends left. You've been cleaned out of whisky.'

'I'll be right down. I'll see you in the restaurant.'

'Okay, see you there. It's all right to be late now and then, remember.'

I put the phone down and sat for about a minute. 'Try this,' said Flora, appearing in front of me. She handed me a glass and pressed my fingers around it. I took a sip, felt it warming going down. 'A is for Ardbeg,' she said. Her face appeared in front of mine, concerned.

'Flora,' I whispered. 'Can I talk to you please?'

We went off to the place we always sought out when we needed to talk – the laundry room, which was situated through the back of the laundry cupboard and behind the Ladies toilets. All the dirty washing of the Whisky Society was brought here to be washed, rinsed and spin-dried. Everything had a thorough airing before being put away again. The room was warm and soapy-smelling. The washing machines toiled away, sloshing noisily. Flora pulled herself on top of the dryer, shuffled her bottom to the back wall and stretched her legs out.

'It's lovely and warm,' she said cosily. 'Come and sit down. Tell me what's been happening. I've been stuck arguing with Freddie Fawcett all evening.'

'Kate saw me with Jack. Kate knows.' At that point the washing machine beside us clicked into spin cycle and everything began to shake. Flora slid off the dryer. 'Kate thinks I should tell Andrew what I've done.'

'You have to tell him now because he's going to find out

one way or another,' said Flora. 'You'll just have to be brave, Emily.'

'I don't know how I'm going to talk to him.'

'You'll have to.'

On my way out I met Kitty, who was putting some gin distillers into their taxi. 'It was a wonderful success,' she said, beaming. 'Wonderful. Flora is feeling rather disillusioned about the mass market forces that rule us all but it was always going to happen. I told her to go and sort out some samples upstairs. She was starting to say inappropriately critical things to the wrong people. You're going for dinner with your charming husband, aren't you? Have a wonderful time!'

I left her waving to me from the steps of the building. In her cloak and red silk dress she took up position like a flag, like a warning sign.

I hurried round to the restaurant on George Street where I had arranged to meet Andrew and I took the lift up to the top floor of the building. It was the same restaurant we had visited for my twenty-third birthday. This was also where he had brought me that very first time we went out together. We had had lunch here and straight afterwards he had gone to see Kate to finish it all between them. I had an awful sense of foreboding as I walked through the door this time.

I hovered about at the reception area, trying to see where Andrew was sitting. It was completely full, every table occupied, and then I saw him. He was sitting at a table quite a long way inside the room. He had his back to me, and while I watched he bowed his head and seemed to crumple up. Something was very wrong. Quickly, I started to walk towards him, and then I saw a woman rise from her place opposite. A woman in a white blouse and a pink tweed skirt. It was Kate. She had got there first. Kate put her hand briefly on his shoulder and left him. She was walking straight towards me now. Her face was flushed and determined.

'You told him,' I said numbly.

'Yes.'

'Why?'

'You didn't want to tell him,' she said, 'but I certainly did.'

She made to walk past me but I put my hand on her arm. 'Kate, you said we could talk.'

'I decided against it.'

'You shouldn't have told him. If anyone was going to tell him it should have been me.'

'I didn't think you would get round to it, somehow.'

'You just wanted to hurt him. And me. You just wanted to get your own back.'

Kate's eyes were very bright. 'You're the one who's been the cause of all the pain, Emily.'

I glanced over to where Andrew sat, hunched in his chair, staring into space, and I felt overwhelmed by guilt and love and anxiety. 'I can't bear to see him hurt.'

'You should have thought of that before, shouldn't you? Go and talk to him. He's waiting for you. You don't need to say much. You can keep it brief. Say, "Look, I feel terrible hurting you, but there's somebody else." He'll understand if you put it like that because that's exactly how he put it himself. I remember very clearly.'

I watched Kate leave. She moved smoothly between the tables to the door. My legs were shaking when I sat down opposite Andrew. At first he didn't even acknowledge my presence. This is the end, I thought. I can't bear it. He seemed shocked, like he'd just witnessed a terrible accident.

'What did she say?' I asked, feeling sick. 'What did she tell you?'

He raised his eyes to mine, and I could tell he looked at me differently. Somewhere between dismay and revulsion. It made me feel faint to realise how he must think of me now.

'She said you've been having an affair. She said your trip to Spain was to see your boyfriend. She said you met him just a

282

few hours ago and you've arranged to meet him again tomorrow.'

'I told him it was over. Andrew, I'm sorry. Please forgive me.'

'She saw you kissing him.'

'I hadn't expected to see him. I . . . ' My words were feeble and I realised I didn't know what to say, how to explain. I felt so terrible that I couldn't bring myself to face him. I stared at the table.

'Did you spend your holiday with him?'

'No, no, only one night. Just one night in Barcelona. That's the only time I ever—'

'You slept with him.'

'Only that one time. I didn't do anything really wrong until then and it was only that one time. I was faithful to you but when I went to Spain I just wasn't sure any more and, and—'

'You really did sleep with him.'

I looked at my husband desperately, and his face was shut against me. 'It was just the once. Please forgive me. It was a stupid thing to do because I just felt guilty and I didn't enjoy it as much as I thought I would.' (Oh God, that came out badly, didn't it?)

'You want me to forgive you?' He raised his voice. 'You cheated on me and you want me to forgive you because you didn't enjoy it as much as you thought you would?' He was shouting now. 'Because you didn't have a really good shag?'

Oh God, how a busy restaurant can fall silent! All the watching faces. I felt so ashamed. There was a roaring in my ears and I thought I was about to faint. I bent forwards, doubled up as darkness blurred my vision. I clung to the table and I didn't faint. I was on my knees but my sight had returned and all I could see was the floor and his feet, his shoes. He stood and I saw his coat as he threw it over his arm and he walked right past me.

In the restaurant, the music returned. They were playing Frank Sinatra: 'You Make Me Feel So Young'.

I saw my husband walk away from me. I heard his footsteps fade as he walked all the way out, through the terrible silence of the audience.

Exit.

'The first of the three distilleries you encounter on the tiny road from Port Ellen to Kildalton Kirk malts its own barley and its whisky is famously smoky. This cask is no exception; a fine, full-blooded example, made more so by the fact that it is still young and vigorous. The flavour at reduced strength is both sweet and acidic'

Cask No. 29·20   *Green Sticks*
Alcohol: 58.6%   Proof: 102.5°   Outturn: 261 bottles

The Society Bottlings, Summer 2001

Chapter Twenty-one

I went home and the house seemed vast on my own. It was such a big house. I walked through the front door and felt immediately how empty it was when he wasn't there with me. I wanted him to come home. I wanted him to come back. When we had first moved here, we hadn't had the furniture to fill the space. There had been all these empty rooms in this echoing house. It had been exciting; there had been so much to do, so much to furnish, to find and to organise. The emptiness hadn't seemed overwhelming at all. We hadn't called it emptiness. I think the word we had used was 'potential'.

I waited and waited and he didn't come back. I stayed awake all night, sitting up alone, and I thought of what I would do if he never did come back to me, if he had left me for good. I wondered where he had spent the night.

At dawn, I walked around the house and opened all the doors and windows. The cat came sauntering in from the garden. He stretched and started rubbing against my legs. I picked him up and cuddled and fussed over him. He purred loudly. I had loved my pet and looked after him. I hadn't abandoned or neglected or hurt him. Well, I had got him castrated, but that was always going to be part of the deal. The cat had exchanged his balls for domestic bliss and, snuggled in my arms, he seemed perfectly contented with his bargain. I gave him his breakfast, his favourite Pussyfood, and he ate it greedily.

I made coffee and took it into the living room and finally shut the doors to the garden. I would have to take Jaffa Cat with me when I went to Flora's. I didn't know if Andrew would be coming back to this house ever again and I had to take care of my cat. I had to get his cat-carrying thing out from the cupboard under the stairs. I had to get my backpack out too. I had to gather together what I needed and go.

I wrote Andrew a letter, in case he came back to the house we had shared together. I told him, over many pages, that I loved him, that I was sorry and I asked for his forgiveness. Then I locked up the house, buried the key in the garden in the secret hiding place we both knew, and I left.

Flora opened her door to me and Jaffa Cat and took us in. She hugged me and sat beside me while I cried. It was the first time I had cried since I saw Andrew walk away. It was strange that I hadn't cried until now. Flora said it was just shock. I realised I had never cried so much in my life. 'Oh Flora, I'm sorry,' I choked. 'And I've always said I hate it when people let it all out.'

'It's okay,' she said. 'It's not surprising you need to cry. You don't know where he is, either, do you? Have you rung anyone to try to find out?'

'I don't like to. I'm worried he might have gone to see Kate.'

I wept some more, quietly and desperately. The cat came to sit on my knee and I cuddled him.

'What happened?' Flora asked. 'What did he say?'

'He left.'

'Do you want to stay at my place tonight?'

'I want to stay with Andrew.'

'He might not want to be with you, though, Emily.'

And at last I realised, with awful clarity, that my sadness at burying my longing for Jack was nowhere near as painful as my despair at losing Andrew.

Flora was practical. 'Are you still going to meet Jack this evening?' she asked. 'Why don't you ring him up now and tell him whatever it is you have to say – that you're really not going to see him again. That way, if you do talk to Andrew tonight, at least you can honestly tell him you're not seeing Jack again.'

I rang Jack but there was only the answerphone. I left him a message to say I couldn't meet him. I couldn't meet him at all. I told him I was sorry. I felt a coward leaving a message like that.

Then I tried to contact Andrew. I wanted to beg him to meet me and let me try to explain, after I had explained so little and so badly. I tried his office. Just his voicemail. I rang the main switchboard, explained it was urgent and asked if he could perhaps be somewhere else in the building?

'Who's calling?'

'His wife.' I'm his wife, I thought. I'm his wife and I've done this terrible thing to him.

'I'm sorry, he doesn't seem to be here. No one's seen him since last night.'

I put down the phone, disconsolate.

Flora said she would pop out to the newsagent and get us both a big bar of chocolate. Jaffa started wandering round the

287

room, mewing. I felt sorry for him, taken from his old home to this new place with no garden doors.

'We can't go back,' I told my cat. 'I'm going to have to find us a new place to live.' He sat and blinked at me a few times in a baffled sort of way and then he opened his pink mouth in a long, tragic, 'Why?'

'Why?' he miaowed. 'Why? Why?'

'You can stay as long as you want,' said Flora, reassuring me. 'I was going to advertise the spare room anyway. I've got a notice up in the entrance of Broughton Real Foods.'

'It's kind of you, Flora, but I really need to sort out a place for myself.'

We ate all the chocolate and I volunteered to go out and buy some more, together with some Kleenex tissues. I borrowed Flora's floppy hat and pulled it down low to try to hide my red, puffy eyes. On the way to the shop I found myself wondering how much rent she had hoped to get for her room, so I made a detour to Broughton Real Foods. There I found her little advert. It was a pink piece of paper with a fringe of little tabs cut into the bottom, each tab displaying her phone number. She was asking for far too modest a sum of rent considering the size of the room, the spaciousness of the flat, and bills were included too. I sighed. She might be a good nose, she might be a connoisseur, but a sales pitch was not her forté.

Room in quite nice flat, it said. No heating in room, but bed has electric blanket. Standard facilities. Would suit female young professional, non-smoker. No pets.

No pets. I thought of Flora's nice furniture and Jaffa's sharp claws. I remembered her smart new sofa and her beautiful embroidered cushions with long silky ties at the corners, and her tassel-edged tablecloth and all the other pretty, irresistible cat toys she had made herself, hand-sewing in the evening over many years and every single episode of *Friends*. Jaffa would shred her handmade world to pieces. I thought of the destructive influence I had become in the lives of the people I loved most and it was hard to bear. I would have to find somewhere else to live and quickly.

I looked over all the other 'Room to Let' notices and pulled off half a dozen fringey phone numbers. There was one that said: Must love cats. It was a shared garden flat inhabited by Young Female Professionals. It had All The Mod Cons You Can Think Of – And Some. The advertised Fabulous Room was available now. The other three in the house were clearly all very happy to live there because it was Probably The Nicest Flat In Edinburgh. If the place was as good as the sales pitch, it could be great. But it was very expensive, bills extra. It was as much as I could afford – and some.

'Must love cats.'

Just how much do you have to love them? I thought.

When I got back to Flora's, she came running down the stairs to meet me on the landing. 'Jack's here,' she said, urgently.

'Did you tell him?' I whispered.

'No. What are you going to do?'

'Talk to him, I suppose.'

He had lost all of the optimistic air he used to have. He looked tired and he stood with his shoulders slumped. When he saw me, I took off the floppy hat and he seemed to get a bit of a fright. I caught sight of myself in the mirror and I could see why. I looked dreadful. Red-eyed and blotchy.

'Oh Emily,' he said. 'Did you tell him?'

Flora tactfully withdrew to the kitchen.

'Andrew found out. It would have been better if I had told him myself, but someone else got there first. And I feel terrible about it, Jack. I felt terrible when I saw how hurt he was.'

'It was never going to be easy for him,' he said, 'but you've made the break now and that's what's important.'

'I didn't want to make the break.'

Jack looked bewildered. 'You did. You just needed some-one to help you do it, someone who cared enough about you to help you. Don't change your mind now.'

'I haven't changed my mind. I always wanted to be with my husband, I was just . . . working it out.'

'And what did you work out? I thought you wanted to be independent and travel and—'

'You're all the things I admire,' I told him. 'You're confident and certain and fearless about things. You know how to wing it. You're all the things I'm not and I was flattered that you wanted me. It was like being paid a huge compliment. And I wanted you to want me, but I can't leave with you. I can't see you again. I've made up my mind.'

He stared at me blankly. 'And that's it?' he asked. 'That's all you have to say to me?'

I nodded. Right then, I couldn't have spoken another word if I'd tried. I couldn't have told him how hard it was for me just being in the same room as him, how my heart was still aching. I couldn't tell him anything tender at all. I had to learn not to give those thoughts away.

He was angry and hurt. He called me a hypocrite. He said I was a liar. He said he was glad he'd found out what I was really like. His voice was hard.

Flora appeared in the kitchen doorway, watching over us protectively.

'I'm sorry,' I told Jack. 'I'm sorry if I've hurt you. I didn't want to hurt you.'

He strode angrily past me and out of the door. I heard him running down the stairs. I stood on the landing and watched him leave.

'You were finding out, remember,' said Flora beside me. 'You were just working through it. You have to try to talk to Andrew again.'

'Come on.' She took my arm and I went back into her living room and sat down.

'Andrew might have gone to talk to David,' she said. 'At least find out if he's been in touch.'

I phoned and David answered. 'It's Emily,' I began, 'have you heard from—'

'He's here, I was about to ring you. I thought maybe you'd want to know.'

'Can I speak to him?'

There was a pause. Muffled voices, then: 'I'd wait a bit, Emily.'

'David, I'm so sorry. Please tell him I love him. Please tell him—'

'Just wait a while, Emily,' he repeated. 'Let's just keep in touch and see what happens. Are you at the house?'

'No, it's locked up. I'm at Flora's.'

'Okay.'

'David, do you think there's any chance he might forgive me?'

He let out a long sigh. 'Put it this way, Emily, it's taken Jane ten years to be able to forgive me. I don't know what's going to happen. I'm his brother and I don't like to see him hurt.'

'No.'

'There are quite a few things to deal with here. Take some time.'

'I'm sorry, David. I'm so sorry for hurting him. I feel like I'm going to be apologising for the rest of my life.'

'I recognise that feeling,' said David.

'Tell him I hope I can talk to him again soon.'

'Let's stay in touch, Emily. Come round and see me and Jane. Let's just take it one day at a time.'

I put off telling my mother and sister what had happened. When I did call them, Polly burst into tears but Joanna took it all in her stride. 'I was expecting it, to be honest,' said my mother, 'especially after our conversation, but Polly is taking it badly. She always liked Andrew, you know. He was always kind to her. She got flowers from him yesterday for winning that part in the musical. They came from both of you, but he had sent them. Wasn't that kind? She was thrilled to bits.'

'I didn't know he had done that.'

'It was just yesterday. I emailed you both at work to tell you she had got the part.'

'I never heard.'

'Well Andrew did and he sent her flowers immediately. I expect he would have mentioned it, if he hadn't had other things to ask you about. So, Kate told him. There was always a chance someone would. Terrible bad luck Jack turning up at your office, though. You would think he would have more sense. You can't have an adulterous affair without careful planning.'

'I didn't plan it.'

'You took a risk,' said my mother. 'We talked about it when you were here. You knew the possible consequences.'

'I can't bear the consequences.'

'You can. You're taking responsibility.'

'I've just made a terrible mistake.'

'You're learning. You'll survive. When I was your age I was making huge, massive mistakes. I had you when I was twenty-one, for instance. But you learn from your mistakes. You'll be all right,' she soothed. 'Just do your best.'

'Was I really such a huge, massive mistake?'

'Oh don't take it so personally, Emily! And no, you weren't such a huge mistake – we had ten happy years after you were born. It was Polly that was the really seriously massive mistake, but I love Polly too, don't I? Look how much I adore her. See how things can work out all right in the end? Oh, Polly wants a word.'

'Polly,' I told her, 'you are not a massive mistake.'

'I know, I know,' she sniffed. 'I'm her consolation prize. Oh Emily, I understand you had to work through whatever it was that was bothering you, but I wish you hadn't split up with him.' Polly wept down the phone.

'I'm going to talk to him soon,' I told her, starting to cry again myself. 'I'm going to get myself a new place to live and sort out some other important things, and I'm going to talk to Andrew soon.'

'How soon?'

'As soon as possible.'

I tried to be patient. Over the next few days, when Andrew didn't want to meet me, David persuaded him to talk to me on the phone instead. It was a short and excruciating conversation. 'I really need to see you, Andrew.'

'There's nothing to talk about.'

I went to see David and Jane and when I met Andrew there, too, it was unbearably hard. He hadn't wanted to go back to our house. He was staying with them until he got himself a flat of his own somewhere.

At about the same time I moved into the flat for cats with Jaffa, Andrew moved into a place in the West End. It was very near his office so he could work longer hours than ever. I heard from Jane that Andrew had been in touch with Kate. They had met and talked. They were putting certain things to rest, she said.

The weeks passed.

I worked hard too. I threw myself into my work like it was the only cure. The pink whisky was proving to be a phenomenal success. We had enquiries from a dozen different countries. Kitty Gillespie was asked to send someone to speak at a conference in Madrid which was all about whisky marketing in the Spanish-speaking world. Since I was the only one at Charlotte Square who spoke Spanish, she suggested I should be the one to go. Flora gave me extra coaching on nosing technique in case I got drawn into any blind tastings, but the trip was really about making a presentation: 'La Whisky Rosada'. I was worried about going on stage to make a speech, but I found that when I had something I really wanted to talk about, it was easier than I thought.

I faced things. I tackled everything head-on. I got busier and busier and the adrenalin rush felt like a controlled, refined, positive kind of anger – something I had never felt before – and it gave me an energy I hadn't known I possessed. It was like a clear, white light. It was something that seemed to appear from out of me and put itself at my disposal.

'This is not a loud, demanding Islay malt; it's the strong, silent type and gently stimulating. In its presence we feel soothed and reassured, lulled into a dream of warmth and home while outside the sea is gathering its strength and the sky is blustery with gales'

Cask No. 53·47   *The Strong, Silent Type*
Alcohol: 56.8%   Proof: 99.4°   Outturn: 205 bottles

The Society Bottlings, Winter 2000

Chapter Twenty-two

David and Jane's wedding took place at a country house hotel on the west coast. It was near the village where Jane had grown up. There were about a hundred guests, all family and friends. I got a very early train across to Glasgow and two connections on the West Highland route before I arrived at the nearest station, and then I took a taxi the last ten miles to the hotel. The wedding was due to take place at two o'clock in the afternoon. Like most of the guests, I planned to stay overnight and leave the next morning.

The setting was very beautiful. The hotel was right on the seashore and the window of my room looked out over a long, gentle arc of white beach and sand-dunes. About a mile away, there were cliffs of red sandstone. Beyond the cliffs there were mountains.

I recognised many of the wedding guests as being old friends of Andrew's. People I had met at dinner parties and whose lives I knew something about. They were all aware that it was now a few months since Andrew and I had split up. Some said hello and asked me how I was getting on. I felt embarrassed because they all knew I had had an affair. They all knew I had lied to my husband. Some people would only exchange nods. Others didn't want to meet my eyes.

Kate was there, with a man I had seen before at David's party. His name was Alex. I didn't know if he was there as a friend or a partner, but from the way they talked and sat together, Alex and Kate were certainly closer than I remembered.

Andrew was at the wedding too, of course. I saw him at the door of the hotel when I arrived, talking to his old friends. It was difficult to meet him so publicly. We nodded and said hello in polite, grown-up voices. We still had not met to talk properly. There was so much distance now. If it weren't for David and Jane I would have found it impossible to see him at all. There would have been no meeting ground, no connection, no one who was able to put us both together again. He had consciously avoided seeing me alone, he wouldn't stay long in the same room as me. I knew that David had spent hours talking to his brother. I knew there had been lots of late nights and long conversations, but I didn't know, and Jane couldn't tell me, if there was any chance that Andrew might forgive me. I knew I had hurt him deeply.

Andrew had been surprised that I still wanted to go to David and Jane's wedding, but they had made a point of asking me and I wanted to see them stand bravely in front of all of their friends and say their vows. All those promises. I wanted to hear the vows spoken out loud in English. I wanted to remember what I had promised. The last wedding I had been to had been my own.

In my room, I prepared myself.

I have a beautiful silk dress which is the colour of clear blue sky. It is my wedding dress. In my hotel room, I stepped into its soft blue and it slipped over my skin like water. In Paris I had worn it with pink roses fastened in my hair. I remembered being surprised and delighted at their scent every time I turned my head.

At our wedding ceremony, I remembered reaching for Andrew's hand and him taking mine tightly, both of us nervous. His hand had felt clammy and our fingers had slipped hotly together. I remembered the Mayor, important in his patriotic sash of blue, white and red, smiling benevolently, reading the first words of the service: '*Mes chers enfants*,' he'd begun. 'My dear children.' And there we had been, so afraid of this new beginning, this fragile infancy of our marriage, taking its first steps. Terrified and hopeful. When we had exchanged vows, the Mayor embraced us, kissing us on the cheek. Three kisses, the Parisian way. I remembered the look on Andrew's face when he realised he wasn't just going to be shaken by the hand. I remembered us laughing about it in the restaurant afterwards. I remembered a pink rose petal falling into Andrew's champagne and him fishing it out and eating it. I remembered, in our room later, the soft, sliding sound of his hands on this silk dress.

I looked at my reflection in the mirror and saw my face, pale and still. I have my mother's big eyes. 'You're such a solemn little thing, aren't you?' she would say when I used to watch her getting ready to go on stage. She would try to make me laugh. 'Say "solemn" Emily. Say it like me,' and she would repeat the word over and over again in a deep, slow, pouting way until it made me laugh. 'Soll–ummm,' I would chant, like a little Buddha cross-legged on the floor.

When I had lived with my husband, there had been times when he had taken my hands in his and said, 'Emily, STOP worrying.' He would say it gently and firmly. He would say it

297

because he had happened to notice that I was sitting very still and silent and staring straight ahead with my hands clasped tightly in my lap. That, apparently, was the only clue he needed.

'Emily,' I said to my reflection. 'STOP worrying.'

I smoothed the soft material of my dress. I would talk to him. We would be able to talk together here. He *would* talk to me again. But what would I do if he didn't want to be with me ever again? What would I do if this was to be the very last time I would ever see and speak to him?

I sat in the back row. An usher asked me to move to the seat reserved for me at the front. 'You're being a witness, remember. You need to be close to the front.' He guided me to the seat next to Andrew. We sat side by side. He nodded at me. I was aware of all the eyes behind us and all the stares and glances in our direction.

Tom sat on Andrew's other side, ready to be his father's best man, and next to Tom sat the bridegroom, David. He was nervous. 'It's really happening,' he said. 'All these people, everyone we know, all our friends and family. Everyone is here.' It was very different to my own wedding.

The witnesses to our wedding had been the people who often stand in at such occasions: the office workers at the Mairie. I had their addresses written down somewhere. I had sent them a couple of photographs of me and Andrew grinning hugely on the steps outside the building. Me with my blue silk dress and pink roses, Andrew with his dark suit and blue spotted tie. I wondered if Andrew recognised my dress now. I folded my hands in my lap and waited.

Music. We stood and the bride arrived, Jane on the arm of her elderly father. She wore a long, straight, cream dress and carried red roses. Behind her stood Sarah in a bridesmaid's dress that I knew had taken much negotiation – scarlet tulle with matching ballet shoes. Creamy roses.

The service began.

I listened to the vows and I thought how saying them must be like reciting lines of Shakespeare that are so well known they're almost clichés, but still feeling the meaning running right through them.

Then we came to the vow about faithfulness.

You could rephrase it and make it sound more frank. You could turn it into: I promise not to have an affair with anyone else but you . . . However, that would cut it down to basics. There was nothing about: I promise not to want anyone else. So maybe it was assumed that that sort of thing could happen, but you just had to forsake the person you wanted. It was a far-reaching promise as it could be broad in its meaning. It could mean: Don't go having coffee and whisky late at night with that other man – that really interesting man you've met – just the two of you, round his place after midnight. You have to forsake all others and if you don't think you can manage it, then obviously don't get married in the first place.

What if, say, you started out confident in your ability to be faithful, happily forsaking all others, and then this really good-looking, desirable Mr Other came along. Say you know you've got Mr Right but, oh, this Mr Other really is fantastic. He is the Other to end all others. I could love him. I could throw away all my vows to Mr Right for just one night with this amazing Mr Other. Not being able to resist temptation is very human. Only an angel can resist temptation (and then only on a good day). So I had had my Mr Other and Mr Right had rightly left me.

I witnessed Jane and David's vows with Andrew at my side. When the time came, we stood to sign our names on the marriage register. He took the pen and signed first, then handed it to me. I signed the same surname. I had been glad to lose my father's surname but it had still been strange to think my name had changed from my father's to my husband's. My mother's name was one that she had made up for herself and changed by deed poll. It was her stage name. She believed you could create yourself anew.

The ceremony came to a close. There was applause. David and Jane were now husband and wife instead of partner and partner. The wedding guests all rose to take photographs, and there was champagne and everyone seemed to breathe a sigh of relief. I went with Andrew to congratulate the happy couple. A crowd quickly formed around them and so we moved on. I followed Andrew to the side of the room.

'It was good,' I said, 'wasn't it? They look very happy, don't they?'

'Yes,' he said. 'They do.' Then he touched my dress, lightly, just brushed it on the shoulder. 'I remember this dress,' he said. And he smiled a little.

There was a big party after the ceremony. A reception with speeches and more champagne and wedding cake. David made quite an emotional toast and Tom had all the elderly females of his family in tears of pride and joy at his little speech about his dad. We applauded him loudly. Andrew and I were surprised to find that we were seated at the same table. We talked with the other guests about easy, obvious, happy wedding things. Tactfully, no one asked us about our own marriage.

The tables were cleared for dancing.

People 'stripped the willow' and 'dashed the white sergeant'. Eightsome reels and flings. I didn't meet a single other partner who knew how to do that thing with the thumbs so you spin round fastest.

I met Andrew in the middle of a more sedate dance. We only got to hold one hand. Later I saw Kate dancing with Alex. At the end she found herself standing right next to me.

'Emily, hello.'

We waited, wanting to say more but not quite sure how. Two well-dressed wedding guests being courteous to each other, making acknowledgements. She was wearing a bracelet I knew Andrew had given her. She touched it as she was speaking. 'I haven't worn this bracelet for so long,' she said suddenly, 'and then I thought, why not? I should wear it. It's very pretty. So I bought the earrings to match.'

'They look lovely,' I told her.

We looked at each other for a moment, face to face. 'I hope you're . . . getting on with life,' Kate said. 'I hope you're well, Emily.'

'Yes and you?'

'I'm happier these days.'

'Good. I'm pleased for you.' I meant it. I didn't want her to be angry or jealous. I didn't want to feel jealous any more either. The feeling had gone now. There was just sadness.

After that final reel, I sat out. I took a cup of coffee to a corner of the room and watched the party from a distance.

And then, he joined me. 'Emily,' he said. 'Do you remember this is how we met?'

We began to talk. And everyone could see we were sitting alone together, talking. We sat with our chairs shuffled together, in this quiet alcove, and people saw us and nodded to themselves and told their neighbours. I could see we were being pointed out.

When the party was over and all the dancing was done, we were still talking.

'I gave you everything I had to give,' Andrew said. 'What more do you want from me?'

'Your forgiveness.'

He was silent.

I watched him stare into the distance for a few moments. 'You want forgiveness?' He held his cupped hands out to me. 'There's forgiveness. Take it. It's yours.' And he dropped the forgiveness into my lap. 'There. Now what are you going to do with it? I'll tell you what would be a good idea – move on, get on with your life.'

And he slumped back in his chair and rubbed his eyes. He looked very, very tired.

'Do you mean it about forgiving me or are you just joking?'

'I mean it.'

I breathed out and began to have some small, glowing hope. 'I can't get on with my life if it's without you.'

'You've been doing just fine,' he said. 'You've got yourself a good job, a nice flat, too, I hear. You've got a great life. You don't need me at all.'

'I do need you.'

'You don't, Emily. You're managing very well without me. You don't need me to look after you, to leave the light on in the hall at night, to give you lifts home when you've been out with your friends. You don't need me so don't say you do.'

'Well if I don't need you, I definitely still want you.'

'Why? What for?'

'Because I love you.'

He groaned. 'Can't you think of another reason?'

'Well,' I tried. 'I just like having you around. I liked how you used to make me laugh and I liked it when you were just there, kind of pottering around or playing music or making a sandwich or playing with the cat. I liked sitting at the table with you and talking after dinner. I liked it when you used to come and talk to me in the bath. I liked being in bed with you. There's all sorts of things – and I haven't even mentioned the times we went out.'

'You'll easily find someone else who can do all those things for you.'

'But I want you.'

'Emily,' he said, leaning forward. 'I want you too. There is nothing I would like more than to spend my days pottering around making sandwiches and talking to you in the bath and especially being in bed with you, but there's no way we can live together again. How do I know you won't go off with someone else?'

'I won't go off with someone else.'

'How can you possibly know, Emily? How can I trust you?'

302

'I love you. If you love someone with hindsight, it's an absolutely undeniable love.'

'You don't make vows with hindsight.'

'Jane did.'

'Emily, we can't try again because I don't have a double helping of forgiveness to offer. I can only forgive you this one time.'

'I know. I understand. And I'll do my best to be faithful.'

'You'll do your best? Well, that's nice of you.'

'And how hard would *you* try? You said fidelity was only for angels and dogs, and angels weren't as good at it as dogs.'

'I was faithful to you.'

'I promise I'll be faithful. I'll remake my vow.'

Silence.

'Do you still love me, Andrew?'

Silence.

'Do you hate me for what I did?'

'I don't hate you. Of course not. I just . . . lost you. You weren't who I loved any more. You weren't the girl I had imagined you to be.'

'I was always me.'

'I used to think you were perfect.'

'I was always just me, Andrew. I made a really serious mistake and I'm desperately sorry. I've paid a high price for it because I lost you. I wish we could try again.'

'I don't think it would work.'

'It could.'

'Why should it?'

We talked for hours, but nothing I could say would make him change his mind. He said he couldn't trust me any more, he couldn't give me another chance. I wasn't the person he had thought I was. He had been in love with his idealised, perfect girl, the only good and lovely thing in his world, and he was grief-stricken that he had lost her. And I couldn't replace her.

'But I'm me. I was me all along and I still love you.'

He said nothing.

'Do you love me?'

'Emily, that's irrelevant.' His words shocked me and I turned away. I felt his hand on my arm. 'Emily, look at me,' he said. 'Can't you see? Of course I love you, but it's all just a terrible waste of time. It's nothing, because nothing can ever come of it.'

'It's everything!'

'If you want my forgiveness, Emily, you have it. But that really is all I have left to give you.'

It was nearly dawn. We were both exhausted, going round in circles. I had said everything I could think of to make him see that I was serious, that I loved him, that I wanted to be with him again and that I would be faithful. In return, he had given every possible reason why our trying again was doomed to failure.

Depressed, we went to our separate rooms. We parted at the foot of the stairs and there was no gentle goodbye, just a tired, sad good night. It seemed there was nothing else to be done.

I went to bed and lay awake in the dawn, listening to the sound of waves breaking gently on the shore. I thought of the sound enduring through aeons of time: the sweeping in and out, the breathing of the blue planet. In the past I had found the sound of waves comforting, but now I felt nothing but a terrible hopelessness. I had loved my husband deeply and yet I had still been unfaithful to him. What kind of love was that? He didn't think there was any point in trying again and why should he? I felt wretched.

Knowing sleep was not going to come, I climbed out of bed and stood at the window. Grey dawn. I stared at the horizon, the mysterious Infinity Point, the place where time and space seem to meet, where eternity appears visible. I could see two boats on the horizon. Little boats too small for such a long journey.

There was someone out walking on the beach. A man with his hands in his pockets, his head bowed. He was halfway along, walking away from me towards the cliffs. No one else was about. His were the only footprints on the sand. I stood and watched and listened to the waves. He reached the cliffs, paused a long time, then started back again. He paced along the beach, all the way back to the hotel, and as he got closer I saw that it was Andrew. He was almost under my window, then he stopped. He stood for a long time looking out to sea, watching and listening as I had done. When he turned to walk into the hotel, I stepped back from the window.

I got my things together and went down very early to check out of the hotel. It was time to move on. I ought to be on my way. I went into the dining room for coffee and there was Andrew. After a night of talking and soul-searching he was finishing off his full Scottish breakfast. He downed the dregs of his coffee and stood up to face me.

'I've been for a walk,' he said. 'It was kind of bracing.'

'I might go for a walk too, before I call for a cab to the station.'

'What time's your train?'

'There's one at eight o'clock. I can get a connection to Glasgow and then on to Edinburgh.'

I looked out the window and the sky was clearing, the mist at the horizon was lifting. He came and stood beside me and we looked at the view together, the waves rolling in from Infinity.

'Do you want a lift?' he asked.

'It's all right, thanks, I'll be fine taking the train.'

'I mean,' he said quietly, 'would you like to go home?'

I turned to face him and saw in his eyes that he wanted there to be hope, and so there was hope. 'Yes, I would very much like to go home.'

'Come on, then.' He offered his hand and I took it and held it fast. Joy and relief, like when we got married.

We set off together. Travelling home. The music on the car radio merged into the weather forecast. Sunshine and scattered showers to drive through together. Some highs, some lows. Changes in pressure. Sun and rain. A rainbow.

Weathering.

Epilogue

'. . . there remains for us only the somewhat risky, yet not unnecessary, duty of attempting to forecast the future of this extensive branch of our native industries. At the present moment, the whisky trade stands in possession, broadly speaking, of the key of the situation. French Brandy is, as an article of general consumption, hopelessly discredited . . . Rum, for some reason, nobody that is anybody drinks. Gin, with all its many merits, fails to gain new drinkers, while the old consumers seem to be dying out. The opportunity for whisky is, therefore, overwhelming. What will it do with it?'

The Whisky Distilleries of the United Kingdom,
Alfred Barnard, 1887

Factual Note

In May 2002, The Scotch Malt Whisky Society
offered for sale to its members a very fine and rare
pink whisky.

It was, by its very colour and style,
a very girlie-looking single malt,
never before available on the open market.

It was widely admired and sold out very fast.

More's the pity that under the terms of a
'gentleman's agreement'
within the whisky industry, the distillery
cannot be named.